VESTIGE

ALSO BY ANTONIO ROBERTS

The Vestige Saga

Vestige: Rise of the Pureblood

Vestige: What Lies Beneath

VESTIGE

What Lies Beneath

ANTONIO ROBERTS

First edition published April 2020. Second edition February 2021.

ISBN 978-1-7347426-6-4 (paperback)

ISBN 978-1-7347426-3-3 (ebook)

theantonioroberts.com

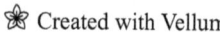 Created with Vellum

CHAPTER ONE

We strolled into camp, rubbing our tired eyes. The fire pit still smoldered from the night before. Romero dozed against the trunk of a tree where I'd left him. The man had the right idea. Sonia poked at the fire, trying to salvage what scraps she could.

Sonia and I were freezing. Our wet toes numbly tingled from the basin and the brook. I gathered some more kindling to get the fire going again. Most of the wood was damp from rainforest moisture, or morning dew.

After we got the fire going, we curled up beside it, shivering for warmth. The wind blew cool and brisk through our clothes. My thoughts turned to the nesting celebration. I guess becoming a woman meant hypothermia in tight, constricting clothes. Myst rose around us. Or maybe it was just plain old mist. At this point, I wasn't sure but whatever it was, my headaches returned. I grimaced

"Hangover?" Sonia asked.

"I'm not sure."

"There's some more blue lotus down the way."

"After your story, no thanks. We need to get out of here. Any thoughts?"

Romero grunted in his sleep. We lowered our voices.

Sonia yawned. "I need some sleep," she said.

"Well, it's been a few hours and it's likely they have the docks under their watch, love. Go ahead and get some rest," I reassured her.

Sonia unfolded her wings and tried to lie down, but she shot up with a squeal. "Bad idea," she whined, rubbing her back.

"How do you feel? Didn't the magic healing work?"

Sonia began combing leaves out of her feathers. "No, it did. I have felt little pain until now."

Romero sat up and trudged over to the fire.

"Well, our conquering hero returns," he said, sitting beside me. "You put that training to good use?"

I nodded.

"Good." His jacket still hung open. His wounds had scabbed or faded as scars, give or take a few gnarly ones.

"How do you feel?"

"Sore, but better. I couldn't help but overhear, but there's another dock on the other side of the island. It leaves a chance they don't have that one under watch, but knowing Jasper, he's too good for that."

I never corrected him. The image of the dead man still festered in my mind. I never wanted to kill again. "Any other way off the island?" I asked.

As Sonia thought, she let out another yawn. "Well, only one. Jasper never liked to talk about his own black eyes. There was a shipwreck he covered up years ago. There may be a life raft or two that we could salvage and paddle to the mainland."

"It'd be quite a trek," Romero mumbled, mostly to himself.

I looked at him with a raised eyebrow. "What's the matter? Too much work for someone of your stature?"

Romero laughed. "You learn fast. I'm proud of you."

"I'm sure if we work together it will be a cinch," I said. "So it's settled—we rest, then we all leave the island."

"Kiera, may I have a word with you in private?" Romero asked.

Out of the corner of my eye, I watched Sonia squirm to find a comfortable position on her side.

"What gives?" I snapped. "Anything you say to me you can say in front of Sonia. We're a team now."

"Look, kid. This ain't no pleasure cruise. We still have a job to do. We're not on vacation, in case you haven't noticed, and I'm still trying to rid myself of the last stray I took in. I don't need another sack of dead weight holding me down."

"Hey!" Sonia sat up with a hand at her side. "I stuck my neck out for you. The very least you can do is show me some respect and get me off this rock. You best watch who you are talking to."

"Or what?"

"Guys, now's not the time for fighting," I interjected.

"Fine. Once we've left this place, we split paths."

"Fine."

"Guys, come on, can't we just—"

Romero stood up. "I'm heading for the ship."

"Good. Like I'd want you around me while I'm sleeping, getting any ideas," Sonia muttered.

I tried my best to get a word in and said, "Guys, can we talk about this?" But they kept arguing. "Like I'd want any of your crusty pigeon mites anyhow."

"Now, that wasn't very—"

Sonia yelled after him, "Hey! Don't you walk away when I'm talking to you. Hey, I'm talking to you!"

Romero stormed off, right on cue. Sonia groaned, rolling over in the dirt. With the crackling of the fire, silence returned once again to the morning. I sat there, warming myself. My head throbbed. I was glad the shouting was over.

SONIA TOSSED and turned all day. I offered what I could for her back, but everything we tried proved fruitless. Plus, a debilitating, throbbing migraine seared my skull to the point of flattening me. I guess I was 'burnt out of juice', like Minnie had said. We slept as best we could on the ground throughout the day. But with our various ailments, we didn't get much rest, as you can imagine.

Too awake to sleep anymore, we discussed what plagued our minds.

Sonia insisted on knowing how I met Romero and "what was his problem?" I put more wood on the fire and brought her up to speed.

I explained everything I knew: the mystery of his name, the flintlocks, Kiera, the airship . . . it wasn't much. The man kept himself hidden away, whoever he was. While that may have not been good enough for her, it was fine for me. He had proven his loyalty, and, even though he'd shown himself as one of the most egotistical, self-centered pricks I have ever met, he had his moments.

Eventually, our stomachs overtook our minds. We had eaten nothing since the night before, so I met Romero by the wreckage, hoping he'd found food.

Sonia led the way. Her sores were flaring up again, so I had to help her along. Not really much I could do but help her balance, really. My head still throbbed, and I was ready to take my saber and lodge it there—anything to relieve the pressure. My brain swelled like it would burst into changeling confetti.

Trapped in the thick roots of the marsh stood a colossal iron vessel. The sides of the hull were draped with ivy and large cracks splintered up the bow. The wind whistled through the shattered windows. Crusted dirt and grime permeated the shards of glass. The boat tilted in the sludge from where someone had lodged it into the undersea bed. A small light flickered in the cabin above deck.

Sonia explained how Jasper had been anxious for another, easier smuggling port. She said that in the dead of night (and despite all reason) he had brought this ship in and crashed it. Tunnels had been dug to the blue lotus grove to retrieve the remaining cargo, but he never came back for it. Jasper had been too ashamed and desperate to hide his failure, so he just left it.

Oddly enough, Sonia was one of the few who had been allowed to go through that tunnel. I imagine the blue lotus groves gave her hope, and a small bit of freedom. When she collected the lotus, Sonia could experience freedom for the first time, even if short-lived.

A small boat sat a great distance off the shore. I had a bad feeling as we waded through the icy water toward it. The water appeared shallow but after about ten or fifteen steps, my foot gave way to nothing. I splashed frantically about. Sonia hoisted me to the edge of the drop-off.

I coughed and choked up water.

"You all right?" Sonia asked, trying not to laugh.

I nodded, holding my chest.

"You can swim, right?"

I shook my head. I had never left the village before, and all this was entirely new to me. And with what water meant in the goblin bildungsroman, why would I ever want to learn? Water was a weapon in the village, and Pater, my "daddy" knew how to use it.

"Right. Well, it's easy. All you gotta do is . . ."

Sonia attempted to teach me how to swim. I was having none of it. She would have to kill me before I went over that drop-off. I tried humoring her in the shallows, but for the life of me, I couldn't stay afloat. You could count the seconds before I would sink back with my head beneath the water. Three, two, one—failure. Over and over.

Eventually, we returned to camp, cold and hungry. Our clothes were soaked again. Sonia limped off, trying to find us something to eat.

I shivered by the fire. Fear consumed me. I was too terrified to attempt anything I had "learned" on the other side of the drop-off.

How are we getting out of here?

By late afternoon, my stomach roared like a lion and Sonia returned empty-handed.

We attempted another healing of her damaged wing, showing little promise.

After I had rung out my hair and dried off, Sonia had the bright idea to try again. I refused, and she went and swam off to the boat by herself.

I stood by the shore and watched. Before Sonia left, I pleaded with her to at least try to get along with Romero. Yet in pure Sonia fashion, she ignored me and waded off.

Sonia disappeared for hours. I walked along the shore to kill time. Gritty sand lined the water's edge where weeds and ferns had overtaken the forest floor. Dead roots and fallen trees lined the way back to the hatch. Birds whistled and chittered from the branches above. I found a berry bush.

The berries shone bright red and squishy. My stomach growled.

Please don't be poisonous.

I took one. My lips puckered, and I gagged. It was bitter. Turning around,

I saw the hatch from where we had come. It was open. Footprints scattered in every direction from it. And worse yet, paw prints. We were being tracked. We had to move *now*.

I hurried back to the shoreline. Shadows stirred in the cabin and I heard faint voices; they were arguing.

We're dead.

A small paddle boat with Sonia in it came my way. I waded out and hopped inside. "We gotta go. We gotta go now."

"I agree. Your 'fiancé,' Romero, is unbearable."

"Fake fiancé," I corrected her. "But no, not that. The Order. The hounds. They're close."

I explained the situation and we paddled back to the hole in the ship's wreckage.

Inside, a room below deck had taken on a lot of water. There was an inch of water in the lowest places, but everywhere else would require us to swim through it like mermaids. Sonia led me through the overturned crates and rotten wood casks to a rusty stairwell. The floor was at a tilt, so I tried to use the crates for balance.

Luckily, the second floor wasn't so bad. A smell of mold and algae reeked inside. Aside from that, it was relatively dry. The metal staircase creaked and moaned. Handrails snapped at the slightest touch. We rose to the top deck. My feet gave way on the damp deck and I slid to the other side. Sonia spread her wings out for an even balance and continued on.

Romero wasn't in the cabin with the helm as before, but in the captain's quarters. When we finally entered, he sat at a desk, going over maps and charts of the area.

He turned around, puffing a pipe. "Ah, our conquering heroine appears to have a new weakness."

"Can it. We have company."

I explained the situation to both of them there.

Romero took another puff. "Way I see it, they can't track us without footprints. As long as we make no signs we are here, we should be fine."

"Are you sure?" I asked.

"Old habits die hard. If those tunnels and this wreck were prohibited, they may be more cautious."

Sonia shook her head. "Are we really going to bank on that?"

"Of course not," Romero snapped. "But I found something that may be of interest. Many things, really."

Beside him sat a stack of maps and books, most of which had remained relatively intact. He pulled out a small, torn map of the shore of Aerogapolis and Isle of Jarbah.

"Like I said, it will be quite a trek to shore. Not easily navigated either. If Jasper crashed, so could we."

"Jasper was reckless and stupid," Sonia said. "As long as we are careful, we should be fine."

They debated the proper route and coordinates and whatnot. All that navigation jargon between the two experienced travelers was lost on me. Nevertheless, the heat ramped up again, and it soon turned into bitter, quarrelsome bickering. My head throbbed—still.

"Can it! Both of you! I've had it up to here with you two. I spent the entire night carrying your sorry rears out of that place, and you refuse to listen to a single word I say. If we're not careful, they'll haul us right back. Your arguing will solve nothing. Sonia's coming with us, end of story."

"Who made you captain?" Romero said, unmoved.

"The same changeling who decided not to leave you behind. You're acting like children. Grow up and work together."

Both Romero and Sonia glared at each other and crossed their arms.

"If you won't do it for me, do it for yourselves. We have a better chance if we work together."

Romero heaved out a sigh and extended his hand in a silent truce to Sonia. Sonia curled her lip and stared at him as if he had just spat in her soup.

"Partners?" he said.

She shook her head.

"Sonia," I growled.

She sighed. "All right, fine. Partners." She shook his hand.

Romero continued, clearing his throat. "Right. Well, I found something else of value that you may be interested in."

He gathered a set of books he had stuck aside: handwritten leather journals and torn, yellow-paged hardbacks.

"Sonia, did Jasper ever say what the cargo was?"

She thought to herself for a moment. "Never. He was usually secretive about that kind of stuff. Only that it was heavy and important."

"Whatever was on this ship, Jasper wanted it really badly."

Romero began flipping rapidly through the sketchbooks. Schematics flashed before my eyes. There were numbers, dates, arcs, and geometry filling the pages. Orange paper glowed by the oil lantern's light in an arcing sunset. Suddenly, he stopped and smacked the book down at a page he wanted.

"Let me read something to you . . .

JUNE 6

I'm writing this should I succumb to the wrong hands. I hear those blue ticks are nasty devils, and it scares me to think about what should happen. I cannot forget my purpose and calling. I have fulfilled my role to the High Wolf.

The Vestige is finally in our possession. Just one more cog in place for when the door should open. The beast shall rise anew. Mammon Fenrir will be most pleased. Should Dr. Henry's theories prove correct, this is indeed one of the seven evils of the old world. There will be no stopping the new order. Oh, happy day. Oh, happy day, I say! The new nation shall be a force to be reckoned with. No longer shall we bow to either Northstrand, Archades, Geneva, or Aerogapolis. . . ."

ROMERO STOPPED. "You get the picture. It continues with much more mono-loguing if you wish for me to go on."

Both Sonia and I exclaimed "No!" at the same time and laughed. Romero flipped a few pages over and continued.

"JUNE 29

Another drawback: I gave into my emotions again today. Cursed feeling clouding my judgment. The confounded Starshell Station complicated matters yet again. Filthy red-coated humes! Wretched humans think they rule the place. Go back to your country and leave my haven alone. Curse them, expanding their reach.

I took to the cover of darkness to protect the Vestige at all costs. Bringing it into port was not an option. Too many wandering eyes. The "Oracle"— bah! Puppet master is more like it. You can't trust them—witches. She's on to me; I can tell.

Despite Sonia's heeding, I attempted to land it ashore in the marsh. Fog clouded our view. The crew warned me of the danger. There was no turning back. We were going to land this if it killed us. In the second or third hour, the hull was breached. I gave the orders to secure the cargo at all costs. Water poured in fast. We sealed the hatches. We prepared for such a situation as this and made for the boats to safety, but suddenly the ship creaked.

A grinding of metal groaned beneath us. I sent the crew to investigate. I didn't care how many men it took. No water could reach the hold.

As they went to inspect the bulkheads to the Vestige, the walls gave way. The springs of the deep burst forth, flooding them in an airtight box. None were spared. I saved the Vestige, but at what cost?

As I recall these events, I must suppress these thoughts, these . . . feelings. Why must it be so difficult? Guilt is a hard emotion. Sonia, you were right, and I've treated you poorly for it. I'm sorry, my dearest. I regret to inform my master of my failure, and the widows of the men in my care. May my labor not be in vain, for there is blood, their blood, on my hands.

CHAPTER TWO

"That explains the shipwreck," I said. "But what does it have to do with us?"

Romero closed the journal. "Don't you see?" he said. "Whatever Jasper was after is still here. This Vestige is some kind of weapon."

"Yeah, but whatever it is, the thing's sealed safe underwater, right? They can't just pull it out."

Romero rifled through the mound of books he'd used for his investigation and pulled out a small book with a blue tattered cover, *Levitation for Young Sparks*. "He'd thought of that, too."

"The sorcerers! Of course!" Sonia exclaimed.

Romero nodded, puffing his pipe. "He was going to make them dig their own graves and retrieve his prize."

Sonia shook her head in disgust.

"We have to save Cheryl," I said.

"Afraid that's not an option," Romero said.

"And why not? We can't just leave the sorcerers. They'll kill them."

"So, you got a plan?"

"Well, no, but—"

Sonia butted in, "To be fair, puddin', Jasper planned to transport them in a couple of days anyhow."

"Where to?" Romero asked.

"Not sure. Up the channel, I believe. I'd imagine on the mainland somewhere."

"Then what do you suggest we do, Sherlock? Keep in mind we have people after us."

"Sonia, you got that stick of dynamite still?"

She pulled it from inside her dress and shook some of the water off it. Where she got it in the tunnels, I didn't remember.

"We're gonna sink it," Romero said.

"You're crazy. Sonia, tell him he's crazy."

"I like it. Let's bury this place with him," Sonia agreed.

My jaw dropped as I turned to her. "You guys are insane. We need to attract less attention, not more."

"Come on, Sinopa, think about," Sonia began. "This will give them more time. They can't retrieve it if there's nothing to raise."

Romero began tucking journals away into his pockets. "That leaves only one problem: we'd be gambling. I'm a gambling man, but who's saying they don't do away with them immediately after we sink it?"

I looked at him, confused. "'Do away' as in . . . ?"

He made a line with his finger across his throat.

"No, no, no, no. They can't do that. I'll . . ." My mind raced, at a loss for words. I thought of Cheryl in a still frame, being attacked. I thought of Simon alone. I thought of Sophia never seeing her daughter again.

Romero handed me the book, patted my hand, and blew smoke away from my face. He circled the room, holding his arms up for show. "Look around you, kid. This isn't a fairy tale. Sometimes the bad guys win."

"But that would be assuming they know this is here," Sonia said. "All the ship's crew died, right?"

"All but Jasper. The water flooded the cabins, drowning the men inside. And, well . . . you know what became of Jasper."

I flinched but Sonia ignored the comment. She continued, "Then we're golden. We can sink it and none would be the wiser."

"No. I can't risk anyone else getting hurt for my sake," I said.

"We'd be far away from the blast if that's what you're wondering," Romero said.

I bit my lip. "Not that. It's—"

"Sinopa, sweetie, this may be our one chance to help them. It may buy us more time to rescue them. And if they die or are taken, well, at least they won't suffer much longer."

I stared down at the cover of the book in my hands, trying my best to block out her words. The cover held a picture of a boy balancing a balloon and brick in the air. Sonia put her hand on my shoulder and comforted me. *It's not fair that they should suffer this way. They did nothing to deserve it.* I gave in to the plan. Anything to grant them relief.

We prepared to leave in one of the small lifeboats. The charges were set. Romero looted the place of anything of value or incrimination of the Order of Archaeopteryx. We had to take them down. I flipped through the levitation book with its faded ink. Sonia searched for any morsel of food or dry clothes. Nothing. My stomach groaned in protest. We piled up all our belongings and readied the oars.

Romero left to light the fuse, seeing as he was the only one who could move quickly enough. There was still some doubt as to whether it would work.

We waited in silence. The sun set in a fiery red ball on the horizon. Our day had come and passed in a blur. Overhead, seagulls screeched.

Sonia and I turned to each other in anticipation. Footsteps raced toward us. Romero leaped into the water, shoved the boat, and climbed in. Sonia started rowing.

BOOM! The ship creaked and lurched. The water rippled. The backside tilted further down, and the port sank to a sharp forty-five degrees. The boat still stood, only in even more disrepair. Only the nose and half the top stuck out of the water in an awkward slant.

We rowed away on a course for the coast. It was worth the try. I hoped it did something to ease their pain. *Hold on, Cheryl, I'll save you. I promise.*

❧

As we rowed further toward the horizon, it became clear we were lost. Of course, Sonia was quick to blame Romero for not heeding her advice, comparing him to Jasper. And of course, Romero blamed it on the lack of proper navigational tools, and here we went again. Not only that but the surf jostled my body. My stomach did somersaults and growled, empty. So not only was I sick of them, but seasick to boot.

I stuffed my face in the levitation book with the oil lantern from the wreck. We would need all the tools at our disposal. Who knew what lay ahead of us?

My eyes strained to pick up most of the words. Reading was never my strong suit compared to numbers and figures. I could work with those, but words—they might as well have been hieroglyphs because I couldn't make them out.

Back at the library, I was too embarrassed to tell Minnie before, but I couldn't read. From Al's bedtime stories, I loved books at an early age. Goblins are excellent storytellers. They'll reel you in and enrapture you in the fewest words possible. That's more than I can say for myself.

It didn't help that I hadn't really gone to proper school, either. At least this book had pictures. Most of the pictures were of the same boy with glasses, showing the right way with a check marked box and the wrong way with a big X crossing it out.

As we rode, a foghorn blew, breaking up the squabble. In the distance, a large row of shadows levitated in the cloud. A blockade.

Before we could turn around, three smaller vessels closed in. Our oars barely pushed the water away as we paddled furiously. Spotlights shot on the boat and a loud voice bellowed over speakers for us to stop. We were surrounded. Uniformed men with crossbows loomed over us.

"You're in Northstrand territorial waters and past curfew. State your business."

Romero motioned for us to let him do the talking.

"Sir, there is an excellent explanation for this."

"Indeed? Cuff them. Bring the smugglers in for questioning."

"No, wait!"

Men rushed the boat. We were all pulled separate directions with our arms behind our backs.

One soldier pulled up my levitation book. "Magical contraband. Very illegal in these parts. What do you have to say for yourselves?"

All three of us stared at each other in silence. We were so close. The men in armor bagged all our stuff in a burlap sack.

"That's what I thought. Take them away."

"No, wait! You can't do this!" I screamed.

Sonia called out from another boat. Romero hung his head in shame. Our boat was brought aboard one of theirs, slowly. The cold gusted and I noticed a small Northstrandian flag buffeting in the breeze.

I stomped on one of the men's feet and rushed the captain. Another patrolman leaped on me and tackled me to the ground.

"I appeal to Master Rudolph," I shouted.

He laughed nervously, "What did you say?"

The captain raised his hand for all the others to stop. "And what is your relation to Master Rudolph, creature?" he snickered.

I was brought to my knees with my horns pulled back to force me to look him in the eye.

"He's a friend. He's expecting me."

"Well, we'll just have to see if your story checks out. Cart them together instead, under armed guard. Leave the contraband with me. Make sure they are well taken care of. No cuffs. You won't want to hear his temper."

The patrols nodded and did as they were told. We were strip-searched with hands in more places than comfortable. Sonia sucker-punched one of the grabby patrols in the search, and they had to wrestle her down to search her on the floor.

Internally, I cheered her on. Romero and I did our best to hide our grins.

Crossbows pricked our backs as we walked beneath the boat to the brig. It was a row of six empty cells with bars dividing each one. Once our cuffs were removed, icy hands pushed us into the cells. Sonia squealed as their fists smacked her mangled flesh. She teetered off balance, limping forward in compliance, but still too slow for our captors. A man kicked her inside the cell; her legs collapsed, faceplanting her to the floor. Her exposed skin oozed against the rusted bars between us.

One of the guards cursed her under his breath as a filthy sorceress mutt. Sonia wept on the floor. I wished the bars weren't there. I'd have been by her side and helped her up. Romero lit his pipe to ease his nerves. I sat on the

VESTIGE

bench. My seasickness had slightly subsided. The bigger boat did the trick, I suppose.

At least we had beds and a roof over our heads. Romero dozed off, paying us no mind. *How could he be so calm in a situation like this?*

Sonia stayed on the floor and wept herself to sleep. As of this writing, it was one of the only times I'd ever seen her cry.

In goblin, there's a saying that 'real men never cry'. They could be kicked in the kidneys, lose a loved one, or hold their insides from spilling out, but real men never cry. There is not much of an equivalent for women.

I've seen people put up with many things: loss, regret, heartache, child-birth, betrayal, and abuse. Some more than others. Sonia endured through it all and stood a bulletproof, blazing bull with all the strength and attitude to prove it. Yet, here, she faltered. I suppose no man's immortal, as they say.

They brought us food, smelled before seen as it should be. Butter and flakiness wafted beneath the deck and mouth watered, pleadingly.

They slid the trays through slots in the bars. It was really only bread and water. Not much of a meal, but I didn't care. I scarfed it down ravenously.

Sonia moaned. She still lay on the floor. I broke off a piece of my bread and tossed it to her through the bars. The crumbs struck her face, and she ate it thankfully. A guard came over to Sonia's cell. *Could she get up?*

"Hey, get off the floor! You're not hurt. Quit faking it! The bed's over there."

Sonia attempted to push herself off the floor and shook her head.

The guard began unlocking her door.

"I said, on your feet!"

He hoisted her by her armpits to stand and she thrust open her wings. A gusting wind echoed in the brig, along with a hard smack on his face. Her wing heaved him clean into the cell door, out cold with a bang. She limped out the door, holding her back. Blood oozed between her fingertips down the open slit of her dress. No wonder she couldn't stand. Let alone walk.

Three guards poured into the brig with cocked crossbows. The captain stood behind them. "It appears I've underestimated you. Cuff her. Bring her upstairs to the dining hall for a chat, will you?"

"Don't hurt her," I begged them.

They placed cuffs on Sonia's wrists. Ropes bound her wings and arms

15

together behind her back, so she stumbled to balance on her toes. The captain walked over and stood in front of my cell. His nose hooked like a hawk or a crow, jutting out of his face. His brow cast a shadow over his sockets in the dim light.

"And why should I listen to you?"

"Because . . . because you'll answer to the Master."

The captain smiled. "Beast, I hardly doubt the Master would be friends with the likes of you. Why, any master wouldn't. But to humor a dead girl's delusions," he turned to the guards, "clean her wounds and shove her back with the others. We can't be too careful. Wash her every last feather. The Master finds anything on me, it'll be on you, understand?"

The guards all nodded their heads in fearful acknowledgment.

The captain continued, "I find you're lying, lizard, and I'll pluck her every last feather one by one. Get her out of my sight." He left, bringing up the end of the train.

Sonia came back an hour later with bandages wrapped up her back and side. They set her on the bed, lying on her stomach, and left. I tried to stay awake to talk to her more, but my strength failed me. Two or three hours of sleep will do that to you. Gravity overtook my eyelids, and my world went black.

CHAPTER THREE

I awoke to more prodding, and a crossbow pointed at my face.

"Get up. We're here," a soldier growled.

They led us out with our hands on our heads. Topside, they clasped Sonia's arms behind her back. The soldiers brought us ashore in a single file line.

The island burned a lush green. Foliage crept over blackened volcanic rock and shale hillsides. In the center on top, the large mound was made of a solid concrete compound. The seams of the granite walls were split with marble columns. Blazing crimson banners hung from stained azure glass. Crowning the top, a giant sea-foam stained-glass dome draped overhead, a castle of colors and cold, hard stone. The island stone was like a massive sea turtle.

Large cougars and lions, carved in stone, lined the promenade at varying levels of the grand entrance. They appeared frozen in the volcanic rock of the empire. Small encampments of tents lined the dazzling granite thoroughfare outside.

Standing at the door under tropical heat, two armed guards were sweating bullets in full plate. The ten-foot, reinforced, cherry wood door lumbered open, leading us into a grand foyer.

Once inside, the entrance glowed in white marble and sandy accents. This room, as with most in the fortress, was walled hexagonally like plates of tortoiseshell. The idea was to be aesthetic and defensive without compromise.

Romero would argue it fails at both. "It has a glass ceiling, for Pete's sake. It's a resort, not a fortress. The chokepoints in the entrances leave much to be desired. The number of walls are too excessively cumbersome for defense, and an eyesore, at best. Each room creates a sense of claustrophobia, boxing you in."

A young-looking receptionist with wheat-colored hair sat behind the counter, filing her nails. *Because when aren't they?* I struggle to remember meeting a single receptionist who was not filing her nails.

Anyway, the guards led us toward the receptionist and escorted us behind the counter.

"We'll see an end to your lies soon enough, iguana," the captain said. He pushed me in front of the receptionist and said, "Abigale, this filthy lot claim to be friends of the Master himself. We both know the masters, and the magistrates, have yet to see guests."

Abigale nodded, put down her nail file, and began going through a large book. "Right. Now, did you say Magistrate or Master?"

"Are you kidding? You're cute. She's cute, isn't she, boys?"

The guards laughed.

Abigale blew her bangs out of her brown eyes with an annoyed glare. "I was just asking a question. I don't see what was so—"

"Master, sweetie. Magistrate Beauregard is far too busy to deal with mongrels such as this. The only imperial blood they probably met is some warden."

At this, Romero's ears perked up. "How is the Magistrate these days?"

The guards laughed. "That's a good one, street rat."

"Don't encourage them," Sonia snapped.

The captain smiled. "If you must know, he's negotiating a deal on the empire's behalf with our consul. Some egghead stuff."

Abigale stopped at a page near the end.

"Ah, yes, a Hazel or . . . Kiera, was it?"

"Yes, I'm Kiera."

The captain choked, seemingly on his own spit. "What? There has to be a mistake here."

Abigale thumbed through the pages again, reading aloud, "'Master Rudolph C. of Capital City'. Yep. It says 'Kiera', right here."

The captain stood baffled. His eyes widened as if Abigale had just turned into a chimpanzee. "Do you have some ID?"

The guards rifled through our clothes till they found the papers that spelled in large black ink, "Kiera Estaban."

The captain cleared his throat. His face reddened. "Right. Free to go."

I cracked a half-smile. He led his troops toward the door like a dog with its tail between its legs.

"Just a minute," I called back.

The captain turned to look. I cleared my throat and gestured to Sonia, still in restraints.

"Right, yes, of course," he apologized and slapped one of his men, knocking his hat clean off.

The guards rushed over to unchain Sonia.

"Don't just stand there. Free the bird," he snapped.

While they unchained her, I stared the captain dead in the eye. His gaze kept darting to the floor, and back to me, and then back to the floor.

"The Master will hear of this," I threatened.

"My apologies. I had no idea an—"

"Yet, we told you and you refused to believe us."

"I'm sorry. It's these men. There are so many and they—"

"Funny, I seem to remember you in command. Whatever happens to you, Captain, would be on them? Hmm? I think it's looking like whatever happened to us will be on you. Don't you agree, boys?"

Two guards stood beside me, their knees shaking. One shook his head in agreement. The captain shot him a piercing glare, and the guard quivered, darting after his helmet to the floor. To this day, I swear that boy's kneecaps clapped like a castanet.

"Don't tell him, please. I'll do anything," the captain begged.

I turned to Romero with a devilish grin. Romero clasped his hands with pride in his apprentice.

"Gee, I'm not sure. That was a very poor way of treating the lady-to-be of Master Rudolph in her time of need."

"Anything. Just name it. I need this job. I *need* this job," he sobbed on his knees.

Snot dripped from his nose. He was an ugly crier.

"I want a fresh set of clothes for my companions and me. We are to stay the night and meet with Master Rudolph."

"A meal would be nice," Sonia chimed in.

"As many meals as you like, ma'am," said the captain.

"Yes, and a dozen plum tarts," I said.

Both the captain and Sonia turned to me in confusion. "P—plum tarts?" He stammered as if to be certain.

Romero murmured through pursed lips, "Don't overdo it."

"And who did you say you were?" he asked.

"I'm the lover and soon 'lady-to-be' of your superior, and you best not forget it. Or maybe I won't forget how you treated my companions."

His entire demeanor changed, and the captain sniveled on his knees before me. "Yes. Yes, I meant no offense. I was merely unaware the Master had time for a wife."

Romero stepped in closer, not letting me have all of the spotlight. "The master's dealings are his own. Why should he answer to you?"

The captain wiped his face, struggling for any semblance of decency. "Yes, Abigale, see that they are taken care of, please."

Abigale, who had been watching all this play out, nodded with a smirk. Her cheeks glowed like puffy white marshmallows. "It would be my pleasure."

"Now go. By nightfall, plum tarts or it's your head!" I shouted.

The captain rushed to his feet, pulling his guards out the door with him.

I shouted after them, "Best make it two dozen," and Sonia doubled over laughing.

I turned to Romero, and he smiled. "We'll work on it," he said.

"What's that supposed to mean?"

"You overdid it, but all in all, not too bad, kid. Good show. Quite the performance."

Sonia jabbed me in the arm. "I thought it was wonderful."

Standing there, I pulled my friends close as I watched the men bolt down the corridor to the door. Romero pulled my arm off his shoulder like it was diseased, and Sophia looked at it and shrugged. We may not have been much, but no one touches my family.

WE RESTED at the fortress for the evening. I spoke with Abigale to arrange an audience with Master Rudolph. She informed us that he was on leave to attend the consul to the academy progress report. She said it was in the mines, up the channel, and that he should return in the morning, or by noon the following day, at the latest.

Abigale showed us to a set of rooms we could stay in while we waited. We thought it best to tell Master Rudolph about Jasper and check what he knew. He was a lawman of sorts, after all. Dinner wasn't until six o'clock, so we had time to kill.

After talking to Abigale, we discovered a clinic on-site that mended our wounds. But first, we were given back our "contraband." I took the book of levitation and tucked it under my arm. Romero took back the journals and stuffed some in his coat pockets and took the rest back to his room.

So, after much wandering of the honeycomb halls, we stumbled upon a room with rows of beds divided by sea-foam curtains. A few men, all bandaged up, lay in hospital beds, but most of the beds were empty. Again, it was more of a resort than a fortress. The clinic was just beyond the ward.

One at a time, we were taken in the back and examined, we girls separated from Romero for obvious reasons. I refused to leave Sonia's side, even though she insisted she was fine. I couldn't help but feel responsible somehow.

A nurse clad in a pink dress and apron, each stitched with a small country flag, examined us. As she inhaled deeply, her hands glowed. She slowly moved them down Sonia's back and torso until they stopped glowing.

"I thought magic was illegal in Northstrand?" Sonia asked, wide-eyed.

The nurse laughed. "Only in certain circles. We've received an education at the academy to earn our nurse's license. I'm licensed to practice magic and medicine."

She made Sonia lie down, and she massaged her spine. I became mesmerized. Each of the cuts pursed like lips as the nurse smoothed and kneaded Sonia's skin straight, like clumps of dough. I had to learn how she did it.

"Doesn't it hurt?" I asked.

Sonia shot me a dirty look.

"Sorry, not you Sonia. Her. I have migraines after using my healing magic."

The nurse shook her head. "Only if you overexert yourself. Gentle movements. Magic's like a muscle you have to stretch."

"Can you show me?"

Her eyes searched, as if someone was watching in the closed room, before she agreed. The nurse grabbed my hands and led me through it. Her hands pulsed, holding mine. Energy vibrated my fingers, turning them freezing cold and then flaming hot. The nurse slowed my movements to control the flow. Magic is hard to describe yet easy to feel. Being a numbers person would explain why it proved so difficult for me.

Soothing thoughts rolled in like a gentle ocean breeze and caused my fingers to glow brightly. I was quick to make sure not to protract my claws. No need to cause more pain.

Sonia's skin rippled and jiggled like gelatin yet remained pliable and stiff. Simultaneously, it stretched more malleable and viscous, like butterscotch pudding. I swore my fingers would sink through to the other side of her body if I wasn't careful.

We started at the top of her back and worked through the skin, rolling and tucking it forward and back. The nurse called it the strudel method. It sounded appropriate somehow. I enjoyed strudel, so it wasn't too hard to wrap my head around.

Soon, only a few scars and scabs remained. There was only so much that nature couldn't do itself.

My headache started resurfacing as my fingers dulled. The nurse sat me down and rubbed her ruby-tipped nails over my temples.

She examined me next. "Any other thoughts what could bring these on? Besides the magic of puberty?" I asked.

Sonia laughed. I didn't think it was that funny. My head throbbed like it was being bashed in with a brick.

"Well, you need to stretch your muscles more, so to speak. It's very natural for you to feel nauseous, sweaty, feverish, and exhausted."

She made it sound like I had the flu, not superpowers.

"You're reaching the age where your body and gifts are unstable—which is not a bad thing. Your powers may even reach their peak and dwindle from here. Who knows? It's hard to say. The arts of the arcane myst fell out of study in light of recent politics. In short, you need practice. Disrobe for me, please."

I rubbed my side where Jasper had stabbed me and shook my head. Aside from a few bruises and coming of age, I was fine.

"Kiera, she's a doctor. She can help you."

I took a deep breath.

"Fine."

Sonia turned away. The way the nurse's face scrunched up while she studied my mangled midriff wasn't very assuring. I hated anyone to even glimpse me like this.

"That bad?" I asked.

She didn't answer. Hands glowed and sewed my intestines. As for my scars and abnormalities, there was nothing she could do. She wiped the sweat from her brow when she was finished.

"This must have been some accident you three were in. Anything else?"

I looked at the book of levitation.

"Could you teach me?" I asked, sliding her the book.

The nurse looked at me and then at Sonia, who seemed just as uncomfortable about the subject as she was. She locked the door.

"Where did you find that?"

"What does it matter? As you said, I need practice."

"This may be Aerogapolis, but this is still Northstrand territory. I could be executed. Both of you could be executed. No, not me. Why don't you seek the Academy? It would be legal there. In a couple of years, you'll be a scholar in the medical myst, nursing, and Northstrandian law."

"A couple of years?!"

"What did you expect? You're gifted, but you're a late bloomer. It's like an instrument, you need to start young to adjust easier."

I groaned, putting my dress back on.

"You best not flash that around."

I looked to Sonia and her gnarled, gimpy wing. "What about her?"

"Well, sewing you up and dulling the pain is one thing. Growing things back takes time. May I?"

Sonia looked at her wing and winced. She fanned them out. The nurse took a small magnifying glass and otoscope and began examining her feathers.

"Well, avian anatomy is out of my expertise, but I'm aware of some. You're lucky you accidentally missed the blood feathers. As far as I know, they'll regrow, but it will take time."

Time was something we didn't have. The order kept those sorcerers hostage, and a group of murderers hunted me down. We didn't have time for me to spend years of training and come back. I hoped Rudolph had a better plan.

"This could be an excuse to practice your healing. Perhaps a nice bath could help," the nurse added. "A hot spring brews beneath the building. A nice soak may help your soreness, for a start."

A bath didn't sound too bad, though. It would be fine; Rudolph would have a plan. I was sure of it.

CHAPTER FOUR

"What do you mean, you're going?"

Romero tried his best to calm me down. "I won't be too long. There is some business I need to take care of while we're here."

"What kind of business?"

"That's a personal question. I don't answer those."

"Can you at least tell me where you're going? What if something happens?"

"Kiera, we're in a fortress of the best trained army in the world. I think we're fine. Besides, myst can't travel over water. There is no way they can even see us unless they were already here. We're ghosts."

"What about your 'fans'?" I asked.

He ran his hand over his stubbly, newly shaven chin. He'd cut his long brown curls as well. "It's amazing what a haircut will do for a mug shot," Romero explained.

I wasn't sure whether to interpret that as good or bad. "Be careful," I said.

"I'll be fine," he assured me. "Have fun with your girly bubble baths."

"Sure you don't want to tag along? You need to rest."

"I'll pass."

"Good. We won't have to worry about skinny dipping, then."

ANTONIO ROBERTS

"It wouldn't have been anything I haven't seen better on someone else."

And with that, he scooted out. He was in for it when he came back.

Meanwhile, I practically had to drag Sonia down the steps to the basement. The springs were divided into men's and women's. Naturally, there weren't very many women on base. Probably for good reason, so it was just Sonia and me. A large wooden screen barred off the other side from prying eyes.

Small red candles lit the interior, and large white sconces lit the white stone walls. The room smelled salty and earthy from the smoky sediment pools. Hints of cherry blossoms rose from the candles. I stuck my big toe into the water first and pulled it out quickly. Definitely hot. Best to ease into it.

"I can't believe you dragged me into this," Sonia said, dipping her toes in the water.

"You'll thank me later. Wash up, rest, and we can leave."

We removed our towels and slowly sank beneath the water.

The water boiled my scales and pores. I can't say I wasn't a little scared. I quickly undid the strings of my glove so as not to wet the fur. I tossed it by my towels and it thumped against the hard cover of the book and my purse. If only I could read. Then maybe I could learn.

"Sonia, I've got a favor to ask you."

"Does it involve getting rid of Romero? If so, I'm all ears."

I couldn't help but smile. "No, not really." I paused and cast my eyes down at the bubbles. I looked up at her again, took a big breath and said, "Do you know how to read?"

Sonia laughed. "Yes, Jasper had insisted upon it. Why do you ask?"

I picked at the dirt under my nails in the water. "Could you teach me?"

"You're like, sixteen, and you can't read?"

"I can read some. Just not very well or fast, or big words, or . . . much."

Sonia's eyes narrowed in suspicion. "Wait, this is about that book, isn't it?"

"Oh, Sonia, please say you'll do it. You heard what she said. I'm only going to improve and feel better with practice."

"No," she shot coldly.

"I'll pay you. You won't be doing it for free. Anything. Just name your price."

She scratched the back of her head. "This isn't about money, Sinopa. You don't understand. You and your healings are fine, but . . . you wouldn't understand."

"Maybe I would if you told me. We're in this together now, Sonia. Like it or not, that means Romero is, too. If you don't want to tell me, that's fine, but maybe I can at least help *you* somehow."

"I'm fine."

"You don't sound fine."

She shook her head. "Drop it, Sinopa. You don't understand what you're dealing with. I've seen sorcerers perform 'acts' that demons would applaud. You don't want to go down that road."

My tail dipped and swayed over the tip of the water. "Then help me to be better than them. Hold me accountable. Help me combat that evil."

Sonia remained silent. I couldn't tell if she was angry or just lost in thought.

"Maybe you're right," she finally said.

I screamed and hugged her. "Thank you! Thank you! Thank you!"

"That's not a yes."

A laugh escaped me, and I squeezed her tighter. "That's not a no, either."

Sonia smiled and splashed me with her wings. I splashed her right back.

By the end, the soak soothed our aching bones. The water did wonders for my scales. We were glowing and Sonia's maimed wing gleamed, washed white as wool, a dazzling dove white. We finished washing up with some small talk and somehow got to the subject of boys.

"Who knows, Sonia? Maybe I can help you get back on the horse."

"I'm not getting back onto anything, or anyone. One marriage was enough, thank you very much."

"But you're free of that horrid monster. Don't you want to find real love and spend your life with someone?"

Sonia laughed. "Keep dreaming. You need to take your head out of the clouds. When you're older, it will make sense."

"What's that supposed to mean?"

Sonia let out a low whistle and picked at a few loose feathers. "Life doesn't work that way."

I thumped her on the arm as she did me. Only, hers hurt. "Whatever. All I'm saying is you don't deserve to be alone."

Sonia smiled and thanked me.

A bell whistled in the hall. Wouldn't you know it—soldiers ran for the pool. They cried shouts of, "Cannonball!" and, "Over here! I'm open!" on the other side of the divider. We grabbed our towels and made for the exit, our silent sanctuary now ruined.

I grabbed my tail with one hand and tucked it close under the towel. It hurt, but it was better than drawing the wrong kind of attention. Sonia reluctantly carried the book and tightened her towels as well.

As we rounded the corner toward the door, the men's side roared in chaos. Large titans wrestled and threw each other into the pool. There were dozens of them.

Out of the blue, I heard a shout, "Look out!"

BOOM! I jumped and squealed. Strips of pigskin hung, dangling and tattered, from my horns.

"Great going, freak. That was our only ball," one man sneered at me.

"You owe us a new one," said another.

We walked past them toward the door, ignoring the confrontation.

"Yeah, you better leave, ya freaks. Who even let them in here?"

Sonia put her wing around my shoulder and told me to never mind them.

"Hey, I'm talking to you," the voice called after us.

I heard Sonia cry out in pain. A rock tumbled across the ground. She fluffed her wings and began marching back. Her eyes burned full of fire.

"Sonia. Where are you going? Sonia? They're not worth it," I called back.

"Stay here," she said.

She tossed me the book and walked over to the pool, tightening her towels around her waist and chest. Like with my tail, her wings made it difficult. The man who had been shouting insults stood taller than her, undeterred.

"Hey, you owe us a new ball," he insisted.

She took a deep breath and put on her best pretty face. "No, I think you owe my friend and me an apology. That's not how you speak to people."

A few of the men laughed.

"I don't owe you jack squat. But say, doll face, you let loose them towels of yours. We can—"

"Doll face?" she growled.

Oh boy, here we go. Grab the popcorn. Now he'd done it.

"You wanna try that again?" Sonia challenged.

The man smirked and shook his head.

"You don't speak to me like that."

A silence started as a circle formed in the water.

"Or what, baby? You're going to nag me to death? Like I'm gonna fight a girl."

"I assure you it wouldn't be much of a fight."

The crowd hyped his burn.

"That's no way to speak to a lady. I bet you're alone, aren't you?"

A few men laughed.

She continued, "You have no manners, but that's okay. I can fix that. I'll even let you strike first," she said, tempting him with the tap of her cheek. "If anyone's the animal around here, it's you."

What is she doing? She's gonna be massacred.

"How dare you insult an officer of Northstrand," he roared. The man lunged forward, throwing his entire body into one shot. I winced and turned away.

SMACK. The crowd roared. I peeked. Sonia held the man's fist with one hand, shaking. He stared in disbelief at his hand. She smiled and slowly twisted his wrist, sending him to his knees. The man clutched his wrist with his other hand, crying out in pain. She tossed it to his side and swiftly kicked him in the groin. The entire audience winced. She grabbed his cheeks.

"Nobody calls me doll face."

The crowd roared in applause. Sonia wiped her wet hair from her eyes. A circle formed around her, blocking my view. Calls were given for bets. Odds were given for anyone who would take on "Ladybird the Destroyer."

Sonia welcomed the challenge. Before dinner she'd won two-hundred-fifty gold pieces in one afternoon, as well as the hearts of the men on base. So much for keeping a low profile. I suppose if it hadn't been us, it would have been Romero.

No one ever crossed Sonia and lived to tell the tale. She made sure of it.

She even advocated for Abigale to be treated better. Bullying would not be tolerated. And after seeing what she did to all those challengers, I'm glad I was on her side, nestled underneath her wings.

CHAPTER FIVE

D inner came at long last. Sonia and I washed up again after taking a bath, strangely enough. All the guys pulled up chairs around her, regaled by her tales. She was one of them now, and two-hundred-fifty pieces richer.

No sign of Romero. I sat alone at my section of the table. I kept glancing toward the doorway, hoping that Rudolph would arrive at any moment.

Yup. Any moment now.

Seconds passed. Minutes. *Who am I kidding? As if someone like him would care for someone like me.* I twiddled my fork in my potatoes after I'd had my fill of them. My eyes wandered around the room. Everyone sat in tight-knit clusters. They were smiling and laughing, all so . . . happy.

I exited to the grand entrance. Abigale sat at her desk, humming. She was just as alone as I was. I asked her if there was any word from Rudolph, and there was none. Apparently, he was scheduled back with the consul by now.

I asked her if she had someone special in her life, and she didn't. Given the lack of respect the captain gave her, I could understand why. I thanked her and went on my way. My boots echoed in the empty hall.

My tongue fixed itself on a piece of corn stuck in my fangs. I stood in front of one of the large glass mirrors that lined the walls. No matter how much I tried, I couldn't remove it from my teeth. I flicked out my beady claws and began digging. I pricked my lip. Blood trickled down my fangs as I rubbed my lips.

Why can't I do anything right?

I stared at myself in the mirror, my frown coated in crimson. I really was a blood-thirsty monster. All I saw was a creature, not a girl or a lady, but an abomination: sad, stupid, and alone. This is what I deserved.

My room lay cold and still. I kicked off my shoes and fell back onto the bed, staring up at the ceiling.

Why am I always alone? Why doesn't anyone like me? What's wrong with me?

I heard faint music in the room next door. It grew louder. So loud I couldn't think. It was Sonia's room. *How funny that she hates being called a slut, yet it seems she just bagged the first boy who was willing.*

I knocked on her door several times but there was no response. Then I heard a faint scream over the music. *That can't be good.* I thumbed through my hair for a bobby pin and picked the lock.

Inside, a horrifying form sat by the fire. An alligator tail, with a cottontail for an end, dragged the ground. Angular six-inch claws ground ferociously at the knob of the chair arms for freedom. An elongated snout spouted from soft cheeks and snapped open with a gaping maw.

Romero stood over the creature with a musket to her throat. "Shut the door!" he screamed.

I slammed the door shut and looked on in horror. "Can't I go five minutes without a disaster?" I cried. "What happened?"

Romero tossed me a vial. "Poison. The Order sent her for us."

He pulled up the prisoner's sleeve and showed me a tattoo of the Order's insignia. The beast's mouth clamped on Romero's wrist like a vise. He bashed her face with his other fist until her jaw sank with a hiss.

"How did they find us so easily?" I asked.

"Gee let me think. Maybe it was the wrestling match that is now the talk of the entire world. Or possibly it could be the grand lady changeling whose plum tarts have arrived."

"Sorry. Wait, they've arrived? Where are they?"

Romero wrapped a pillowcase over his wound. "In the master's chambers. Where else? It was a grand spectacle—them bringing four dozen tartlets to the master suite. Meanwhile, that bird of yours, Sonia, vanished after flirting up a scene. That's not important, though. This thing just tried to kill us, and we can't rely on her. What are we going to do with it?"

"I thought you said this place was safe. How did something like that slip through?"

"Easy," he said as he reached for her breast pocket. Instinctively, he pulled it away, only barely avoiding her jaws.

"Second thought, we'll fix this right now."

He told me to hold the front of the chair down as he undid his belt. His boxers had little red hearts on them.

"That's a side I never wanted to see," I joked.

He kicked off the pants and readied the belt. "You should be happy you got to see this much. There have been women who would have killed for me."

I rolled my eyes. "Lucky me."

"Ready?"

I nodded.

He threw the loop over the creature's neck, and I held the chair down. The beast howled and shrieked, lashing out at the surrounding air. Spit and drool splashed me in the face. Romero pulled the belt tight, strapping its neck to the chair.

The prisoner kept her soft voice, despite all her grotesqueness. It was feminine and rang clear as a bell. Her cries tugged at my soul—I had to look away.

"This doesn't feel right," I said. "Even if she is of the Order."

"Maybe this will change your mind." Romero reached into her pocket and pulled out an ID labeled "Staff." In it was the picture of a young maid with mahogany hair and hazel eyes. The label read "Changeling," yet her face was entirely human. She was young and beautiful.

"This is your beast," he said, holding the picture beside her for me to see.

I was flabbergasted. "How?"

He walked over to the nightstand and picked up a belt of vials. "It just took one. She could have used them on any of us. Still think she is so innocent?"

The doorknob jiggled.

Two voices giggled close to the door, and Romero sprang to action. He pulled the chair away from view and signaled me to the door. Looking through the peephole, Sonia chattered close to a guard who cradling her neck. Ironically, it was the same man she had decked in the balls by the pool earlier. She began unlocking the door with one hand.

"What do I say?" I whispered back to Romero.

He desperately attempted to gag the beast quiet. "Stall her."

"Sinopa?" Sonia called from the other side.

Oh crap, she heard me.

"What are you doing in my room?" she asked.

I turned to Romero, again unsure of what to say. The beast was now shredding through a pillow, shaking it like a dog toy. "Tell her my pants are down."

"Don't come in. Romero's pants are down," I repeated to Sonia.

"What?"

"No, no, no," he cried, shaking his head. "*Your* pants. You're changing."

The creature started making velociraptor-like noises under the pillow he held over her face. The other pillow lay burst open on the floor.

"Sorry, *my* pants. I'm changing. Long day," I feigned a laughed. "Know what I mean?"

Totally not selling this any better.

"You and Romero? What are you doing in *my room*?"

Sonia pecked the guard on the cheek, waved him away, and banged on the door.

"Sinopa, open this door right now," she demanded.

I pressed my back against the door with all my weight. I could hear her fiddling with her key on the other side.

"What now?" I asked.

Romero shrugged.

The beast had now eaten through the pillow. Feathery mounds bulged in its lap.

I stood no chance when Sonia shoved at the door. It crashed open and sent me flying ten feet back. Sonia stood in the doorway, veins bulging. She scanned the room, taking it all in: the open wardrobe in disarray, crackling fire, and finally the eldritch spawn writhing in her coat of feathers.

"What the heck is that?" Sonia shrieked.

I held my head from where the door had struck it. Sonia turned the lock shut.

"Can't we go twenty minutes without a disaster?" she sighed.

"That's what I said."

The beast growled at us.

"Afraid not," Romero said, passing Sonia the vials. "I believe these to be the culprit."

I studied them, too. There were labels on some that read, "Property of the Grand Academy" and "Triune Treaty Research Society," accompanied by the seal of a stairway extending into the heavens, bordered in olive branches and three stars.

"Luxembourg Laboratories, no doubt," said Romero.

"How do you know?" Sonia asked.

"A man of my stature must keep tabs on his patrons, for pick-pocketing."

Sonia rolled her eyes.

"I've seen nothing like this," I said.

"Neither have I," said Sonia. "Was Jasper involved in this?"

"Well, judging by the marking, the vial came from a Triune Pact that established the Royal Research Society to begin with. Geneva Paradiso, Northstrand, and Archades joined forces in the last war. But as far as how they got a hold of this . . . is there something you're not telling us, bird?"

"Why would I hide something like this?" Sonia replied.

"I can think of loads of reasons."

"What's that supposed to—"

I butted in immediately, "I think what Romero is trying to say is that we should know the facts before jumping to conclusions, right?" I elbowed him in the ribs. "Right?"

"Precisely," he agreed.

Sonia rolled her eyes, unconvinced.

He continued, "Who is this 'High Wolf' Sinopa mentioned? Who is the Order? What do you know?"

Sonia crossed her arms in a huff. "I wasn't involved in many of Jasper's dealings. At first, he'd take me on business, and we'd see the world. He wasn't always a madman. It was one of the few things we enjoyed together. On one of our travels, we found an archaeological site. We met a nobleman who was in charge of the project that studied the ancient philosophy of evolution and the origins of changelings. His name was Ernesto Jericho Fenrir. Jasper called him Ernie."

Romero smiled. "Naturally."

"Ernie was a fanatic; obsessed, really. Sinopa, if you thought Jasper was crazy, you ain't seen nothin' yet. This man's insane. He and his colleagues believed the old society could be restored. Technology and medicine would bring a new renaissance. That's where it all started. They studied and practiced ancient medicine.

"Ernie believed the ideal man evolved. The being known to the ancients as the archaeopteryx was the supposed missing link. He could rise past their humanity and inhibitions into a super race. Sound familiar?"

"Just like Jasper," I said.

"Jasper and I visited him and his wife a few years before Jasper became indoctrinated, and—"

The prisoner started shrieking, blocking the sound of Sonia's voice. Romero pulled from his pockets a small vial of white pills. He opened it and tossed one down her screaming throat. The beast began to choke, and her eyes dilated.

"What was that?" I asked.

"Just another trick of the trade, an expensive trick, mind you. Sleeping tablets will do wonders both in evasion, information, and relaxation. You experience a lot of things in my line of work. Make sure you take note of this, Kiera. I'd hate for my knowledge to be lost on you."

"You can call me Sinopa. You don't have to call me Kiera anymore."

Romero smiled. "No, I think it is rather fitting, and you need to remember your role."

The monster's head reeled and slumped at its side.

"Go on," Romero said to Sonia.

"As for what happened to Ernie or who the High Wolf is, I'm not sure. I heard stories of Ernie, Jasper, and Cutswell in the Order, but I wasn't allowed to attend their meetings."

"Where did their meetings take place?" Romero was quick to ask.

Sonia shrugged. "Hardly the same place twice. After they got word of the Oracle watching on the island, the meetings at our bar stopped. I assume they went underground. Jasper's clothes were always covered in dirt when he returned home. I suspect they were upriver by the way he talked," she said.

"Who's the Oracle?" I asked.

The two of them looked at me with disbelief.

"What do you mean, 'who's the Oracle?' She's the Lady of Jarbah, the Blue Lotus queen, the Belle of Aerogapolis Bay. Any of this ringing a bell?" Sonia looked incredulous.

I shook my head and began to speak when Romero put his hand on my shoulder.

"You will have to excuse her. Farm girl didn't get out much."

I glared at him.

"Remember the temple from when you arrived in Aerogapolis?" asked Romero.

I pulled his hand away. "That's her? You're telling me she's real?"

"Of course she's real!" Sonia snapped.

Romero continued, "Sinopa, the Oracle is one of the most powerful and respected figures in the known world. She holds control over myst like to no mortal ever has, and she rules the waters of Jarbah."

"People say her sight goes beyond water and moonstone," said Sonia.

"If she's so powerful, why doesn't she do something about this? Surely, she's seen the sorcerers, right?"

Sonia's voice broke, "She has. Several times, actually."

I took a step back and remembered the wall, and the rows of heads hanging over the bar, Jumbo especially. No doubt Sonia did, too. Now she murmured to herself. She walked over to the bed, taking a moment to compose herself. She had said before that they were a monument to her failures.

Romero took me aside while Sonia fixed her makeup. He spoke quietly to drive the point home. "The gist is you best not speak lightly of her. She also holds religious authority. You may upset someone."

. . .

BEFORE I COULD APOLOGIZE, there was a knock on the door. Romero drew a flintlock at one side of the door while I checked the peephole. A short, wispy brunette stood outside with a bottle of champagne, a deck of cards, and a plate of fancy hors d'oeuvres and cheeses.

"It's Abigale," I called back.

Sonia sniffled, "What does she want?"

I winced. "I maybe, kind of, invited her to play poker or something?"

"What? Why?"

"Well, she seemed lonely. And everyone here mistreats her, so—"

"Do away with her," Romero barked.

"I'm not killing anyone else," I shot.

Romero facepalmed. "I meant, get rid of her."

Abigale knocked again. "Kiera? Are you in there?"

I wasn't sure what to say, but anything was better than the undressing excuse. I couldn't just ignore her.

"Kiera? I was hoping we could . . ." Abigale paused. Then, she faintly breathed, "Never mind."

I opened the door and called after her. Romero cursed me from behind the door. I pulled her inside and Romero locked the door. Abigale dropped the tray onto the floor at the sight of the creature. Romero caught her as she began to faint, and we set her down on the bed. The little angel lay fast asleep beside Sonia, who dried her eyes.

"Now what?" I asked.

Romero sat down and lit his pipe to think. "Well, we have a few options. We have a small chance of stealing a boat, but I'm not particularly fond of shackles."

"And we need to wait for Rudolph. If anyone can help us, it's him. He has influence and an army at his side," I said.

Romero blew a long puff. "Forget-me-Nots come to mind." He pulled a few small, crystal blue spheres from his coat pocket. Small metal legs extended at his fingertips.

"Don't. She doesn't deserve it," Sonia said calmly.

"You have a better idea?" he asked.

"No, but I've seen what this can do."

He looked at me, and I nodded in agreement with Sonia. Romero sighed and tucked the blue spiders away in his cloak.

What other trinkets did he have? The man was starting to scare me.

"Well, there is always a ruse for every situation." Romero huddled us together and told us the plan.

Thus, I began my descent into even more darkness.

CHAPTER SIX

The next morning, Abigale awoke at the base hospital, not Sonia's bedroom, as planned (thanks to Romero's pills). Piles of roses, cards, and chocolates sat by her bed. She was hailed as the hero who stopped the planned assassination of the master, magistrate, and the consul.

How we pulled it off is a feat Romero is truly proud of. First, Sonia gussied herself up and fetched her 'lover boy' to the scene. Guards questioned Romero and me to confirm our alibis and the heroic tale of how the simple secretary had saved us all.

I'm not allowed to disclose all my tricks of the trade, as Romero would put it. A girl has got to have some secrets. It keeps things interesting. I will say what Romero told me, though. He said that people will listen to what they want to hear. If I could work with that, I'd have them in the palm of my hand. Translation: learn their desires and exploit them.

Naturally, being Little Goody Two-Shoes, this didn't sit well with me, but I tried my best. I played up the guard's fear. His fear of being upstaged by a secretary helped keep his mouth shut, not to mention merited Abigale the respect she deserved. At the very least, I was glad to have used these lies and powers for some good.

The only problem was that Abigale knew the truth. We would have to convince her to keep her mouth shut. That was Romero's role; one he proudly kept tight lips on, I might add.

Last, that left me. I now had to commit to my role as the master's bride-to-be. They sent me to his chambers with my things.

Armed guards stood outside my door in full salute. I was unsure whether to return it. My hand slowly shook to my brow. The guards smiled and let me inside.

The room appeared three times the size of the room I'd occupied. A grand piano stood near one wall. Marble tile lined half the room, cherry hardwood lined the other. A vanity sat by the door with a small brush and the four dozen plum tarts packed beside it. I stuffed my face ravenously with two at a time. Crumbs and cinnamon sprinkles littered my dress.

I searched the walk-in closet for a robe. Inside stood a spare suit of his armor, freshly polished. He was so tall. I felt minuscule beside it. I found a red robe monogrammed "RC." Until this point, I hadn't heard his surname. I lit a small lantern and explored his chambers.

The window allowed in a cool ocean breeze on a stuffy night. The room opened onto a balcony. The moon rose once more, breathing out over the empty sea. Its reflection rippled through the rough waves, shimmering and distorted.

I wished someone were here to witness this. I engaged in the usual teenage fantasies about Rudolph: how romantic the moon had been to spend with him, the firmness of his touch, the gentleness of his voice. All that fake, corny crap.

Hanging above the wall, a row of portraits displayed the previous masters before him. I followed them over one by one. A few names repeated, like a dynasty. Cottontail was one of them. I laughed to myself at how ridiculous it was.

I scanned over the Cottontails. The first one was a changeling! Cornelius Cottontail the First was a changeling. I followed it on down the line, coming to one I recognized, "Rudolphus Valour Cottontail II." Rudolph was a changeling, too! Or at least he descended from one.

Oh, happy day! There is hope. There is a chance he could fall for me.

My heart leaped. I twirled and danced, in love—infatuation really—with the idea. I brushed my hair and cleaned myself up in front of the mirror. He should be here by noon tomorrow.

Royal purple satin sheets lined the bed. They smelled just like him, lye soap and baby powder masked with cool, brisk hints of cologne. My tail wriggled and flicked at the thought of him. I guess that's kind of creepy, looking back now.

I lay back, sighing at the canopy above the bed. Tomorrow I would see my beloved, and he would see me. We'd save Cheryl and the others and live happily ever after. I could hardly sleep at the thought of it.

Come morning, everyone awoke rested and renewed. Everyone except Sonia, that is. I think a spat erupted between her and Tom, AKA lover boy. Long story short, she kicked him out late that night. Didn't surprise me, with his track record.

That morning, I impatiently paced the lobby hoping Rudolph would arrive. I volunteered to take Abigale's duties while Romero "worked his magic." I thought he hated magic.

A courier rushed to the desk, searching for Abigale with urgent news for the captain. I sprang into action. I grabbed the letter and vowed to hand it to her. After the messenger had left, my claws shredded it open. Bits of paper fell like joyous snowflakes.

It read:

To Grand Protector Heimer,

Requesting immediate reinforcements to the ivory front tunnels.

URGENT- Consul Beah's party, as of late, has not returned from excavation examination. Natives are growing increasingly hostile and uncooperative. Consul remains safe in the care of Magistrate Beauregard.

Requesting a search party and funeral arrangements for Master Rudolph Cottontail's unit, and additional security team for upcoming festivities underground, further negotiations of said research cargo . . .

Judge Cobarde

My heart sank. Dreams faded, and my tail slumped to the floor. He wasn't coming. Our only hope was crushed, and my soul with it. He was likely dead, meaning Cheryl and all those poor sorcerers would be, too. I fought back tears, rubbing the parchment between my fingers.

Footsteps approached. I tucked the letter away. Sonia came in, rubbing her eyes and yawning. She told me about her night and all the details about how "men are jerks," and "don't let your guard down," and "they'll only leave you broken." The last one was beginning to feel true.

We fetched Romero to tell him the bad news. Whatever "spell" he had cast over Abigale must have worked. Her cheeks were rosy and her smile bright, behind the desk once more. Romero informed us he'd gotten us a ride back to shore. When asked how, he replied with, "A gentleman never tells."

I loathed his teachings. His lessons transformed me into something manipulative and controlling. I bent people to my whim and it made me powerful, invigorated. My wit grew quickly, knowing what made people tick.

I was a goddess, yet I couldn't help but feel dirty. Puppeteering with people's heartstrings—it felt just wrong. People's fears, goals, emotions, and desires are not to be played with. I was as bad as Pater.

Yet Romero did it all the time. Romero did it right in front of us. He sweet-talked Abigale to gain the information he wanted, and all the while swiped the papers right out from beneath her blue eyes and button nose.

He borrowed Rudolph's armor to fit in as an escort to the shore. Sonia was "given"—forged really—new papers claiming to be my handmaiden, much to her scowling chagrin. Can't say I blamed her.

We forged a second set to further prove my boast as engaged Lady Cottontail, now that I knew his elusive last name. I wondered why he didn't use it as much. Most people referred to him only as Master Rudolph, not Master Cottontail. Strange. Oh well.

We spent one last night at the fortress before departing in the morning. Despite what Sonia had said before, she begrudgingly taught me to read the first few pages of my book. I picked up on about half the words. She told me I wasn't as bad a reader as I thought, whatever that meant.

On board, Romero gathered our heads together for a meeting on the ship.

"Now what?" Sonia groaned.

"Unhappy to see me?"

Sonia was quick to affirm it.

"I'll be brief," he began.

Yeah, right.

"Let's go over the plan again," said Romero.

"Why? We got this," Sonia moaned. "You're treating us like we're children."

"I don't want any slip-ups this time."

My eyes darted away because I knew he was referring to me.

He cleared his throat and continued, "An entrance to the ivory caverns opens in the city's square, but security is tight, so—"

Sonia yawned, "Get on with it, gramps. Why should I care? I'm splitting ways once we reach the shore anyway."

"You are?" I cried.

I felt I had just lost another friend. First Rudolph, Cheryl seemed good as dead, and now Sonia was leaving me, too. Could it get any worse? Wait. Don't answer that.

"Sonia, please say you'll stay a while. We could use your help."

"Hate to say it, puddin', but there doesn't seem to be much we can do here. The sorcerers have no hope now. We have no one who will believe us, and no one with the power to do anything about it."

"But where will you go?"

"Beats me," she said. "Home, I guess. Anywhere is better than here. Too many things I'd like to forget."

I looked down at the floor. All I could manage to say was a small "oh." I told her she was more than welcome to stay with us, and Romero rolled his eyes.

To tell the truth, I zoned out most of Romero's lecture after that. It was something about the tunnels, and why and how we were going there; it didn't make sense to me.

I had just begun to like Sonia, since I'd been getting to know her better, and here she was ready to ditch us. How was I supposed to learn how to read now?

The waves chopped beneath us. At least my stomach didn't feel too bad this time around.

"Just one more thing before we make landfall," said Romero. "Our goal in this is stealth. The less we draw attention, the better. Questions?"

I raised my hand.

"Yes, Kiera?"

It bugged me that he still called me that name. "Yes, you lost me. Could you repeat the plan again? From the top?"

Romero groaned.

As he repeated himself, Sonia left, presumably for some fresh air. More likely so she wouldn't be bored to tears. The plan still made little sense, as he hadn't dumbed down any of his wording and phrases at all. He might as well have been teaching me quantum physics.

Upon telling him again that I still didn't get it, he gave up.

We reached the port by noon. The city was just as we had left it. Aerogapolis loomed in the shadow of the midday sun. Bustling busybodies rushed past us to greet the fishing boats and haul the packed crates ashore.

Two guards, both changelings in form, inspected the boats. Luckily, we had not done anything to arouse suspicion. Romero, sadly, abandoned the armor. He looked fetching, if I do say so myself, but it turned too many heads.

I forgot how colorful everything was outside the islands' green and gray. Clear azure breakers crashed onto the beaches. Redbuds, cardinals, and violet crocuses climbed the cliffside. Yellow paper bulletins hung from poles—advertisements mostly, but two in particular, caught my eye.

One was my wanted poster. There was another beside mine of a young woman with blonde curls. She appeared to be quite built in the jaw and shoulders. Two giant white wings rose behind her.

In bold it read:

WANTED!
Sonia Pidgeona Strignolli Scales for murder. Picture as shown.

*Last seen fleeing with another female,
a scaled changeling 4'2", 120 pounds.
Reward for tips leading to an arrest.*

I pulled Sonia by the arm to show her.

"I'm . . . a felon?" she cried.

Romero loomed over us from behind.

"Should have seen that coming. You put him down. I guess what they say about wives 'out to get their husbands' is true. Who knew you had it in you, though?"

"What are you talking about? I didn't kill him," she said.

Romero turned to me with a smile.

I looked away.

"Now, that . . . that's a surprise," he said. "My little baby bird is all grown up."

"Please stop," I mumbled.

He ignored me.

"How'd you do it? Felt good, didn't it? You gave him what he deserved."

"He deserved it, but—"

"Easy. Not so loud," said Sonia. Her head swiveled to see if anyone was watching. "Not so loud out in the open."

"So now what?" I asked.

"Right. It's your first time. You've got to lay low. I know a place. I'll take Sonia to Hazel's. Lay low, lose the heat there. I have a plan; I'll be back shortly."

With that, Romero darted off, tugging Sonia by the arm.

"Wait! What am I supposed to do while you're gone?" I cried.

Romero called back, "Nothing stupid!"

"Stay safe," Sonia called out.

They drifted away before my very eyes. I was alone now. My claws and I read the wanted poster again. There was no way I was that fat and that short! I crumpled it up and tucked it away.

We were felons. Great. Just what I needed: police and criminals alike were after me all over again. *Just when you think it couldn't get any worse.*

I sat down on a bench to wait.

Poor Sonia. She's now caught up in all this. I hated to see her go, but now she didn't have the luxury to leave. At least we could be felons together.

CHAPTER SEVEN

I did as Romero had taught me. My hood was up and my head was down. There was no need to arouse suspicion. *Hurry up, you guys.*

My stomach growled. I rifled through my bag of plum tarts and began to eat them, one by one. It's hard to be on the lam with an empty stomach.

At least an hour went by and I grew increasingly bored by the minute. Several words of the levitation book tripped me up, so I put it away. Now wasn't the time, anyway.

Eventually, I decided to go for a walk. Humes and changelings laughed and visited. A jovialness unmatched by Aerogapolis breathed here. In hindsight, the poor souls didn't know the horrors beneath their feet.

The occasional guard gave me a nod or passing glance, but I just kept walking. I made my way over to the Cornerstone arch when I noticed something. The whole time, a clanging sound had been following me. I felt eyes burning through the back of my skull. I was being followed. I tugged my hood up further.

I kept my head down and continued walking. I bobbed in and out of crowds, hoping to blend into the chaos. The clanging raced closer.

"Halt! Stop where you are!"

Crap!

"Hands where I can see them."

I complied. My hands slowly raised on their own accord.

Romero is going to kill me. I must think fast.

The clanking came closer. As it came near my shoulder I turned and raised my knee. With a warrior cry, I struck whoever had risen against me. A blood curdling dog yelp rang out, and a guard was on his knees.

It was the dog changeling from before. His face fluffed in a dark chocolatey fur, with mismatched eyes.

"Oh my gosh, I'm so, so sorry."

The dog held his groin and rocked with his tail between his legs. I had hit him just beneath his breastplate below the waist, the one place he didn't have armor, oddly enough.

He wheezed, "What was that? I was just going to say hi."

People stared at the scene playing out here on the pier.

"I'm sorry. Are you all right?" I asked.

He whimpered with a nod. I dropped to his level and handed him his helmet that was lying dented on the ground, just as dented as his breastplate. He placed it on top of his head, lopsided. The visor strap flapped open and shut. No wonder he'd made so much noise.

"Mike, right?"

He shook his head and the helmet nearly fell off. "Max, but you can call me Mike if you want."

I caught the helmet again before it hit the ground. The metal was cold. Max. I knew that name—but from where?

Memories trickled back. I remembered the hardness of a chair and the pressing of icy metal on my skin. This dog stood on his knees, begging someone to choose him instead.

My head pounded.

"You were that boy. From before . . . at the guardhouse . . ."

His ears perked up. "What guardhouse?"

"You don't remember?"

He shook his head and pointed to the bandages wrapping the left side of his noggin and said, "I woke up in the police academy's hospital. Beyond my dog tags, I don't remember much

Max had taken on a fate worse than death, in my place. He would never be the same man I first met.

48

Amnesia is a terrible ailment. Sometimes memories come back over time, and others not at all. It's not like in stories where you can get bonked on the noggin again and recall everything. Life doesn't work that way. If I were to stab you twice, the cut wouldn't magically heal itself because the knife sliced the same spot.

"You rescued me," I explained.

"Rescued?"

"You were a hero."

His eyes widened and ears perked. "I was?"

His tail wagged up a storm.

Hmm, I could work with this.

"I don't remember any of this. What else do you know about me?" he asked.

"I suppose I could tell you, but where's the fun in that? Let's go for a walk."

"Walk? I love walks."

I smiled. *What dog doesn't?*

"Come on, I'll show you around. Fill you in."

I took his arm. His ears tucked back. His padded hands (I called them paws) pressed soft and sweaty. *Still bashful, I see.*

But this Max was different. He was less reserved. This new Max had a few screws loose. He was dumbed down they'd turned him stupid. His mind acted on instinct and spontaneity, with little thought behind his actions. I guess you could say that's what made him fun, though.

We walked along the pier together. I had the perfect cover, as before. The wooden beams became white sands. The waves crashed into the beach, and seagulls screeched overhead. I took a spot in the sand, taking a load off.

Max nestled beside me. This other side of him was almost cute, even if he was a bit clingy. Once I was certain we were alone, I explained what I knew.

"I really did all that?" he asked in amazement.

I nodded.

"Wow! Wait, but that can't be right. Cobarde's a judge. He's a good man. The chief says so, and the judge even checked on me in the hospital."

"He probably planned to do you in."

Max frowned. "Kiera, that's terrible. He'd never do that."

"My memory's foggy, too, but I know what I saw. Here." I pulled out my forget-me-knot. "He used one of these on me, and probably one on you as well. If we can just find yours, maybe we can get your memory back."

He took it and held it up to the light. The sun refracted off the blue glass.

"There has to be an explanation for this. Maybe next time I see him I'll ask."

"I wouldn't."

Max's ears perked in curiosity. "How come?"

"Just be careful. Don't trust him."

Max's stomach growled.

I smiled and offered him a plum tart. He scarfed it down and licked his lips when finished. I gave him another, and he stood upright.

"So, how'd it go with Jasper?" asked Max. "He's quite the figure around here."

I forgot we told him that. Gotta change the subject. Quick.

"Good. You sure you're okay?" I asked, referring to the bandages wrapping his head.

He nodded and scratched the back of his head.

"The doctors said I hardly need them. I can take them off this afternoon. So, uh," he tucked his arms behind his back, "you in Jarbah long?"

"For a little while, yes. Why?"

"Well, I was wondering, since you are still in town for a while and you're the only girl I've met, and if you're free to, um . . ."

"Go on," I encouraged.

He pulled two tickets from his pants pocket for the guardsmen's gala.

"The army is holding a small banquet and a private tour of the Temple Forty-Two. If you're not busy, I'd be more than happy for you to go with me."

I smirked. "So, what, like a date?"

Max fumbled for a moment. "Well, not unless you want it to be. You could see Cobarde for yourself."

He panted and turned his head expectantly.

This could be the perfect way into the tunnels. But an entire room full of police? I might as well have been wearing an "arrest me" sign.

Max came on a bit too strong for my liking. Not in a bad or creepy way (like Jasper). It was more like an innocent kid who didn't know any better. Kinda cute, actually. Even so, a bit weird.

One of his ears cocked sideways all the time. At first, I thought it was just a nervous twitch, but that's just how it naturally sat. His eyes blinked, mismatched cerulean and copper. He stared at me with a goofy grin that I couldn't help but laugh at.

"I'd love to," I said. "Could I bring some friends? Maybe we could make it a double date."

Max barked, wagging his tail. "Sounds great! I can pick you up at six."

I gave him Hazel's address, and he went on his way. Max raised one last howl in delight with a skip, clicking his heels together. I smiled, waving goodbye.

I turned to see Romero behind me who had been watching the whole thing.

"Having fun?" he asked.

"How much did you hear?"

"Only all of it. Well played. I taught you well. Come, we have much to discuss."

What am I doing? I don't like Max. Do I?

"I don't feel right about this. This is playing with people's emotions."

"What's the alternative? You said it yourself before, goodie-two-shoes; people's lives are in jeopardy."

"I guess you're right," I replied.

"I know I am. Come, we continue your training. Let's knock him dead."

"Metaphorically, I hope."

"Jasper, right. My apologies." He put his hand on my shoulder, leading me through the cornerstone arch. "It gets easier, trust me. Now, about that training."

&

YOU CAN IMAGINE how thrilled Sonia was that I volunteered her for this.

"What do you mean, you got me a date? I was gone for thirty minutes!" she roared.

"I promised you, remember? You'd help me read, and I'd help you get back on the horse. Now shut up and pick out something to wear."

Romero brought my trunk from the Sirius, and Hazel loaned us her pearls.

My only qualm about getting all gussied up was that I couldn't bring my sword. What good was having a saber without being able to use it? And the heels—I wasn't going anywhere in them ever again. If I didn't hear an earful once from 'fashion police officer Sonia', I heard it three times. I can still hear her now.

"This is a gala, Kiera, not a hiking trip. Ditch them rags. Wear something nice."

If this turned south, and I expected it to, I wasn't running for my life in heels again.

I brushed my hair and turned to Romero. "What about you?"

"Don't worry about me. It's you two who need all the help you can get."

"Gee thanks," said Sonia.

Sonia stood in the doorway. Her dress glimmered a dazzling sequence of the colors of fluffy clouds. The top opened in a V around the neck, and in the back as well to accommodate her wings. Her golden hair curled down in ribbons. Sadly, nothing could ever cover those scars on her back and bare arms.

"How do I look?" she asked.

Romero turned around. "Well, you clean up nice," he said.

"Who asked you?" she sneered.

"Calm down. I was only teasing. You look absolutely stunning."

"Why, thank you, Romero. It means a lot coming from you. So you *can* say something nice."

He brushed her off. "Don't get used to it. You're missing something."

"Oh, whatever. Get out of here. I need to help Sinopa get ready."

"Good luck with that one," he said.

"Hey! What's that's supposed to—" The door slammed behind him.

I had half a mind to storm out of there, half-dressed and knock some sense into him. I'm sounding like Sonia now. Scary.

I hate to admit it, but he was right. Sonia looked like a doll as she was, so it wasn't hard to make her look angelic and enchanting. I was another story. I looked like the experiment of a bored taxidermist in drag.

First, there was my skin. Crusty brick scales look good on no one. No lipstick would match my skin color. Blush was out of the question.

As Sonia was the "expert" on such matters, she wasn't as discouraged. In fact, she fancied the challenge. Here was the most unattractive specimen, a beast really, in her grasp, and she had to make it shine.

Romero made wisecracks from outside the door about how it always took women so long to get ready. Sonia stuck her tongue out at the door and returned to work on my dirty rat's nest that I knew as my hair. I wished I had hair like hers—clean, shiny and alluring—but mine kinked around my horns in muddy red knots.

We exchanged as she removed the rats. Words best not repeated. She told me to soak my hair while she fetched something from Hazel. *This had better be worth all the manhandling of my scalp.*

She returned with a second brush, and my blood boiled. I resisted the urge to claw her eyes out, as I was anxious to leave. I snuck some nibbles at a plum tart when she wasn't looking.

After much more waiting than I could bear, she turned me around in front of a mirror.

"Voila!"

I hardly recognized the girl who stood before me.

"Do you love it?" Sonia squealed.

I didn't know what to say. I was speechless. My hair sat up neatly, away from my horns, with two curls poking at my cheeks on both sides. I wore a lavender satin dress, with a long twirly skirt and white frills, resting below my knees. My "goods," as she called them, sat tucked away behind white lace and red ribbons. Sonia tied two white bows around my waist and placed a cerulean blue bow in my hair, flashing attention to my eyes. It was to "bust out my big guns, both barrels," as she put it.

"Say something!" she cried.

"I love it."

I was beautiful. Hazel and Romero were waiting downstairs.

Hazel and Sonia seemed to hit it off and talked mostly about clothes. I saw a familiar face out the corner of my eye. Young Simon sat on a stool, slowly nursing a nearly melted sundae. I snuck up and tapped his left shoulder, then jumped to his right side, teasingly.

He spun, confused, and returned to his ice cream. I tapped him again and smiled.

His eyes lit up. I sat beside him, and we talked for a while.

"Still no sign of momma," he said.

I remained silent and glossed over the topic, and I did not ask about Sophia. The look in his eyes said enough. We talked about magic. He was more than happy to show me what he knew. Believe it or not, he wasn't a half-bad teacher. Very patient.

Levitation, he explained, was one of the easiest and most delicate balancing acts of magic to perfect. He then boasted in his expertise and showed off, juggling the ball bearings. It was nice to see a smile on his face.

As far as I knew, his entire family was as good as dead, both Cheryl and Sophia. I promised myself that if no one else would look out for him, I would.

Six o'clock came and a carriage, of all things, stopped in front of the inn. It was fancy, I had to admit. Max stepped out and opened the door. His dented breastplate was now polished, and worn over a black suit and bowtie.

At the sight of me, he stopped dead. Sonia entered, and Max still stared.

"Something wrong?" I asked.

He swallowed and tugged at his tie. "N—no, not at all."

"Well, let's go, then."

He cleared his throat and grabbed my hand, helping me into the carriage. His paws were soft and sweaty. With that, we were off. Dressed to kill again. This time, hopefully, only metaphorically so.

CHAPTER EIGHT

I swear, one of the hardest things about travel is making it interesting. No wonder everyone glosses over it in books.

Our trip was one of the most awkward experiences I have ever had. Sonia sat stiff as stone next to her date, avoiding conversation as best she could. I recognized him as the Kingsman from the night watch.

It didn't help that Max kept giving me passing stares. I suggested we open the window. Maybe some fresh air would lighten things up a bit. That was one way to put it.

Feeling the breeze, Max shifted in his seat. In under a minute, he hung his head out the carriage, howling for the entire city to hear. "Boy, guys, this is great! Don't you just love the wind in your hair! *Aaaaaooooohoo!*"

The three of us stared at each other in disbelief.

Max began shouting at people on the street, "Oh my gosh, we're in a carriage! Hey, you over there! Yes, you. I'm in a carriage. Don't you wish you were in a carriage? *Ow—ow—aaaaooooohoo!*"

My face turned pink.

Sonia patted me on the knee. "You sure know how to pick them," she teased.

The Kingsman laughed.

I pulled Max from the window and shut it tight.

"What's the matter? Did you want a turn? By all means, you have a go," Max said, panting. His tail wagged a mile a minute. His fur looked like he had been through a windstorm.

"And mess up my hair like you?" I teased.

I licked my thumb and wiped bug bits from his face.

"You've always looked fine to me," he mumbled.

I smiled and pulled a small brush from my bag. Max sniffed.

"Did you bring more plum tarts?" he asked, leaning over the bag.

"As a matter of fact, I did."

Sonia laughed. "Why'd you bring food to a banquet? Isn't that against the point?"

Max huffed next to my purse. "I say she's got good taste," he said.

"Thank you."

I began rifling through my bag for the tarts, and Max practically drooled. Sonia kicked my foot.

"Ow!"

"Sino—I mean Kiera, a word, if you'd be so kind?"

She pulled me close, with her hand cupped over her mouth in a whisper. Max stared, tilting his head and perking his ears. Her date didn't seem to care at this point.

"What are you doing? Don't feed him."

"Why not?"

"It's just weird. You're encouraging him. Why are you making this more awkward?"

"You're the one whispering when he's three feet away."

"Relax, he can't hear me. You're just making this harder on us."

"Oh, quit being such a drama queen."

"Hear me out. You feed him, he'll get attached, and do you really want that thing following us around?"

At this point Max spoke up, "I can hear everything you're saying."

Sonia turned scarlet.

"Can I have a plum tart or not?"

I picked up the small sack. My fingers plucked one out and handed it to him. "Maybe I want him to," I retorted back, without blinking.

Behind my back, Max gingerly grabbed the pastry with his snout, not his hands. He quickly chewed and swallowed it down without even savoring it.

I brushed away a few crumbs from his whiskers and cheeks with one hand. His tongue then found its way to my fingers. I bit down on my own, so as not to scream.

Sonia nodded with a look of, "I told you so."

Worst carriage ride ever. I can only think of one worse, but that's a story for another time.

We soon came to a stop in front of the gate to the tunnels. Patrols inspected the carriages at the front. When they came to our caravan of dignitaries, if you could call us that, they waved us on. It was a good thing, too, as you shall soon see.

As we entered the tunnel, the carriage got dark. The light drifted further and further away. Then, as the gates shut, darkness. The Kingsman lit a lantern, and the cabin dimly glowed.

Once lit, I could see Max eyeing the window again. His paw slowly reached out to open it, and I smacked his thigh. Lightly, of course. I'm not a monster, remember. He looked at me and I told him to sit—and he sat. Again, I've always loved dogs.

Out the window, sconces sporadically lit the halls for our arrival. The entire tunnel flickered like a poor man's runway. The air sunk ten degrees cooler. Our cabin jostled up and down on the bumps as we descended deeper into the cave. No longer were we coasting on the richly paved streets.

The carriage stopped. Attendants with lanterns opened the doors and led us into the tunnels. Max and I locked arms. Sonia and her date exited first, and we followed. The hallway ran forever in the dark. It would be easy to get lost. The cold air rushed around my bottom as Max's tail wagged near mine.

Eventually, the tunnel split in two. The left led to the banquet hall, and over the right hung the tourism signs of Temple 42.

Naturally, they led us to the banquet. The trickling of water echoed all around us. From stalactites hung a red welcome banner. Northstrand and Aerogapolis flags hung out front. This must be the place.

Inside, the room was packed full of men in uniform. At least half the police force gathered here. A large buffet spread across a table on one side of the room. Candle lamps stood at four corners of a large open dance floor.

ANTONIO ROBERTS

Beyond it, a large stage rose from the floor with seats for those of nobility. Names marked each seat. Master Rudolph's was empty.

I imagine this is what school dances were like. Angela finished school. I quit early to help our old lady run the bar in Nantucket. She never forced me to; I just hated being in a place where I was regarded as an idiot and a freak.

Strangers jovially beckoned to talk with Max. He quickly became the life of the party to most of the Aerogapolian cloth. Northstrand men in armor were everywhere.

As her date left to fetch us drinks, Sonia began eyeing the exit. I yanked her arm. "Oh no you don't. You are staying right here."

"Oh, come on, Sinopa. This place is crawling with guards."

"You're not leaving me here with him. Besides, this could be a perfect opportunity for you to shine. Get back on the horse, you know? Get out there. Dance. Flirt. Mingle."

"I'll mingle all right. I'll be mingling myself into a jail cell," she said, tearing her arm away.

Just then, her date returned with drinks. Sonia politely sipped hers before someone clinked a glass for attention.

A large, bloated tick of a man waddled to center stage.

"Brave soldiers of Northstrand and honored guests of the Aerogapolian and Jarbah police, I, as the lord Consul of Northstrand, express my most sincere gratitude."

Small applause rose, and he hushed it before he continued. "I'm honored to announce and introduce my beloved compatriots: Judge Cobarde Estaban, of whom I am sure you all are aware . . ."

Cobarde came out, raising a call for more applause and was met with a few sparse claps.

"Protector Heimer, chief of the Star Shell fortress . . ."

Salutes and glares mixed among the crowd as he entered.

"And last but not least, Magistrate Beauregard, the arbiter of nations presiding over this fateful union of diplomacy."

A tall man walked across the stage to his seat. There were neither salutes nor applause as he entered. His face stretched long and clean-shaven. His eyes burned like fire. In the front, his buzzed hair stood at attention and was braided down his back. I locked eyes with him for a moment as he sat down.

I have seen this man before somewhere. But where?

The consul drew me out of my thoughts with the announcement, "I regret to inform you that Master Rudolph could not attend tonight's meeting. Magistrate Beauregard has volunteered to assist me on the rest of my visit to your lovely city."

Like hell, he couldn't! What'd you do to him, you fat toad?

The rest of his address had an air of dignity and judgment as he stared down his nose at us. The panel's food came first and was tested for safety. Once it was all clear, a line formed around the buffet, and they set a table. Max grabbed my arm and raced so we could be first in line. It was hard for him not to be excited at the mention of food after listening to that windbag.

As we got a place close to the front of the line, a lumbering tank of a man stood behind us, clearing his throat. "Hey, mutt! Back of the line! Your kind's served last."

Max looked at him, confused. "I think you don't understand, sir. I'm Max. I'm a bastion of the Aerogapolian police."

"Listen, I don't give a fine frick who you are. Get out of my spot."

I grabbed Max's arm and pulled, trying my best to persuade him to leave quietly. Max continued in his ignorance. The goliath got increasingly more frustrated. He shoved Max into the table. Max stood to his feet and growled. If it hadn't been for a voice calling from the back of the line, he'd have been a pancake.

His chief at the back of the line called for him. I pulled at his arms, leading him away from a fight. His hair bristled underneath his suit, prickling my fingers.

His chief was an elderly, dark-skinned man. His suit was well decorated with medals and badges under a black leather breastplate.

He explained to us how changelings weren't exactly accepted, even here. He seemed used to explaining this to Max and surprised at having to explain it to me.

"And what are you doing here?" he roared at Max.

"Coming to the banquet like the rest of the guards on duty, Master sir."

"I specifically told you not to come. How did you even get the tickets?"

"I bought them off the pier, and for a bargain, too. It only cost me two hundred silver each. Now I can be here with you like a good watch guard."

Max's tail wagged. His eyes glowed and his tongue lolled sideways as he panted.

"No, Max, that's a bad dog."

"What?" His voice broke in a whimper.

"I said, that's a bad dog, Max. A very bad dog."

Max's lips blubbered to object, but he walked away. His head hung in shame; his tail sagged.

"Why did you tell him not to come?" I asked.

The chief placed his hand on my shoulder.

"Look at him."

Max's ears perked at a distance. Then they tucked back, and his eyes blinked, staring at us longingly.

"The man's a total wreck. The dunce can never do anything right. For the few days he's been in my care, he's been an absolute nuisance. If someone like the Magistrate, Consul, or even the Judge sees him, I'm ruined. I'll tell you what. You seem like a nice girl. Here's two silver. Get rid of him, will you?"

I turned over my shoulder to look back at Max. Tears welled in his eyes. The chief didn't even try to hide his words. Max heard everything, even from a vast distance across the room.

"Keep your money. We're leaving."

I grabbed Max by the hand and led him out the door. *Who needed this stuffy gala, anyway? Look what it made me do—it got me in a dress and ribbons.*

Nothing good could come from that. Dress-up was for children. My friend's feelings were more important than the chief's image.

CHAPTER NINE

D roplets trickled down from the ceiling. The air ran thick and frigid as if it saturated the entire cavern in moist, misty drizzle.

My feet chafed. I took off my boots, and my toes immediately sank in the drenched sandy floor. Max took off his bowtie and cast it into a puddle.

I asked him if he was okay and he remained silent. "We can go back, you know. We don't have to listen to him."

He wiped his nose and sniffled. "No, that would be a bad dog thing to do."

I squeezed his hand. "You're not a bad dog to me."

"Thanks. I want to be part of the force. If I'm not part of them, who am I? I joined to help people . . . I think."

"You don't have to be a guard to help people."

"But that's not it. There must have been some reason I joined. I can't remember."

I shook my head. "They're the reason you can't remember. Why would you want to be like them?"

"But that's just it, Kiera—I don't believe you. A true man of law would never do that."

"Well, then, he's no true man of the law, is he?"

Max growled and whimpered as if he would cry again.

"Look, Max, if you want to be a lawman, that's fine. You are the best one you can be. Be better than him, and don't let those jerks stand in your way. Just be careful. Bad company corrupts good character, and I'd hate to see you end up like him."

Max wiped his eyes. "Be better than him?"

"Exactly."

"You really think I can?"

"Positive. Come on, let's get some fresh air and have some fun. This is a gala, remember?"

Max nodded.

"We still have those tickets to the temple if you want to go," he suggested, "or do you want me to leave, too?"

I grabbed him by the crook of the arm. "Of course not. Lead the way."

I knew I was supposed to be using him and all, but it was hard not to feel for the guy. He tried. No matter what, he also failed. Worse yet, I knew exactly how he felt, having been tossed aside like that from my tribe. He wasn't much to look at, or smell for that matter, but I don't know . . . Max was sweet.

"Sure you're not hungry?" I asked.

His stomach growled. "Maybe just a little. You still have them plum tarts?"

We sat down by a pool and ate. It was nice that someone else could appreciate good food when they found it. Heaven knows Romero wouldn't even try them. Sonia saw my tastes as childish.

"You know, Kiera," Max began.

I never corrected him about my name.

"Your friend was partially right. In dog culture, when people break bread together it's a sign of unity. It's like family. We're packmates now, like it or not."

Way to make me feel more awkward, buddy.

"What about you? You got a family?" he asked.

I shook my head. "No, not really. I have a foster sister and that's it. I never knew my parents. You?"

I was desperate to make this conversation less uncomfortable. I didn't 'like' him, or that's what I told myself, and he was digging deep.

"My memory's foggy. I never knew my parents either. I have a sister and brother, though, and a dozen or so wild pups that just about kill their uncle every time he visits. Every time, they dogpile me in one heaping clump of fur. Every single time."

I chuckled.

"They leave me exhausted."

I put the bag of tartlets away. "I think you're moving too fast. I hardly know you."

"No, we pack changelings have a nose for character," he said.

If he had a nose for character, he'd know I wasn't interested.

"Your friend was only half right, remember? It's still your choice. But you're still a friend to me."

I smiled.

Aw, it hurt so much.

"Thanks, packmate," I said, grabbing his paw.

I couldn't say no.

He led me down to the hollowed-out section of the cavern. The limestone ground ended, replaced with a solid black surface. Not cobblestone, sand, or cave floor. Some material known as asphalt or assault or something. The tour went on as you'll see.

Large lanterns, run by the same windmill power, lit the temple and its grounds. It was a temple unlike anything I had ever seen.

The grounds splintered in cracked silvery concrete beyond the blacktop. Overhead, was a roofed pavilion. Eight rectangle altars stood upright.

Immediately, a man with a long white beard rushed out to meet us. He dressed strangely. His pants were comprised of a tattered blue canvas, almost like denim material. He wore a white tank top and a gold chain, and over that, a long overcoat.

"Greetings, travelers. I'm Herodotus. I'll be your tour guide for this evening of the fantastic Temple Forty-Two of the year 2076."

"What's with your clothes?" I asked.

"You know what this is? We believe it to be what all standard men of the year wore. Isn't it grand? Now, right this way. There is so much to see."

I leaned in and whispered to Max, "No wonder they're all extinct. I'd die of embarrassment, too, looking like that."

Max snickered.

Herodotus waved us over to the altars under the pavilion. "These altars, we believe, were for many purposes, but cleansing before entering is believed to be the first use. As you can see here."

The tall platforms stood upright like a cabinet covered in soot. Beside the altar ran a rubber hose and a handle. Different offering suggestions were placed on the buttons of ancient machine.

Also etched into it were faint words like "no smoking." Herodotus was happy to explain that this was to help ensure the sanctity of the sacrifices as they were slaughtered, and how he knew the hose could also be used for bathing. The end of the hose could have very well been placed in a victim's mouth for human sacrifice to the god of Pepto-Bismol. But he was quick to stop there as he was "getting ahead of himself."

The old man squealed and ushered us over to the temple gates. "Hurry. Come."

The roof of the temple rose flat and arched like a ziggurat. A gleaming yellow and red sunburst stood high above with the number "42" written on a large metal sphere above the temple. Prices for what were assumed to be "the wash" hung below.

The few remaining windows stared back at us with warped bull's-eyes in the glass. Those in the doors had been blown out. Upon opening the door, a bell rang to celebrate our presence.

"Welcome to the Temple Forty-Two!" Herodotus shouted.

Once inside, the glossy white floor shone our reflections while rows of empty shelves stood barren and alone all around us. To our left, we saw a tall counter with a guestbook and registers on it, and stacks of small cartons behind it. This is where the ancients paid the temple tax and penance granted by the god of Pepto-Bismol. As the large idol cutout said, "It provides maximum relief for all your needs."

The cartons were believed to contain sticks of relief. A stick's white end symbolized the purity of life, long and wishful. The gold, tarnished butt represented the tarnished reality of life taken into the body. They were believed to have been smoked like the vapor pipes of today.

The sticks proved toxic and were considered a rite of passage for those eighteen or older. Pepto had granted favor only to those willing to burn away their lives, take in and breathe the ash of purity. Lung cancer seemed the price to pay for their salvation.

Along the back wall was a vat of churning cylinders with silver udders beneath them.

"Behold! The cryo-communion vats," Herodotus cried. "These cylinders' frozen liquid are known as 'radical!' by the patron polar bear. It served delectability to all followers of Pepto-Bismol."

To the right stood blue stained-glass lockers for the priestly garb and consumables. The lockers were chilled to become one with the Pepto-polar bear. Also, it helped them stay "cool." It was customary to believe that the temperature of the body held the key to prime sexual attraction. One's "coolness" aided daily social hierarchy, while a person's "hotness" repelled predators, rivals, and potential mates. They truly were a barbaric and primitive-minded society.

Feasting was also a big deal, according to Herodotus. They had three kitchens: Men, Women, and Family. Stews and soups were boiled in large porcelain cauldrons. The pure white cauldrons were handcrafted to serve as the thrones of the great purifier and exfoliator of men. All men shall be flushed bare before him.

Unlike the women's, the men's kitchens baked special cakes in open ovens, possibly for a rite of passage. After all, nothing highlights manhood like baking over a roasting flame.

Not a scrap went to waste at the temple, either. After meals were finished, the remainders were flushed to offer themselves to a higher purpose.

I had to admit it was fascinating how they could tell all this just by looking at it. It almost made me wish I had finished school and learned more about the ancients. Wouldn't Angela be jealous?

Herodotus began preaching from the remains of the sacred texts, promoting Thanksgiving before the coming apocalypse known as Black Friday. While it was interesting, it sounded more like a load of hoo-ha, if you know what I mean. When he demanded us to "repent and consume the radical nectar," I grabbed Max by the collar and we were out of there.

CHAPTER TEN

W e sat outside on the stoop, arm in arm. Max seemed to agree that it was all a load of baloney when I explained it to him. He let forth a series of high-pitched squeals and quickly put his hand to his snout. His laugh sounded like a psychotic baby. *And I'd thought his toothy smile was frightening.*

"I'm sorry," he began apologizing.

"It's okay to laugh. You just startled me, that's all," I said, thumping him on the shoulder.

He remained unphased. I guess I still punched like a girl, or at least not like Sonia.

The air blew salty. Dense myst started rising around our ankles.

Not again. Not now.

I tried my best to remain calm. Deep breaths, in and out. My eyes opened and my night vision kicked in. *Oh, well, I'll take that over migraines and blackouts.*

The walls around the cavern were piled high with rubble. This just wasn't a "temple." It had been an entire city.

I blinked and tried to let my eyes adjust. Off in the distance, two changeling men in uniform approached carrying torches and a vellum poster. Two to be precise: one highly-detailed blonde female changeling, and the other a crude, chubby female changeling with brick-colored skin that totally didn't look like me. No, I'm not projecting. Shut up!

They questioned people as they left the temple and received nothing but shrugs.

Time to bounce. I gotta scrape up Sonia and leave. Maybe we can sneak around them.

"Max, I had a great time tonight," I began.

He nodded.

"These ruins look enchanting, don't you think? Care to go on a little walk?"

His head cocked toward me. "Walk?" His tail wagged.

"Sure, why not? I can't see no harm in—"

"Oh boy, I thought you'd never ask. I knew there was something good in you. Thank you very much, Kiera. I love to walk. I walk all the time."

Max rocketed to his feet in playful bounces. I looked on in terror of what I had just gotten myself into. He glanced at me with a toothy grin and saw me cowering.

He cleared his throat. "Sorry." He straightened his back, broadened his shoulders, and held out his arm in a debonair façade. "Let us walk."

I gulped and put on my best fake smile. Over my shoulder, the torches of the bounty men approached the temple. *Getting lost with a loose cannon is better than locked in a dungeon, I guess.*

Max commented that the mounds of rubble looked like piles of cookie crumbs and the brick walls seemed to have been tossed all over like chew toys. He thought it remarkable the temple stood as well as it did.

"Wait, you can see in the dark?" I asked.

"Some dogs can, yes. It looks like flaky biscuit crust spread across the kitchen floor."

"Are you ever *not* hungry?" I said and laughed.

"Sometimes."

"Okay, name one thing that you like that doesn't remind you of food."

Max thought about it for a bit as we walked.

"See? Told you, you can't. Just like—"

"You."

"What?"

"That's my answer. You."

I curled my hand around my finger, desperate to change the subject. "Surely you don't mean that."

"I can prove it. You don't remind me of food. Your eyes are like blueberries, soft, sweet and deep blue. Yet they're wide like robin's-egg-colored teacup saucers. And what better to go with tea than your sugar plum skin and nutmeg-on-toast hair? Yet, your hide is rough and more jagged. By all means, you're more like a pineapple than a plum."

"A pineapple?"

"You know the fruit?"

I had never seen a pineapple before. His words pulled me closer to him. No one ever spoke to me that way before. Even though every metaphor was pertaining to food.

I reached up and wrapped my wrists around his collar. "Tell me more. How am I like a pineapple?"

"They went this way!" I heard a voice call.

Max yelped as I yanked him behind one of the ruined walls. The torchlight loomed closer.

We're trapped. They're going to find me. I'll be in a dungeon and possibly fed to this disgusting High Wolf like an hors d'oeuvre.

My breathing intensified.

"Everything okay, Kiera?" Max's voice ruffed in soft and burning warm R's.

I was too panicked to appreciate how cute it was that he mispronounced my name. It was terrible for me to bring Max into this. He may have been stupid, but his heart was golden.

"No, I'm not okay. Now keep quiet."

"Relax, Kiera. They're just simple bounty folk. You've got nothing to worry about. It's not like you're a pirate or anything."

I then remembered my training. Romero had shown me several ways to use "my luck charms" to save my skin. I had objected to all of them. I'm not a monster. I'm not a puppet master.

"You have nothing to worry about. I'll just go talk to them and—"

"No!" I grabbed Max by the arm.

The men's footsteps approached closer. Max stared back at me with confusion. My back was to the wall. Prison or playing with his heart.

"What's the matter?" he asked.

His head cocked. His ears tucked back. My vision saw nothing but silhouettes around him. Nothing but him. He stood at the center of my vision. My arms lassoed around his neck. He tried to speak, and I snapped his snout with one hand.

I shushed him, "Not a word."

Torchlight glowed around the corner. I stared into Max's frightened, mismatched eyes. I couldn't risk him getting hurt. Could I really do this?

My breathing soared. I took a deep lungful and went for the kill. I closed my eyes. My lips thrust into his, and what followed was one of the worst kisses of my life.

Whiskers rubbed against my cheeks. His lips were furred and flopped like rubbery chicken skin firmly over mine.

So many emotions at once: guilt, worry, compassion, disgust. His lips bristled, moist and rough. Heaven knows how anyone is supposed to kiss a man with a wet nose. And don't even get me started on dog tongue.

Ick! There are things in this world you don't want to experience. The rough, rubbing texture of a fishy dog tongue is one of them. Few things are as disgusting as they are affectionate. Who knows where it had been?

Max whined, and I stroked his ears back. I peeked my eyes open, and the men cursed in disgust and left. Just as planned.

I looked at Max. Tears welled in his eyes as he cried. My claws had burrowed bloody divots in his snout as I held his mouth closed. I immediately released it.

"I'm so, so sorry. Are you okay?"

He rubbed the cuts on his snout, looked at me, and smiled at the realization of our kiss. He let loose a wide-eyed howl.

I clamped his snout shut again. "Max, look at me. Look at me, Max. I'm going to let go now, but when I do, I need you to keep quiet, understand?"

He nodded with worried eyes. I smoothed damp blood on my palms. Not again.

"I shouldn't have done that, Max. I'm sorry."

"No need to apologize, Kiera."

"No, you don't understand. None of this is right. I'm not Kiera."

Max's head tilted again in confusion. "If you're not Kiera, who are you? Who else would you be, packmate?"

"Please don't call me that."

I slumped with my back against the wall, ready to cry.

"We're not packmates, then?" He sat beside me and pulled his arm around me.

"We are, but . . ."

His eyes glowed ghostly white in the dark. He stared expectantly. I heard footsteps coming our direction. I was ready to give up. Prison and death didn't seem so bad compared to hurting him again.

"Look, Max, you're very sweet, but maybe we are taking this too fast."

Max chuckled. "We?"

I scooted away from him. "Sorry. I'm confused right now."

"I think so. How couldn't you be, Kiera? That doesn't make much sense, packmate."

Footsteps suddenly raced around the corner. A figure appeared, heaving. It looked up at me, shining me a torch in my eyes. It was Sonia.

I stood up. She dropped the torch and hugged me. "Thank goodness you are all right! We have to go now."

I looked over my shoulder at Max, who was still very much confused.

"Just a moment," I said.

"What's the hold-up? Ditch the mutt and let's go. I took care of my man."

Max growled, stepping forward. "What do you mean, 'took care of'?" he asked.

"You mean like . . . ?" I made a slitting gesture across my neck.

"Oh, no, nothing like that," she said.

I sighed in relief.

"Look, Max, I have to go now, okay?"

"Where are you going? I don't understand, Kiera. Can I come?"

My first instinct was to say no. I didn't want to be around him anymore.

"No, Max, you have to stay here. Stay safe, okay?"

Sonia tugged at my arm to leave. Max began to follow.

"Max, stay!"

"But—"

"Stay!"

He whimpered, staring up at me with puppy eyes. Sonia and I raced off from the ruins. A somber howl echoed from the cavern walls. My head and heart ached as I agonized over Max, and everything that had just transpired.

Max, if you're out there somewhere hearing this, I want you to know that I'm sorry. I'm sorry for playing with your heart. Sadly, you would only be the first and not the last. You would become nothing more than the initial cog of a manipulative machine, readily replaced. I had now become a monster, a vampire, who sucked upon the souls of men. I made many like me.

Since then, I've been with man after man, and many men before you. Sadly, you weren't my first kiss. That was taken from me in the bonds of slavery and cheap flings, for someone's pocketbook.

But, if it's any consolation, I want you to know something. Although you weren't my first, you were the first I chose. The first I was allowed to choose, and if I could do it all again, after seeing every dead-end of my wandering heart, I'd still choose you.

I'd choose you every time. My first choice, my last choice. I'd choose you.

Max, I'm sorry. I'm so sorry, packmate.

CHAPTER ELEVEN

I would have turned back if Sonia had let go of my arm. We barreled toward a sign that read, "Restricted. Keep out." Somehow that must have meant "welcome" to us. I pulled away at the mouth of the cavern.

"We can't just leave him like that," I complained.

"He'll be safer and won't slow us down," said Sonia.

"Yeah, but . . . ," I sighed, "I feel terrible."

"Trust me, you're doing the right thing, even though it's hard. He'll move on and be a tougher man for it."

"And if he doesn't?"

"That's his problem, not ours. Come on, Romero's waiting. Let's move before those goons circle back around."

Sonia grabbed my arm and began pulling me along again.

"Romero?" I asked. "How'd he get past the gate and the guards?"

"Your fiancé's full of surprises. Ask him."

I rolled my eyes. *As if. Ew. I wish she'd stop bringing that up.*

"The smug rat likes to keep these things to himself," She continued.

We found Romero leaning in his usual stance with his back against a wall and arms crossed. "Took you long enough. I swear, it takes women forever to get ready for anything," he said to himself.

"Can it, thief," Sonia snapped.

"Ouch. Such harsh words, considering you've never actually seen me steal anything. Unless it's the hearts of those around me. Then, ha, guilty as charged sweet-cheeks. You've caught me red-handed."

"Oh, grow up," Sonia scoffed.

"So, what's the plan?" I asked, trying to break it up.

"Right, you weren't listening," Romero said. "What do we know about the labs and the drop off location of the prisoners?"

I shrugged.

"They're both upstream," Sonia said.

"Exactly. Take a look at this." Romero pulled out a letter of transport for a military port at the base of the canyon, receiving redacted shipments. "The government's hiding something, and I think we're about to find out what."

"Then what are we waiting for? Let's go," I said.

Romero smiled. "Where's the hesitant farm girl I once knew?"

We walked to the end and found a shaft with a wooden lift, painted green. A series of ropes and pulleys, and believe it or not, a myst turbine, held it in place.

Romero stopped us from going forward. "Careful, this is an ancient machine, a Machina, according to Northstrand. It must have been commandeered by the research team."

"Who did they steal it from?" I asked.

Romero inspected the mechanism. "For your sake, let's hope you don't find out. You are dealing with your average smugglers, here. This is their turf. This is uncharted territory. These are circumstances outside national law."

"So?"

Romero paced the platform. "Machina, of any kind, is forbidden. Remember? Murder could be overlooked easily. Your bodies would be beaten and broken, and nobody would bat an eye. That would be the consequence if they even find them. Now's the time to turn back if you're having second thoughts. From this point on, there is no turning back."

He stood in front of the elevator looking at us.

Sonia and I gaped at each other, bewildered.

"I've come too far to give up now," I said. "The sorcerers need our help. And I made a promise to Cheryl, High Wolf and Order, or not."

"We're dealing with more than just the Order on this one," Romero said, holding up a journal.

Sonia was next to speak. "I've been held back by fear too long. Let's give these bastards what they deserve. I don't care who they are. I'm done living in cages. No one's going to place a bounty over my head, and no one's going to hold me back. These people must be freed."

Romero nodded.

"Then it's settled. You've been warned."

"What is down here, Romero?" I asked.

"Beasts and creatures of the myst. Evils beyond your wildest imagination. The molemen of the Plymouth Saratoga village, known for their magic of immense power, sealed deep underground. Above ground is the Triunity research facility. Sorry, I mean *a* Triunity research facility."

"You mean there is more than one?" I gasped.

"Afraid so. Enough talk. Who wants to go first?"

Sonia volunteered.

The lift teetered under her weight. Romero explained it could best hold one at a time. Someone needed to operate the winch at the bottom or the top, to lower the lift. Then Sonia would need to activate the winch at the bottom to return it to the top.

Romero hovered over the engine. "Birdy, before you go, I'd like a word," he said.

"Now what?" she squawked.

"This may be the last time we speak. And, if so, I want you to have something to remember me by."

"If you touch me, I swear—oh my gosh, they're beautiful!"

Romero had pulled a corsage, pin, and a band from his coat. "Remember when I said your dress was missing something? Here you go. We haven't always seen eye to eye, but I want you to know that, despite being the most enormous pain in my side, you have my respect."

Sonia giggled and held her arm out like a queen for Romero to slide it on. Then he returned to the controls of the engine and winch. "Ready?"

I could see Sonia's heart pounding through her chest. She clenched her fists and swallowed, then closed her eyes and nodded.

The machine hummed. With a loud bang and puff of smoke, air siphoned into the cylindrical turbines. The floor of the lift shook and lowered her slowly down.

"Catch you on the flip," I shouted.

She nervously nodded.

The machine hummed further and further below the ground, out of sight —even my sight.

We waited for the lift to rise. It was just Romero and me.

"Sinopa, I want to ask you something important," Romero said.

His voice turned grave and serious. He didn't even call me Kiera. "Kid, I may not be around to protect you and teach you forever."

"Oh, shut up," I said.

"In case something happens, I want you to take care of something for me. Watch out for Beauregard."

"What?"

"Remember your promise?"

"To help you find your girlfriend?"

Romero nodded.

"I want you to promise me, if I'm not around, watch out for him."

"Is he involved in finding your girlfriend?"

He nodded again.

"Forget the first one, okay? This is the only one that matters. Beauregard is one of the most powerful swordsmen who has ever lived. Do not fight him. You understand?"

"I guess so."

He clenched my shoulders and shook me. His nails dug into my skin.

"This is not a joke, kid! He will kill you if given half a chance."

"Ow! You're hurting me. Stop."

He let go. "Don't let what happened to her happen to you," he said.

His eyes bulged in anger. I had never seen him like that before. I froze in fear. Distant humming began rising from the shaft.

He undid his buckle and handed me my saber from his waist.

"In case things go awry," he said, tossing it at my feet.

"You're not leaving, are you?" I asked.

Romero wouldn't look me in the eye.

"We made a deal, didn't we? I don't plan on leaving, but a good chess player always has a counter-strategy."

The lift rose to a stop at the top with a hiss of exhaust.

"There's your ride. Enough talk. Your people need you, Kiera."

I tightened the sheath around the bow of my dress. My flintlock was tucked under my dress where no one would think to look. Romero readied the next lift. I couldn't resist giving him one last hug before I went.

He started the lift and shouted down after me, "Remember our promise."

I nodded.

The lift shook beneath my feet. It rose up in a hiccup and dropped. Not slowly like it had done for Sonia. The floor dropped beneath me. The wind blew through my hair in a free fall. I screamed, flailing my arms until the lift skidded in midair.

Sparks flew from the rails. My body thumped against the floor. There was a large bruise on my side, but I was alive.

Romero shouted something inaudible, then the lift slowly coasted down like before. I scrambled to the guard rail on my knees. My fingers clung to it for dear life. The elevator squealed to a stop and let loose a puff of exhaust at the bottom.

I held my chest and sighed in relief at the bottom. No more wounds. My head was attached. There was the faint smell of sulfur and rotten eggs, but besides that, things were looking all right.

I heard a slow clap down the tunnel. A torch hung over the entrance to the elevator. Beyond that, pure darkness. I really wished I could work the logistics of this dark vision. Gosh, I hated puberty.

Beyond ten feet of the last trace of light, I saw gray shades on the cavern walls. White figures emerged in the darkness. Helmets with jar-like apparatuses covered their faces.

Cobarde led them to me.

"Well, look what we have here. A couple of trespassers, no doubt."

Sonia's body was tossed before me. She fell, limp. Her skin felt cold but she was breathing. I drew my sword. "Stand back! I'm warning you."

"Oh, please. Put it away, beast," scoffed Cobarde.

"What have you done with the sorcerers?" I shouted. My feet stood firmly between Sonia and them.

"What on earth are you talking about, beast?"

"I am not a beast. I'm talking about the sorcerers you are bringing to the labs. Those you're using to raise the Machina."

"She's delusional. Take her with the others," Cobarde said, throwing down his helmet.

A yellow powder shot through the air. I realized the things on their helmets were gas masks, but it was too late. My lungs collapsed. I wheezed on the ground, gasping for air. Sonia, already incapacitated, was dragged away. I tried to scream out for her and only managed to swallow more gas.

Tears formed in my eyes. They stung. I wept, screaming for it to stop. Then my body slumped over like a grazing cow. I gasped, desperate for air, any air. My throat burned, full of deadly poison.

The men grabbed my arms and thrust them behind me. They tried to raise me to my feet. My entire body drooped. My muscles quit on me.

The men shouted at me to stand up. My face was bashed into the rock floor when I "refused." I was physically unable to stand. They smashed my nose into the stone again. Any air I had escaped me. My toes went numb. My eyelids grew heavier.

Not again. I had to stay awake. It couldn't end like this. I had to rescue Sonia. I had to free the sorcerers. I would have my innocence, and they would have justice.

My lungs gasped for air. My head spun and my eyes closed. I blacked out.

I AWOKE SOMETIME LATER to the sound of water. Fear jarred me awake. My head shot up. We were led into a train of men. Cobarde took to the front. Men dragged my feet in the dirt. Sonia dangled over another's shoulder.

"Too easy! Those government toys worked wonders, for a first try. It's too bad Rudolph's not here to save you," Cobarde said, with an evil laugh.

"So, where are we taking them?" one of the men asked.

"The sewers aren't far. Mother Marilith has great plans for the pink one. The bird's just fuel for Camp 937. Run her along the mill. She'll burn, like the rest of the corpses."

Not if I can help it.

I refused to go down without a fight. Only my hands were bound. Big mistake. My tail cracked a man on the back of the head. I caught the other in the face on the recoil. I sprinted as fast as I could, thrusting out my chest.

"After her! We use the bird as bait if need be. I need that one alive."

My night vision did hardly anything in this blackness. Rocks clattered behind me. My foot slipped and I ate dirt.

Cobarde laughed.

I rolled. Before I knew it, I couldn't stop. I'd rolled off the path and crashed into rocks and crevices, stopping on flat ground. Above me, torch-light approached. I resigned to my fate. I'd done my best.

The ground shook. I scanned around me and saw nothing. It did it again. A stone jumped by my side.

"Faster, before it finds us," commanded Cobarde.

Rumble. Torchlight raced down the hillside. Stones clattered and fell.

The ground rumbled again.

I was a sitting duck. I couldn't even stand. I pressed my ear down against the ground. Something was moving.

Rumble.

It was moving fast.

Cobarde cursed his men to work faster. The guards climbed down as best they could.

CRACK! The ground split open beneath me. Dust clouded all around. Screams rose. A warm breath cleared the smoke and breathed down my neck. The men shook in their armor. A long pink tongue cracked like a whip. The nearest guard dropped numbly. Growls above me vibrated the floor below.

Suddenly, my legs dangled in the air by the bow of my dress. Slobber dripped from the thing's mouth. I saw a flash of scales. It yanked me under-ground. Dust kicked in my face. The ground sealed behind us. Two large claws raked dirt in front of us. I coughed, hyperventilating on soot. Light poured through a wall of rock. The beast built up steam. I braced for impact.

Boulders rolled onto the floor in front of us. I opened my eyes.

Its lair was decorated. Oriental rugs spread across the floor. A small chimney rose in the corner with a crackling fire. A set of books sat on a wall.

The beast set me down. Its teeth rubbed and sawed through my ropes. Its tongue dribbled over my wrists, and my fingers strangely tingled in its saliva.

When I was free, I crawled away from the creature. It sat like a squirrel, nibbling at my frayed cords. A blanket of fur lined its plushy underbelly. Golden giant scales, like a pangolin's, lined its back. Lanky, slender 'sloth-like' fingers popped from its snout one by one. Its beady eyes blinked at me.

It began speaking in a type of sign language I didn't understand. Naturally, I was terrified. The beast gave up and tapped at the tube hanging from its collar. I approached with caution. I gingerly reached for its throat. The pangolin-like creature blinked motionlessly. I popped the tube open and its load tumbled out onto the floor—a letter and a tiny book.

The beast licked my face and balled up, purring by the fire.

The Pocket Edition Guide on the Arcane and Post-Post-Apocalyptic Beasts, Volume Two.

On the cover was a picture of whatever this abomination was. *Thank goodness for those precious few reading lessons from Sonia!* I sat next to the fire for better light.

The ground shook. I jumped back. The beast had rolled on its back and looked at me expectantly. I hesitantly began giving it a belly rub. Its leg twitched in enjoyment.

I began reading the letter to the best of my ability.

"Dearest Kiki,

"This is a letter."

You don't say.

"Thought you'd heard the last of old Minnie, didn't you? No, this old girl still has some fight in her.

"I found some information that should prove useful, and it's been a nightmare tracking you down with your moonstone. So I had to do things the old-fashioned way and bust out my bloodhound. I suspect my book has aided you, yes? What am I saying? Of course, it has.

"First of all, this is Boris, my steel weevil better known as a pill-bear. He's my mister fluffy pants and loves to snuggle, and I don't wanna hear about him getting a single scratch. You got me? I tucked a sign language manual on the mantle and treats in the lockbox. I'm counting on you. He's another secret between friends, mind you.

"Anyway, Cobarde has it out for you. He's insane. The disappearances have a connection to him somehow. All signs say he's working with the wyrm. Max is in grave danger."

That would have been nice to know earlier.

"I have my eye on your little deputy, for the time being. Oh, he's just so cute that I want to explode. Should a hair be plucked from his head, they'll have to answer to me and pay tenfold, rest assured on that."

That's probably how she found me, come to think of it—through scrying Max. Oh my gosh, what did she see?

"Just a refresher, dearie, because I'm sure you've read my book by now."

Ha, that's funny.

"Wyrms gather clusters of men in their harems. They could have thousands after you. For what, I'm not sure. Not even they seem sure.

"Fun fact: mariliths and wyrms are not as interchangeable as you might think, even though both are serpents born of fallen Coatls.

"Mariliths, unlike wyrms, possess a distinct lifelong pact to a single person. Two hearts are linked in lifelong connection and separate bodies. Anyone could be her double. Trust no one, and above all, avoid their eyes."

Boris nipped at my hand like a cat. I yanked it away.

My gosh, Minerva was long-winded even in written form.

"There are glow gnomes below the city. Go there. Boris knows the way. He's getting husky from their food. They'll aid you there; tell them I sent you. I'm uncertain how long this will take to reach you. Once you've reached Plymouth Saratoga, please send my Boris back to me. I fret incessantly over my little Roly Poly. Best of luck.

"Love, your friend, Minnie.

"P.S. Knock 'em dead, love."

Boris rolled over and squeezed into a ball around me.

"Hey, let go," I said.

He yawned. He blinked.

"Boris, don't you dare go to sleep."

He smacked his lips and rested his head on his paws.

"Boris the bear, mole thing—whatever you are—you stop that right now."

He began to snore.

I sighed.

It looked like I was going to be here a while. At least I was warm and comfortable with a roof over my head, and I wasn't alone. It beat being chained or dissected by some giant snake, that's for sure.

Hang on, Sonia. I'm coming.

CHAPTER TWELVE

I sat by the fire for half an hour, uptight in my pill bear nest. No matter what I tried, nothing woke him.

I guess it was time to catch up on my reading. As Boris continued to squeeze in on my waist, I struggled to wrench my purse free, hoping to extract the levitation book from it. But the purse wouldn't budge; I was stuck with my new book from Minnie. Most of the words proved too big or in another language. Minnie had annotated some of the margins.

It was like flipping through my pill bear instruction manual.

Boris grumbled in his sleep and squeezed tighter on my legs.

"Ouch, Boris, wake up."

I punched his hide. My fist buckled and popped. Pretty sure it hurt me more than him. My legs tensed, ready to pop. Any harder and he'd break my bones.

I panicked, flipping through the book. There had to be something in here. I caught a page with a diagram outlining the anatomy of steel weevils. Minnie's scribbling pointed to a spot behind the ears. *This pressure on my legs is unbearable.* It was worth a shot. I leaned over as far as I could and barely reached his head, let alone his ears.

My nails scraped his hide. His ears rose and tucked back. His tongue rolled out like a carpet on the floor. His leg twitched and his back stretched. I scrambled free and sighed in relief.

"Boris the weevil," I snapped.

His eyes blinked open and glared at me in annoyance.

"You could have killed me. Wake up this instant. My friends are in danger, and you *will* take me to them," I demanded.

He exhaled and shook his head.

"No? What do you mean no? Pick up your fat butt and move."

Boris groaned and nodded back to sleep.

"That does it." I charged and pushed on the giant pangolin-thingy's back with all my might. I used my arms, back, head and horns, but nothing would budge him.

I slid down his side in frustration. He farted.

"Ew! You're such a child."

Boris gave me the bird. That sign language I understood.

I gave up and left in search of the lockbox Minnie had mentioned.

On the dark side of the room stood a queen-sized bed, a door, and a tilted painting.

Behind a painting. How original.

I pulled it off the wall and my suspicions proved correct. Minnie had engraved the combination on the side.

Inside the safe was a bag of biscuits, a fur coat, an oil lantern, and a set of magazines.

I immediately threw on the fur coat. The underground froze me to the bone. Minnie's mink coat was touchably soft. I figured she stowed it away for emergencies such as this.

I grabbed a magazine or two out of curiosity and made my way to the bed. Boris was lucky I was tired, too.

"If my friends die because of you, you'll be sorry," I told him.

No response.

I slipped under the covers and worried over Sonia and the sorcerers. Their lives were in my hands. This was about more than clearing my name. This was about justice against Cobarde. That monster hurt me and countless others. Whoever was funding him and pulling his strings was going down. Period.

I fell fast asleep and awoke in the middle of the night to the splitting of wood. Boris had crawled into bed and broke the posts at the foot of the canopy bed. I was too exhausted to be upset. Come morning, he licked my face awake.

"All right. All right. I'm up. You didn't want to wake up for me, but I guess I have to get up for you." I wiped the weevil drool from my face. The heavy animal pinned me under his down blanket—again. "Boris. Get."

He shook his head.

"Now. Get up. Now is not the time to snuggle."

He shook his head.

Stubborn brat.

"I'll do anything. Come on, please move."

His ears perked up. He signed with his fists toward his mouth.

"Food? Sure. I'll give you treats if you take me to the gnomes. Deal?"

Boris slid off the bed gently, so as not to hurt me anymore, and raced on all fours to the painting on the wall. He did small leaps and circles around it, waiting for me. I guess he just needed the proper motivation.

Weevils aren't stupid. They're smart enough to learn sign language. Don't think he didn't plan this ruse from the start.

I trudged out of bed. My back and legs still ached from running a few nights before when we were in the jungle; but overall, I felt more refreshed than yesterday.

I rubbed my eyes, opened the vault, and threw Boris a biscuit. It crumbled to pieces on the floor and he heartily licked it all up. Nothing went to waste. I pulled out the lantern, and a magazine to flip through during my breakfast.

Most of the articles were lost on me. I found one magazine at the bottom of the pile with the tagline, "Deer Dominatrix: Bad Girl Tells All." On the cover, Minnie wore a fur coat in a seductive stance. *Only* a fur coat. My stomach churned. I felt sick.

Needless to say, both the coat and the magazine went into the fire after that.

I wished I could bleach my eyeballs. I could have happily lived my entire life without that mental image. Well, now I knew why she had locked them away.

Sadly, the pasty sight of a saggy-skinned old lady in lingerie would be the first horror here to plague my mind. I'd rather freeze than contemplate what she did in that coat. Whatever treatments she took must have worked well to hide . . . that. Clothes help, too, of course.

Boris watched the coat burn beside me.

"Now you're going to tell Minnie, right?"

He shrugged, signing to the bag of biscuits. I tossed him another one and he caught it midair.

"Right?"

He nodded.

"Good boy." I tossed him another for good measure. He signed something to me I didn't understand. I just had to shrug and shake my head. He gestured to his stomach and rubbed it in a circle.

"No, Boris. That's enough treats. Minnie sent you to take me to the gnomes. We had a deal."

Boris moaned in frustration. He crept over and picked me up.

"Hey, what are you doing?"

My legs slid down into a pouch of skin, like a kangaroo. It enveloped me, warm and soft like a blanket. Only my head stuck out. I shuddered in disgust.

He smirked down at me while standing on his hind legs.

"You're just lucky I'm cold."

Boris attacked the wall and clods of dirt flung through the air onto an oriental area rug. He scooped hand over hand, rocketing us through the tunnels at breakneck speed. It was a good thing he was a gentle giant.

Pouch travel was as interesting as it was uncomfortable. His muscles tensed all around me in a fuzzy meat shield. It brushed against me, warm and soft—yet also itchy. The occasional pebble popped up, hitting me in the face, but at least I was safe.

While cozy, it definitely wasn't comfy. The bounce in his trot jostled me dizzy like a merry-go-round. I might as well be riding another boat. I sensed at any moment he would spit me out onto the rocks.

My claws in his underbelly didn't help our situation either. He would stop and nip at my fingers, then charge forward to make up for the lost time.

Boris had a sense of drive and purpose. When a new charge set before him, he barreled like a freight train and there were no breaks, no detours, no delays. You got with the program of his master or he dragged you kicking and screaming. No compromise.

Soon the giant weevil inclined. I choked and coughed at the soot in my face. But it was better than the dirt before. The walls turned smooth. They were freshly dug. He bolted on all fours. I buckled into the pouch. Light raced at the end of the tunnel.

Boris leaped. I fell out. He curled around me. We rolled end over end in a ball. My stomach somersaulted as I turned end over end inside the weevil's shell. My heart raced. My breaths blew hot back in my face. The ball of us slowed and rolled to a stop.

Boris uncurled and I slid out, nauseous and head-spinning. I stood up on wobbly legs and hurled, crumbling down to my hands and knees.

I wiped my lips. "A little warning next time would be nice."

Boris playfully jumped in circles around me, shaking the ground. He tugged at my arm.

"Boris stop. I need a moment. I'm sure it's probably miles away still and—"

He tilted my head up with his claws.

A glowing city wobbled sideways a short distance away in my blurred vision. We were here.

Boris stood over me, waiting for an apology or another biscuit. I wasn't sure.

"Sorry for doubting you."

I tossed him another biscuit. He crunched down on it while I caught my balance. He helped me to my feet and we approached the shimmering ruins in the distance.

It turned out it wasn't just the dizziness. Large metal structures bent and warped, standing at slants of twisted steel and glass. The entire city illuminated the clearing like a massive beacon.

Boris kept pace beside me.

"So how did you meet Minnie?"

He stood on his hind legs and started signing.

"Right. Can't talk."

I considered using the manual but thought better of it. It wouldn't do much good since I was such a slow reader. Besides, we were already here.

Outside the city limits, rapids swooshed by the city's water wheels and turbines. Plots of corn cooked under solar lamps. Single steel weevils plowed the ground like oxen, and others played tussling about like tiny tumbleweeds.

"Family of yours?"

He nodded and signed something I didn't understand. He tapped his thumb on his forehead with his fingers straight, like a fan or a rooster comb.

As we reached the city lights I froze, paralyzed with fear. Everything glowed and pulsed. That strange electricity ran here and thrived. They had constructed the village from the hollowed and broken monuments of the ancients. Towers stretched long on their bellies of shattered glass windows. These had been known as skyscrapers. The glow gnomes lived in the bellies of whales in more ways than one.

The ancients built mighty towers that clawed at the heavens. They had become gods in their own eyes and produced Machina. Then nothing.

Here they lay split in half. They crept low and bit the dirt. The shattered sides snaked in cubes stacked sideways.

Overlooking it all, two buildings' collapsed ends formed a steeple held aloft by joists and rusty makeshift supports over a singly-preserved school-house. It was the only stone building left standing in the undercity of Plymouth Saratoga.

Boris's nose nudged my behind. I cracked my tail like a whip.

"All right. I'm going. Watch where you put that wet nose."

We strolled down the street. The floor of the cavern squashed beneath my feet like sand. Not sand. Ash. It was impeccably soft, hence the fertile crops.

The homes shone bright, but no one seemed to be inside them. No one came to the windows. Not a silhouette or shadow moved inside the rooms. Just empty husks boxed us in with honey-colored windowpanes. Hexagonal tunnels cut through the path to the steeple.

A well-lit courtyard stretched before us. Buildings trapped us in a hive of electricity. Small figures with radiant pale skin roamed the area.

At the sight of me people quickly dispersed, grabbing their children and fleeing back to their burrows like rabbits.

A siren roared. Boris hoisted me into his pouch and raced for the steeple. As we reached the steps, men with onyx blades rushed to meet us. Boris skidded to a stop and growled.

A man walked to the front with a hand up to halt the movements of the others. His hair appeared to have migrated south to his lengthy beard. His walking stick appeared to have been a lamp of some kind in the past. Their clothes were strange—similar to some of Herodotus's recreations, only worn and scavenged. Some wore just what they needed. Others had fashioned clothes from weevil and wolf hides, for warmth.

The men above us had bows at the ready. A few to the front had weevil skin plated shields and blades of vibrating metal. The elderly gnome reached the bottom step and signed something to Boris. Boris backed away two steps and responded. Sweat dripped from my brow. *What were they saying?*

The elder nodded and shouted in an ancient language.

A beardless gnome raced out to meet us. He bore a leather breastplate and a sword at his waist. A reflective red shield was attached to his arm and a long-barreled rifle hung from his back.

Boris signed to him as well.

The young gnome looked at me in the pouch and spoke. "You're a friend of Minerva, the lady of thunder?"

"Lady of thunder?"

A few gnomes shuddered as I spoke and nocked their arrows. The elder calmed them.

"Are you or are you not?"

"Yes, but—"

The young man shouted in an ancient tongue back to the army. They gathered away from us and cleared a path. Just the elder and the man in leather remained.

"My name's Lot. Any friend of the librarian is a friend to us. Come with me. We have a stew going."

Boris followed. He glanced all around and deemed it safe before letting me out of the pouch.

I was given a bowl and they filled me in about Sonia.

"I'm sending a search party out this moment. The surface dwellers have grown more aggressive as of late. My men and I were preparing to storm one of their strongholds before you arrived."

"Good, I'm going with you," I said.

"No, you stay here."

"Those men tried to kill me. They will pay for what they've done."

"Spoken like a true hume. Listen to you. Vengeance, greed, lust. All these things brought wars, and the destruction of the ancients who built these structures."

"This isn't about revenge. This is about doing what is right."

"Is that so?"

"What's that supposed to mean?"

"It means I don't believe you."

I put my hands on my hips, "All right, then, how are you so high and mighty?"

"My men are dead. Nothing we can do will bring them back, but I can save those who are living. You're staying here and that's final."

"You're not the boss of me."

"If the lady thunder wanted you here, here you shall stay. She has brought vast knowledge to our village. I think she knows more than you do. My best men shall protect you. Boris, see that she stays put."

Boris nodded and hoisted me off the ground. Lot stood up to leave.

"Hey, mister, don't you walk away when I'm talking to you. Boris, put me down."

"Every second passes, and another dies. There's a looking glass in the stables," Lot called over his shoulder.

"Hey! Come back here. You're going to take me to Sonia. Hey!"

Lot's form faded away.

Boris carried me, kicking and flailing, from his mouth. He brought me to the stables to spend the night with the rest of the steel weevils.

I pouted in the straw while Boris guarded my pen. This was his new charge: making my life miserable. Any time I so much as sneezed, he was there to check on me. He babied me.

If I tried to leave, he'd catch me before I even got a running start. Then he picked me up, dangling from my bow, and brought me back to my room. I was grounded, and he made sure I knew it. He scolded me in sign language each time, paced in a small circle, and then napped, blocking the door.

Come evening, his ears perked up at a whistle blown in the distance. A few lights dimmed, signaling the evening curfew. Off in the distance stood another pill bear with a ribbon around her collar. Her frame bulged wide and muscular. Her stomach hung fat and round. She was alone, sipping a drink in the dark. Boris stared and whined.

I crept closer, thinking this could be a prime escape. She turned and saw him and signed something. He signed back, turned to see me, and growled. I shot back to the corner. When he turned to look again, she had disappeared.

"Friend of yours?" I asked.

He glared at me, curling into a ball.

"I'm taking that as a yes. Go talk to her. I'll be fine."

He shook his head.

"Fine, Mister Grumpypants, don't listen to me, then. Look, if I'm going to be stuck here, at least give me something to do. Where's that mirror Lot mentioned?"

He growled, baring his teeth. Not once did he lose his temper until now.

"Fine, I promise not to leave if you fetch the mirror."

He stood up by the door. His eyes stared menacingly into mine.

"Go on. Get."

He signaled his eyes were on me. I crossed my legs with my back against the wall, bored.

Moments later, Boris dragged in a rusted version of Minnie's looking glass. I tossed him another treat as thanks and tried to decipher how to work the device.

Let's see . . . magic is fueled by mysts and emotions.

We were underground with plenty of evening mysts. So, what emotion? Reminiscence? Was that an emotion? It was the best I had.

Boris held onto the sides and I tried my best attempt. Mysts channeled around me. Clouds of smoke syphoned around me from the ground. The mirror fogged. I focused on Sonia. I recalled her blonde curls, red gown, and white angel wings, one of which was gimp from my failure to save her in time.

My head pounded, but I didn't care. I had to know she was all right. I had to know I wasn't a failure, and someone else hadn't died because of me.

I felt my body rise up as the mirror pulled me in. I shot through solid rock to meet Sonia.

CHAPTER THIRTEEN

I awoke as a translucent 'ghost' beside Sonia. Ropes bound and gagged her.

I looked around and saw rows and rows of tall, steel cages. They were sitting on carts, next to crates and barred cells, all crammed together. The area was dimly lit by tall torches. But inside the cages and cells? I blinked. The prisoners weren't sorcerers—they were changelings—of all sorts and sizes.

What's going on here?

The bleating of sheep, whimpering of dogs, and moans of despair echoed off the cavern walls into nothingness. They cried for help, and no one came.

I took a deep breath. My focus was top priority. Scrying is dangerous and demanding. If I lost contact with Sonia, who knew what would happen.

A boot kicked the bars of Sonia's cell. She jumped and nearly fell over.

Cobarde sneered over her.

"Looks like you found where the missing people go. Thought you could escape the law, didn't you, beast?"

He kicked and prodded her from outside with his boot and a metal poker. She was nothing more than an animal. Her foot slipped out from under her, and she rolled, unable to sit up on the cage floor. My spirit form swatted right through him.

Cobarde laughed. "It's too bad your little friend isn't here to save you."

She tried to insult him through her gag, but it came out garbled and muffled, indistinguishable.

Nobody hurts my friends.

"What's that? You're going to have to speak up. Oh, wait, that's right. Animals don't talk. But don't worry, my little lamb, it will all be over soon. And when it is," his smile widened, "no one will hear you scream."

She sobbed on the floor as he strolled away. I tried to untie her, but my hands slipped right through. I was only there in spirit.

A shipment was loaded onto a carriage. They put Sonia in a sweaty wooden crate, with a small breathing hole at the top.

The carriage jostled all the way to the slaughter. My spirit body form stayed in the tiny box with Sonia. I tried to comfort her but she didn't even know I was there. She couldn't see or hear me no matter what I tried.

We had come so far to come so short.

The carriage stopped and doors slammed. We must have arrived. Sonia's world consisted of one distant breathing hole that her bound ankles and thin legs could never reach. Her beautifully dressed bangs were matted to her forehead. Soot, pitch, and muck soiled her gown. From the look in her eyes, she had already died inside.

Come on, Lot, where are you?

I heard whirring and grinding outside the box. Axes were being sharpened. The crates were torn open. They placed Sonia into a line.

A rubber conveyor belt fed into a large mill saw. Guards pulled changelings to the belt, asking for any last words before placing them on it. The belt rocketed them into a series of grinding metal teeth. A loud scream echoed in the air, followed by an impatient, "Next."

Those who tried to run were shot. There was no escape.

I examined the lines. One line over, Sonia was just another soul awaiting her demise. She turned my way. Vomit, or bile, covered her shirt.

If only she could see me now.

I perceived our eyes lock, if only for a moment. The butt of a crossbow bashed the back of her head. The guard shouted at her to keep moving. Sonia would die here. And all I could do was watch. Helplessness hung over me.

Where was Romero?

I noticed other strange figures in the lines about to be executed. Pale men and women. Their bodies malnourished. Their hair unkempt. Their clothes matched ragged versions of those the tour guide at the temple wore. They stood at my height. Certainly not like any humes I had seen before. These had to be more glow gnomes.

The lines dwindled as the day stretched on, and my stomach growled. I had to pull myself away.

My muscles and brain ached. I took a brief rest before scrying again. I wouldn't sleep a wink all night.

Back to the scene, the guards seemed bored. The elderly moved to the front of the line. Long anticipation dragged on for hours, and now even longer.

Finally, it came time for the moment I had been dreading. I dreaded it more than my own death. Sonia's heels plowed in the sand as they pulled her over to the belt. Her wings knocked the guard over. A second guard trotted over to assist. Crossbows pointed at her back and her head.

She awkwardly slumped down halfway on the highway of death. I couldn't even bring myself to cry at this point. My tears had dried up. The belt started. Sonia's wings cracked both the guards. A bolt shot into the crowd. The belt turned. Sonia narrowly rolled off, inches before the blade would slice through her.

Shouts echoed above the rocks. Boulders came crashing down on the conveyor's blades. More of the pale human-like figures leaped down, tackling the guards. Arrows shot all around us. Many of the lines tried to run

Screams echoed through the cavern. Then a blast. I recognized it distinctly. A gunshot. My eyes turned for some glimpse of Romero. Instead, a man with a red octagonal shield engraved with an ancient language and a flintlock, long like a broomstick, stood on the belt. It was Lot.

"Surface dwellers, do not be afraid! You shall be fed to your death no more."

Men moved through the rows of bodies, untying those alive and gathering those that weren't. I saw a guard lying in a pool of blood. The bullet sank straight through his armor only a few feet from me.

"You have a choice. You can leave the faithful ones and try to find your way home. I wish you luck." Lot's eloquence surprised me, for a glow gnome. "Or you can come with us. And live among us free, and without fear of the surface dwellers. If you so choose, follow the man with the horn."

A tiny gnome raised a small box with a square horn. Static crackled from it, then a blaring victory siren. Weary faces gathered, following him. I mustered all my remaining strength toward the belt. As my psyche waned, my spirit flickered. Sonia lay in the dirt. A pale man cut her ropes free. She spewed vomit spewed.

They turned her on her side. Two men hoisted her up and carried the unconscious Sonia over their backs, shouting something in another language. Lot appeared by her side.

Despite my fatigue, I wrestled with the mirror and the myst to keep scrying. I stayed beside Sonia every step toward the village. Nothing would escape my sight. Sadly, that went for one of their torn loincloths as well. As the road got dark, I noticed their skin radiated in dull, faint pulses like fireflies. Their bodies were bioluminescent.

They lay Sonia down on a torn fabric mattress. They draped a wet towel over her forehead. Moist droplets formed on her skin in a cool sweat and her hair still stuck to her face. My ghostly fingers sunk through Sonia's hand. *They will pay for this dearly.*

I collapsed from exhaustion.

CHAPTER FOURTEEN

Turns out I slept a full twelve hours after scrying. The intense magic drained me of all my strength, and it was a wonder Boris hadn't paced a rut over me. To my surprise, he'd been relieved of duty and was nowhere to be seen.

Sonia continued to deteriorate. We had trouble getting her to hold down fluids. The nurse of the tent, Meryl, insisted I fetch her something solid to eat, but I struggled to leave her.

Why does everything bad happen when my back is turned?

Lot, the gnome with the red shield, entered the tent.

"Excuse me, Miss Changeling. If you have a moment, there's something I wish to discuss. Something that may aid your friend."

He handed me a bowl of soup.

I held it with suspicion. The thick broth churned like gravy. It consisted of fish, mushrooms, and potatoes.

Strange how nice they are us Changelings. What's their angle? He held open the flap of the dust tarp. I told Sonia I'd be back soon. Her glazed eyes blinked at me. I don't know if she even heard me.

The ceilings rose a mile high here and were smooth as glass. I guess I wouldn't like to live under the threat of giant stalactites of death either. The townspeople hurried about with smiles and joy for those returned. Their tattered rags covered next to nothing. All their homes lay in crumbled ruins, yet they were happy.

The elderly creatures scowled at me as I passed by. *Looks like I'm not welcome here, either.*

Along the edge of the camp, a wooden structure rotated in a circle, over and over. It was an old waterwheel in the underground river system that powered a myst engine. A series of tarnished copper cords ran like tree roots from the camp, and there were two large, red lamps. The lamps provided heat and light over a row of vegetable gardens, and one for what they called "vitamins" for the children to sunbathe in.

"Miss Changeling—"

"I have a name, sir. Call me Kiera."

"Kiera, my apologies. It has been ten years since we have had friendly visitors besides the refugees. I feel we got off on the wrong foot. I'm Lot. We've been called many names, as I'm sure your species has, too. Molemen, glow gnomes, and glow nymphs, but we call ourselves the Faithful."

"What are you doing down here?"

Lot chuckled. "Same as you—trying to survive. Many rulers have risen and fallen. They have persecuted my people for thousands of years. Faith and religion are still outlawed, according to our visitors above.

"That much hasn't changed since the Great Mushroom War of the ancients. They forced our ancestors underground to flee those who would destroy us, and when the sky turned red with fires from the heavens, we were what was left beneath the earth."

"That was centuries ago, though," I said. "Why struggle down here?"

Lot shrugged. "This life is all we know. Should one of us leave and not come back, it would break our families. Besides, some sky city people came to live among us. Our community has thrived ever since."

He led me to a large fern with milky residue and white fruit, like cauliflower, but teardrop-shaped, like a pear.

"This fruit we call 'hot water hyssop' or 'ghost fruit'. It will lower your friend's fever. Take the leaves. Its sap may restore her feathers."

Now *that* I had to see.

I plucked the fruit and branches as directed and remained silent most of our trip back.

"Your people, changeling, have been a tremendous aid to mine, and for that we are in your debt."

My ears perked up. "There are other changelings down here?"

"Yes, the refugees we saved from the red flag nation. There is also a colony deep to the south, in the center of the canyon where the myst runs thickest."

I assumed the red flag nation meant Northstrand. "Could you take us to them?"

"We could try, but the trip will be difficult in terrain and perilous in obstacles. The men we saved you from seized our tunnels. Best make sure your friend is up for the task."

I agreed.

We returned a few hours later with the hyssop and fruit. Sonia's fever left her, and we rubbed her gimp wing with the palms and sap. I also used my magic, for good measure.

Despite my disbelief, some fledgling spines rose where there were none before. Around Sonia's scar tissue and burn marks, new plumage grew. Her second wing was thicker.

I gave Meryl my brush as payment. I should mention that a scouting party had looted belongings off another wagon. Lot had returned my bag and saber to me, much to the grumbling of the looter who had claimed them.

"What caused her illness?" Lot asked.

Meryl held up a small vial of foam from Sonia's mouth.

"Poison. Only a small dose, seeing how she's alive. Somebody must have slipped it in her food or drink," she said.

Lot turned to me and asked, "You know anything about this?" I shook my head. "She's eaten with me every time except for—that's it! Oh my gosh, the banquet! Someone must have poisoned the banquet."

I was glad now that Max and I had skipped the meal. Sonia must have been poisoned from the drink her date brought her. I wondered if he was even alive at this point. Isolated and cut off from help, they were probably all dead by now.

Sonia groaned and shifted in the bed. I patted her on the shoulder and told her to rest well. She grumbled some remark about how these dates of mine would be the end of her. I knew that, from then on, she would be all right.

But what about Boris? It wasn't like him to abandon his job. Well, I didn't find him until much later.

In the corn field's edge, two steel weevils curled together. A farmer tiptoed with a yoke toward the couple, and Boris charged him away. The yoke flew into the dirt and the gnome sprinted back to the village.

One the way back, Boris locked eyes with me and charged again. I blindly raced as fast I could. The ground shook. Boris gained on me. His sharp tongue paralyzed my legs, and I face-planted on the ashy ground.

The steel plating rose from his shoulder blades. Boris's behemoth-like shadow cast over me.

"Boris. I'm sorry I left. I—"

I skidded across the silt as he dragged me by my boot to his nest in the corn. I cowered, expecting him to eat me. My thoughts were erratic due to lack of sleep. *Do pill bears eat meat? What would Minnie think?*

Boris released me and I leaped to my feet dusting myself off. There in the clearing lay a less-bloated pill bear with four kits, suckling. This was the same lady weevil from the night before.

Boris nudged me with his nose, excited over his litter. His eyes watered. The lady weevil panted and growled. I dropped to my knees. Boris signed something and licked her snout, and her breathing slowed. I didn't understand. My breathing still slowed from fear of being eaten.

Boris grabbed my hand and put it over her belly. The lady weevil shrieked and squirmed. One baby was stuck inside.

"Calm her. She'll squish the babies," I instructed him.

Boris lay beside her, boxing the wandering kits in a sandy circle between them. Their bread-loaf-sized bodies shivered in a bright fluorescent pink. His paw held hers and he licked her face again.

Growing up on the farm, I'd helped sows deliver piglets a few times, but this . . . this was no sow. One false move and she'd flatten me—and the little ones. But if I didn't deliver the kit, one or both of them could die.

Boris turned to me with longing eyes—desperate. I thought it shocking, though, that he would trust me. Two days ago, he wanted nothing to do with me and I actually thought he might devour me. Perhaps we both misjudged each other.

I sighed. "All right, I'll help. Calm her down, okay? We gotta keep her still. Does she have a name?"

Boris flicked me the tags on her collar. "Penelope." *What a pretty name.*

"All right, Penelope," I said gently.

Her ears flicked up and she looked at me.

"Everything will be all right. I'm here to help you, but you gotta stay calm, okay?"

Boris licked her face and translated. Penelope focused on him.

I washed my hands and arms in the river and went to work. Boris held Penelope's claw. I reached into her womb. Penelope wheezed, but no movement. So far, so good.

It had been a while since I had delivered a newborn. If memory served me correctly, a common complication in sows formed when the womb horns crossed. This was likely from her weight.

My hands searched for the kit's head. Penelope's muscles contracted, squeezing on my arm. She squealed as my hand found something soft. She started to rock.

"Penelope. Hang in there, Penelope. I'm almost done. You're doing a great job."

Boris spoke in low moans and groans. He soothed her in their secret language. My hand found the tiny snout. Now that I knew where the kit was, I was able to reposition it and turned it headfirst. The walls contracted. The baby came. I fell backward with a slimy steel weevil in my arms. Boris raced to my side.

The newborn was small and thin. Insignificant compared to the others, it was definitely the runt. It didn't move.

"I'm sorry, Boris. It looks like—"

The kit cried. It was alive.

Boris dashed laps across the floor. He started at the cornfield, ran to the stables, and back and forth again. I rested the baby girl beside her mother. Penelope nodded in thanks, out of breath. Boris raised a howl over Penelope. Her eyes glared at him as she limply licked the youngest dry. He nodded and helped her.

Boris signed again to me. It was here that I understood what he meant. He placed his thumb to his forehead with tears in his eyes. He was a father.

I wondered whether Minnie knew. She always had the looking glass, but whether there was a range I didn't know.

He scooped the rest of the litter in his pouch for warmth and took up her yoke in the dirt. This was his charge now, to nurture and protect their cubs, and like the rest of his duties, there was no looking back. I supposed Minnie would understand.

Penelope gave birth once more. She had a grand total of six pink Roly Polies.

⁊⦿

SONIA and I spent the rest of the evening at the gnome village. Come morning, Lot himself was to accompany us, with a small force, to their sister tribe, who had traded Machina with Aerogapolians before the Northstrand occupation. They knew of the tribe as the Ammonites.

Lot seemed uncomfortable answering further questions about them, like why they split, who are they to him, etc. Sonia was quick to excuse me because I "never shut up." *So glad to have her back.*

It was a three day walk to the Ammonites, avoiding Cobarde's men. Steep cliffs surrounded us at every turn. Some cliffs we descended with ropes; others we avoided altogether.

When we made camp for the night, Sonia made good on her promise of teaching me to read the spell book as we rested by the fire. Turns out the gnomes weren't fond of magic either, though, so we kept it to a minimum after they had gone to sleep.

Deep in the hollowed bowels of the earth, darkness surrounded us like nothing I'd ever known. No sun. No moon. No time. There was only the expansive shade of stone. My night vision aided me only ten feet in this much darkness. Torches became our lifeline, and campfires along the route marked our every decision. They gave stern warnings to any of us if the lights should ever go out.

Another type of darkness lurked in these shadows. We set watches each night to look after the fire and wake the others, should a dark one wander into our camp. The gnomes told me the dark ones were called "wendigos" and told me nothing more.

A third and final darkness seeped from the ground: myst. It lined the walls of the cavern and clouded our vision. We took extra precautions, ensuring the torches never went out. The myst seemed to follow me more than others. Even at night with my moonstone ring, I heard voices. My mind became a network in my sleep. I heard voices all around me.

I recognized the grizzly old voice. It rose to the back of my ears and tunneled its way into my skull. "Don't be afraid, my daughter. You are almost home. Come to me. Yes. Yes, come home soon. Daddy longs for the one he lost."

I inspected my ring. Not a single visible crack caught my eye. They could be watching us and we didn't know it. This could complicate things.

𐆛

As MENTIONED BEFORE, the army and police seized most of the gnomes' tunnels, lifts, and camps, complicating travel further. So it came as a surprise when we stumbled onto a ruined camp. There were signs of them were everywhere: trash, footprints, and discarded tools. We even discovered a carriage.

The large coach stood on chocks. The wheels disintegrated when touched. An advertisement for a seamstress wrapped around the outside. Had it been up top, it would have been nothing out of the ordinary.

A few gnomes gathered close with excitement. They smirked at the idea of cracking it open like a piñata.

Lot struggled to maintain the peace. "We don't know what's in there," he said.

A gnome leaped forward onto the steps. "We will once we open it!" He shouted with greedy lust. He flung open the door.

Lot shook his head. "That could have been booby-trapped, you know. It's not like them to leave it unlocked. Crossbows cocked, all of you."

They did so. The smallest among them climbed the steps and scrambled inside. Then he stepped back out. "Boss, you might want to see this."

As the door opened further, a faint mist seeped out. Strangely, I didn't feel cold anymore. I had a bad feeling about this.

Two gnomes played sentinel outside. Everyone else piled in. Even Sonia seemed curious.

The coach was cramped. Benches, dressers in disuse, and even a piano greeted us immediately. To the right, a frail form sat cuffed to a quilting rack. Her gnomish body rocked and drooled. Her eyes stared out into an endless void. Spittle streamed down her cheeks.

Lot dropped to his knees beside her, at a loss for words. His voice broke. "Fidelity. What have they done to you, my baby girl?"

She stared off in space, unable to acknowledge his presence. Saliva spilled down her chin like running water. Her tattered clothes did little to absorb it. The smell of feces reeked from her corner. Whatever they had done to her, she was now an overgrown toddler.

I turned away to explore the rest of the cabin. My body grew warmer. Sweat beads gathered on my brow. *How am I sweating underground?*

Beyond the overturned furniture, someone had been working. The stench of oil and grease made me gag. Scraps of metal clustered beside tables. Gears, maps, and charts cluttered the work benches.

A large mechanical machete lay before me. The edge appeared scarlet. Books and papers littered the floor. The last table sat clean. Somebody left in a hurry. A map of the sewer system hung on the wall. Red yarn and thumb-tacks cast a scarlet web.

Only, they weren't thumbtacks. As I picked at one with my fingers, the metal pin whined. Images of the guardhouse integration room hit me. These were forget-me-knots. Cobarde had stuck them in the wall as cheap push pins.

Lot cleared his throat. His hands slid from Fidelity's face as he kissed her forehead.

"We best be moving on," he said sadly.

"You know what must be done," cautioned one of his men.

In my vision, I saw myst rise beneath Fidelity.

"Right. The one I knew is as good as dead."

A myst wolf's head hung over her with hungry eyes. His fingers practically clawed at her scalp. It was ready to gnaw at what was left of her. Sweat dripped from my brow. My knees shook.

Its grizzly voice spoke. "Yes, kill. Kill. Eat!"

Lot's voice broke. He turned away. *How can he not see it?* "Make it pain-less, okay?"

The wolf chuckled. "Fight. Kill. Eat. *Feed.* Must feed."

"Stop!" I shouted.

Everyone turned to look at me.

I wiped the sweat from my eyes. The wolf was gone. The myst died. They all looked at me confused.

Am I hallucinating? It never spoke to me in the daytime before.

I struggled to find my words. I pulled out my own forget-me-knot.

"We can save her. Look. These spheres. If we can just find the right one. There is a chance we can save her."

A gnome spat an expletive that was not worth repeating if I understood it. The others joined in as a chorus.

Lot examined it for himself.

"Silence! All of you. This is my daughter, you snobs. I have to try. I owe her that much. We have to try. All right, Kiera, where do we look?"

I brought them over to the workshop, and we scoured every bench, desk, nook, and cranny. Few forget-me-knots turned up.

My head throbbed during my search. Not a single soul showed any sign of seeing the wolf but me. My nerves were on edge.

How could he talk to me? Especially now that I'm awake.

Whatever this was, its connection with me was getting stronger. It sounds strange, I know, but I could feel it. The way it spoke rang clearer. Its form stood sharper, and its enticing pull wrapped tighter. I heard its voice in my mind. The line blurred between sleep and wake. I imagined I wanted to rock almost as much as Fidelity. My search was stunted.

I removed some forget-me-knots that strung together the red cords. None were hers. They were all changelings. I pulled another off the wall, howling reverberated through my mind. I heard a familiar yip. I peered through the glass ball and saw Heimer cracking a whip in a mirror, and a chocolate shep-herd crying in pain. This was Max's memory.

In a small sack on the desk, at least seven of the spheres belonged to Max. I stopped counting after seven. They had sapped him of everything: childhood, schooling, and family. Nothing was sacred. He'd given up so much to save me. Poor Max. It hurt even worse leaving him.

I gathered them all and stuffed them close to my heart. A cracked sphere on top trickled iridescent fluid. I may never know how much Max lost. Looking at the spheres and the drooling sack of bones in the corner, I hated Cobarde even more.

I questioned how Lot could be so stupid. These men deserved to suffer. Cobarde, Heimer, the High Wolf—all of them. They deserved far worse than living scot-free. Call it revenge if you like; I was going to give it to them. I'd give it to them all.

No spheres turned up for Fidelity. A cryptic note titled "Auld Lang Syne" mentioned the spheres, but nothing else. The gnomes and Lot continued to argue over what to do with Fidelity. I read the same expression on his face that had been on Boris's. He was a desperate father willing to do anything to save his daughter. I united with him in refusing to let them put her down.

Sonia had gotten bored long ago and fiddled away at the piano. She snatched the note from me and studied it. When her song stopped, we heard a metal click.

"Ahem. Y'all might want to have a look at this."

A compartment in the piano had opened and revealed a fish tank full of cloudy crystal spheres. Thousands of memories swirled in gray glass tadpole eggs.

After much searching, Lot finally found one belonging to Fidelity from images of her inside it. He brought it over, and the tick pierced her skin. Her eyes straightened. She fell over and convulsed.

"What did you do to her?" Lot shouted at me.

I backed away. I wasn't sure what I'd done wrong. Sonia stood at the ready to defend me.

One gnome gestured to her cut. Black ichor poured from her bite mark where blood should have been.

All crossbows raised and fired. I turned away. A bestial shriek roared, and then silence. Fidelity was no more.

Lot marched out of the cabin without looking back. He wouldn't say a word to me the rest of the day. Come night watch time, I wanted to apologize, but he stopped me before I began.

"It's not your fault. She was bugged and rigged to blow. They got what they needed from her. I saw it in her memory. She was bait, left there to kill me or any poor gnome who tried to save her. Did you see the sludge that poured from her blood?"

I nodded.

"She had saryx disease. I'd rather she died my daughter than lived as a monster. It starts in fevers, powers, manifestations, and soon you're unrecognizable."

I was too afraid to ask what he meant.

I agreed it was better she live on his memory. We couldn't have saved her. It broke my heart to acknowledge it. As I held Max's spheres over my heart, I was determined to never let this happen again. I'd save him. He'd be fixed, and good would win. That is . . . if he was even alive down here.

CHAPTER FIFTEEN

Each night, my migraines continued to pound as I tried to sleep. The beast continued to call me as I tossed by the campfire light. That didn't help sleep, either.

At the time, I couldn't understand why we needed so much light. I could see in the dark, and it felt childish to fear imaginary boogeymen. The little glow gnomes might as well have been jumping at their own shadows. It was no wonder they were stuck underground.

On the third day, we exited a cave into a long open valley. Columns of limestone rose hundreds of feet to the ceiling. Lot told us not to make a sound. When I asked why, he threw a hand over my mouth.

Strange clicking echoed in the dark. Water fell in steady drips from the ceiling. The wind faintly whistled in the distance. One gnome took the lead, drawing a sword.

A few pebbles fell from the ceiling. I looked up as bats rushed toward us. I screamed as their wings smacked me in the face. Two of us dropped our torches and were left in the dark.

A gnome trembled alone in the dark. His hisses echoed off the walls. "No. Not like this," he muttered to himself repeatedly. He rushed to cower beside me.

The leader with the torch turned around and called back, "Relax. We have nothing to worry about."

Suddenly, screams echoed in the dark. When I turned around, the anxious gnome was no longer at my side. Lot lit another torch and tossed it to me. Only a severed leg remained of the poor fellow. Lot grabbed the fallen torch and a blood-covered maul and handed them to Sonia. More hisses and screeches circled us. I could see shifting shadows. Teeth gnashed and clacked together in the dark.

We drifted near the lead guide in silence, ever vigilant. Sinewy fingers descended from the ceiling. A silver thread shimmered in the torchlight. An entity of eldritch form caged the gnome leader in spider legs. Reptilian claws latched onto his face. The creature had a serpent's head, and with one massive bite it severed the gnome's head from his shoulders.

"Run!" Lot shouted.

A scout raced ahead, then froze in place. The flames of his torch licked silky webs, and between the columns we could see the beast. It appeared a hollow shell of a man, spliced into a spider body, with eight legs and reptilian claws. Its claws squished the scout's head inward like a cherry tomato. We turned around. A small light shone at the end of a tunnel. It was our only chance.

Lot took the lead, racing toward the tunnel's end. Clicks and screeches rattled the walls. Stalactites fell around us. Crumbling bits of rock smacked me in the chest. I kept running. My eyes watered with dust and clay. Wendigos screeched and galloped toward us. *Seriously? That's a wendigo?*

One man looked back and froze in place. The beast latched onto him. I dared not look back. We kept running. The tunnel entrance grew closer—I could see the light.

Stumbling out to the light, we found ourselves on the edge of a cliff. We were in the canyon's divide below Aerogapolis. A rope bridge stood before us. Roars echoed in the tunnels behind us. Lot ran forward onto the swaying bridge. The wind roared in the canyon. I followed Lot and stopped halfway as the boards splintered beneath my feet.

The creatures hissed. Coal black pupils eclipsed their eyes. Their legs curled and bent slowly. Their eyes shut. They roared in several directions.

"Echolocation," shouted Lot. "If you don't move, they can't see you."

Immediately, the wendigo's head turned toward Lot. Sonia raced onto the bridge. They could still hear us. They started moving in the direction of Lot's voice. One moved forward and pushed another off the edge. Its body flailed. A splash echoed in the channel below. Another swatted and attacked the bridge post, mistaking it for prey.

Sonia shouted for everyone to run. A wendigo leaped onto the tops of the ropes after us. Boards broke beneath us, splintering. They fell like dominos.

The bridge shook as another wendigo destroyed a support post. The bridge tilted. My hand burned as I gripped the ropes. I hobbled forward. The second rope collapsed, and the bridge swung. Wooden slats crashed into the wall. The wendigo roared just behind Sonia. Her wings swooshed her up above me. She grasped onto the overhead boards. One broke, sending her dangling one-handed. Lot grasped a finger of her free hand. She grabbed his arm with both hands, and he hoisted her back over.

The wendigo skidded downward, catching itself on the wall. It now crept after me. They called for me above. I summoned all my strength. The rope ladder swung in the strong bursts of wind. Hand over hand, I climbed. The shrieks of the wendigo reverberated off my skin in volume. The twisted fingers barreled after me. Three more feet. Almost there. Just one more rung.

A board cracked. The vise grip of the beast yanked my ankle toward it. Lot threw a rock at it. Its face caved in at the temple. Its body went limp, legs curled beneath it in a shriek. The wendigo fell end over end like a maple seed into the drink below.

Sonia grabbed my left hand and Lot grabbed my other, and together they pulled me over the lip. My heart drummed in my chest. My chest heaved.

As I stood up, Sonia threw her arms around me. We all looked back to the opposite cliff. The two remaining wendigos paced the edge, puppy-guarding the other side. There was no way back now.

I looked to Lot. Blood oozed from a gash on his forehead.

I panted, out of breath. "Torches. Got it. No complaints here."

CHAPTER SIXTEEN

W e marched along the tunnel, nearly reaching the Ammonite tribe. As we approached on the cliffside overlooking the camp, lights beckoned us from a distance. Solar heat lamps, just like we had seen before, lit a small cornfield. People scurried about their business just as before; but, in this place small wagons moved through the camp. Tents comprised most of the village minus one large stone building. Northstrand flags hung on large posts.

We turned to Lot. His face was sullen.

"What have they done? They've betrayed us all."

"What do we do now?" I asked.

Lot ignored me and marched down the hillside. I turned to Sonia, and she shrugged. We stuck to the shadows while he openly walked right into the camp. *What was he doing? He's gonna get himself killed.*

I rushed after him and Sonia yanked me back around a pillar. Her eyes narrowed, and she lowered her torch. "What are you doing?" she scolded.

"Going after him."

"Leave him. Let's find your friend and get out of here."

I nodded.

We snuffed the torches and left them behind the stone for later. Then we hunched down as we began infiltrating the camp. Our movements were slow, and we remained low to the ground.

The camp grew much worse up close. Prisoners worked in the camp. In the fields, a young lynx lady picked corn. Chains jingled around her ankles. Two beagle-men took turns mining the cavern walls in a chain gang. A cheetah girl jogged in a steel cage, turning a large wheel that powered a massive generator.

Not a single cage in sight. We stood outside a tent and listened in.

"This is not the way of our people," said Lot. "You know better. I raised you better."

"Raised me? You banished me. You've lived with your head in the sand, Father. This is the future where we can be something greater. We can have power and take back the land that was stolen from us. The Machina and sciences can be used for good this time. We can cleanse the earth of wendigos and saryx disease."

"They are the very ones who made them," argued Lot.

"Lies! Lies! All of it—lies! Get your head out of that thousand-year-old storybook and wake up to the future, Pop," the voice said.

Its footsteps approached, and we darted around the other side. A glow gnome with a deformed face and red cape exited the tent. After we made sure he was gone, we rushed in to see Lot.

I whispered, "Psst! Lot. Psst! What are you doing? Let's get out of here."

He looked at me blankly.

"What are you doing?" I asked again. "Did you find the way to the changelings or not?"

"Sorry. It's just that I always feared this day would come. I just wish my own flesh and blood didn't have to be the one who would carry it out."

"What are you talking about?" I said. "Let's go."

"Yes, you must go. Leave these caverns and never return."

"Did he hit his head or something?" Sonia asked.

Lot banged his fist on the table. "Don't you get it? They found it. Your people found the door. Evils shall be unleashed that were previously sealed away by the ancients. Let us pray it is not the spore."

"We're not leaving this place without Cheryl," I said adamantly.

"You'll never reach them. The lift only works one way, and a man named Beauregard took it to the bottom."

Footsteps approached the tent.

"Quick! Hide!" Lot whispered.

Sonia and I ducked behind some supply crates.

"What are you doing here?" a voice began. I recognized it as Heimer. He spoke calmly, and his voice was not as harsh or accented as Cobarde's.

"It's okay. He's with me," said Lot's son. "We were discussing family matters."

I peeked around the corner. There were three guards, Heimer, the deformed gnome, and a silhouette of a man on the other side of the tent. Someone else was listening in.

"Here's the map of the caverns. The smugglers' den is at the bottom here. The Magistrate is negotiating with them at the research lab. So if we can circle around, our little bargaining chip will remain safe, and reinforcements can gather there to assist the magistrate. Cobarde cannot reach the quarry before we do. Is that understood? Aerogapolis cannot complicate matters any further."

The gnome interrupted, "Fine, but do you really think they'll take the bait?"

"Positive. The things will scream bloody murder once they see their compatriots in chains."

"Listen to you two," Lot scorned. "'Let's bring out and throw the innocent blood as bait.' You should be ashamed of yourselves! That's heartless and stupid. Moe, I raised you better. You know it's not that easy. You know what's down here as well as I do. They'll never make it. And, furthermore, you'll never open the door."

Chink. A sword unsheathed. "Is that a threat?" said Heimer.

"Merely stating the facts. You're hopelessly short-sighted. Only a pureblood changeling can unlock the door. One of the seven Vestiges may be in your midst, but without a key, it's a dud."

Sonia and I turned to each other at the mention of the word "pureblood."

"Poppycock! The purebloods are just legends," scoffed Heimer.

"Pops is right on this one," Moe interjected.

"Don't tell me you believe in fairytales, too. The architects would never entrust the protection of the Vestiges to something so vile even if they existed."

"*If* they existed?" Lot roared. "There are ruins of the city at the base of the mountains. You can see it for yourself. The faithful intermarried with them in eons past."

The room got suddenly quiet. I peeked around the corner. The two guards and Heimer were missing. Lot looked my way, shaking his head, while Moe grinned. I shrieked as my tail was yanked. Heimer squeezed my throat and pulled me to my feet. "Well, a couple of eavesdroppers, eh?"

Two men pointed crossbows at Sonia. She raised her arms, and we were brought to the center of the war tent.

"Don't hurt them," said Lot.

"Quiet, old man!" snapped Moe. His face glowed more than usual. "What do you suppose we do with them? Whips? Knives? Cutting wheels? We can kill them now and no one will ever know."

Heimer waved him to stop. He said, "We do this civilized-like. Who do you think I am? Cobarde? We make an example of them and push forward. Call an assembly. We'll behead them in the square. Make sure changelings know what happens, should they step out of line."

A man stepped forward around the corner. "And scene," he said. There was a saber at his waist. Clots of clay soiled his long button coat. Soot scuffed his skin and emerald eyes caught the lantern light.

Romero gave us a playful wink. "That was quite the performance, if I do say so myself. The girls will come with me."

"This place is restricted. Who do you think you are you?" said Heimer.

"I think I'm the one who has just uncovered news the consul will be glad to hear. You can let the girls go. They will accompany me, of course."

Heimer drew his sword. The cool steel gave my neck goosebumps.

"And why should I?"

"Archie don't tell me you don't recognize me," Romero smirked.

Heimer raised his sword and pointed it at him.

"Speak plainly. Who are you?"

"Now where's the fun in that? I know I've been away a very long time, but this is an urgent command from the consul himself. These two shall accompany me to the quarry."

Heimer lowered his sword and ran the edge down the back of my neck, but only enough to break the skin. A warm trickle dripped down to my breasts, and as my heart thumped in my chest, it took every muscle not to scream. Heat flushed my face and cheeks, and I begged myself not to cry. I bit my lip. I couldn't show fear.

"That's strike one. I have no commanding officer. Strike three, I run 'em through."

"What are you doing? Gamble with your own life," I said to Romero.

"The beast speaks the truth. Have you any proof?" Heimer said.

Romero bit his bottom lip.

Heimer pulled me into a chokehold and drew his blade in a sawing motion at my throat. Guards moved, flanking Romero.

"That's strike two. I'll ask again. Who are you?"

I looked up at Romero. His eyes met mine, and he shook his head.

"My name is Magistrate Leopold Xavier Vaughn Friedrich Henry, the second."

One guard took a step back. Another kneeled. Sonia and I stared at him, confused.

"Have you any proof?" asked Heimer.

Romero began to reach into his jacket, and a guard stepped forward with his weapon drawn. "Testy, aren't we?"

Heimer signaled Romero to continue.

He flashed an ID that displayed his pedigree on the back.

The guard saluted him.

"The Leopold I knew died in the war. His body was buried at sea, so we could lay no memorial."

"And I'm telling you, Archie, it's me."

Heimer sheathed his blade. He removed his helmet and saluted as well.

I looked up at Romero. His demeanor had now changed. He stepped forward and shook hands with Heimer, now Archie, and drew him close. Romero's face grew firm. His conceited aloofness had left. His eyes were unsteady, as was his posture. Romero was no more.

THEY PREPARED A MEAL FOR US. Leopold had a lengthy backstory about how he had cheated death. I could tell he was full of it. Who knew that our Romero was a magistrate, one of the highest lawmen, this entire time? Was this a ruse? I was certain this was some clever angle of his. It wasn't until I asked him in private that the truth became clearer to me.

I confronted him before dinner in his tent. He was presented with armor and finer clothes. I hardly recognized him without his jacket.

"Why didn't you tell us?" I asked.

"You never asked."

"I asked your name. Don't you think that's something we would have liked to know? Like, 'Oh, hey, by the way, I just so happen to be a powerful lawman; no big deal.'"

"Some things are best left buried, kid. Didn't I try to tell you that about magic and family?"

"But you're a friggin' magistrate, for crying out loud. You hold one of the most powerful positions in the world. You're free to do whatever you want."

"Free? Kid, there's nothing liberating about it. When you are bearing the fates of nations in conflict as an intermediary, assisting endless and fruitless conflicts time and time again, and are burdened with aristocratic snobbery, then you tell me how liberating it is. It's not what I wanted—at least, not always."

"Oh, come on, you get to rub elbows with all the right people. All those with money."

"Ha. Don't get me started."

"There had to be at least one time you were excited about it."

"It's the path chosen for me. I never got a choice," he explained.

"Who chose it, then?"

He walked away, and the tent flapped behind him. That was the only answer I got.

After the meal, we were able to rest. Thanks to Romero's new persona, they gave us bedding and proper supplies like torches, matches, and food. I'd still be willing to argue that my pastries were enough for me. Even though I offered them to both Sonia and Leopold—that name was going to take getting used to—neither would take them.

Fine. More for me.

The changelings were explained as either criminals, runaways, or vagabonds. I wasn't buying it. Cobarde hadn't known anything about the sorcerers. If we played our cards right, maybe it wouldn't complicate things to ask Heimer.

He remained behind to oversee the camp.

Since the sorcerers weren't in their possession, we would head to the quarry. Lot stayed behind. He insisted on talking some sense into Moe.

We parted ways and entered the mines once more, together as a team. With Leopold's new authority, they had given him passage and manpower at his disposal.

We took three changeling captives with us. Heimer told us to execute them immediately should they become irritable, citing it as a trigger of something supernatural or infectious. He also mentioned that he wanted to be rid of them. I blew it off, merely thinking Heimer was just a racist. My foster mother had always said to never look a gift horse in the mouth.

Anyway, after we left I complained it wasn't fair that we should force the changelings to come with us. Leopold remained silent about it until we were at a good distance. Thirty minutes later, he grabbed their tools and handed them to us. Leopold gave the order and Sonia's sledgehammer shattered their chains.

"As of this moment, you are free," he told them. "You can join us, while we offer protection and food as equals, or try your luck making an escape to the surface. You're free to do as you choose. If you're going to leave, though, make haste. I have no patience for traitors."

Immediately, one prisoner scrambled to his feet, leaving his friends behind. The poor sap didn't even take a torch.

The other two stared down at their broken chains and wept. We gave one back his pickaxe. We gave the other a torch because Sonia refused to return the hammer.

"But he can swing it better," I argued.

"I'm not going down here with those wendigos, or whatever, with only a torch again. Besides, you really gonna trust them with our only weapons?" Sonia asked.

Romero butted in, prying the hammer from her.

"They'll take the lead in front. Unless you want to face your fears, that is?"

She glared at him and crossly released the hammer.

We traveled the rest of the evening into the darkened tunnels. The path wound and rose with a foul odor. Behind a wall ran the Aerogapolian waterway and sewers. This will be important later.

❦

WE CAME to a stop for the evening and made camp. Romero took the first watch while the changelings took their long-needed rest. Sonia and I resumed my schooling.

"What do you expect to pull off in a week, kid?" Romero teased. "People spend their entire lives trying to learn even the basics."

I stuck my tongue at him.

"Give her a chance," Sonia defended me. "She's been practicing."

"Now this I have to see," he scoffed.

Deep down, I knew she hated magic as much as he did. I couldn't understand why. We flipped through the pages. I studied the pictures and breathed.

Happy thoughts. Happy thoughts.

Myst manifested around the cave. My lungs expanded. The air suffocated me. It was foggy, moist, and smelled faintly of citrus. It shrouded my scales in tiny clouds, sitting on my skin. I was a tiny bog beast.

I raised my glove at the pebbles that lined the cavern floor and focused. My throat burned, but I tried my best to ignore it. I focused on the rocks.

Happy thoughts. Happy thoughts. Light and airy. Come on, happy thoughts. Ice cream. Friendship. Plum tarts.

The rocks vibrated and rose. The gravel clattered and scraped near me in a rising blind. My face lit up. Sonia's did too. But when I turned to Romero, he remained unconvinced. Slowly, my rocks began to fall. One by one they sagged and scattered, raining down like hail. My blood boiled and my fists clenched with frustration.

Who does he think he is?

The stones burst into tiny firecrackers. They splintered in shards like scattershot.

My throated scorched. Myst siphoned around me like a cyclone, swirling around my wrists. My muscles tensed.

Sonia shook me by the shoulders. "What are you doing? Stop." Her eyes bulged and her skin blanched.

I exhaled, and the myst dissipated. My knees buckled; my breaths were heavy. I could feel another migraine setting in. The changelings anxiously searched for trouble with weapons drawn, and Romero stood over me across the way. His face scolded me with silent disappointment.

"I can't do it. I'm sorry," I panted.

"You were doing so well. What happened?" Sonia asked.

Pebbles lay before us on the ground in a circle. The crunching of footsteps neared us. Two leather boots stood in the circle of light. I dared not look him in the eye.

"Stand back. She needs air," said Sonia.

"You'll never master this. What did that accomplish, tell me?"

"Back off," snapped Sonia.

"You lack self-control. I expected better from you. You've shown promise, resilience, and endurance. But you will never master sorcery. You will never be like her. You chose that name, Kiera, but you are unfit to wear it."

"You with your secrets!" I screamed. I stood weakly and launched an uppercut toward his chest. He caught my fist before it reached his face.

"You still punch like a girl."

He twisted my arm and held it behind my back. He raised a dagger to my throat. I continued to wail on him with my free hand.

"Who is she? What else are you hiding? You're so full of it! Who do you think you are to talk down to me?" I screamed at him.

"You best watch your tone, kid."

"Romero let her go," Sonia said, calmly grasping the handle of her saber.

"'Kid, kid, kid.' There you go again. Newsflash, Romero—or whoever you are—I'm seventeen."

"No, you're just some dumb kid who has no idea what she's doing, running away from her problems, and getting into trouble and politics that are none of her concern. You don't want this life."

"Who are you to tell me what I want and don't want?"

The two changelings circled in.

"Romero, let her go now," ordered Sonia.

He pulled my head back and slammed me into the ground. Rocks cut my lip and cheeks.

"Because I'm you," he said. He stomped on my back and knocked the wind out of me, yanking my tail and holding me in place.

Romero drew his sword, and Sonia drew hers.

"Don't you dare hurt her," she threatened.

"You want answers, beast? I'll give you answers. At seventeen, the son of nobility was forced to become a magistrate. I was forced to leave my life, my home, and my friends all behind to train as a soldier, a diplomat, and a spy.

"Years of vigorous training came to breed nothing but pain, solitude, and isolation. It was all to be tested at the war between nations. They forced me, a spy and arbiter, into a war I didn't want or believe in. So what did I do? I ran. I ran away from it all. I faked my death and became a mercenary. I sought to explore the world and discover who I was for myself. Sound familiar? I've been down this road, Sinopa."

At that, tears welled up in his eyes. He lowered his sword, and he loosened his grip on my tail.

"You don't want this life. You'll experience nothing but loneliness and regret for involving other people. Like Jasper, you'll lose yourself and the people you once knew. Don't lose sight of who you are."

At that, he raised his boot. I turned over and wiped the blood from my face. He held out his hand to help me up. I stared at it blankly, refusing to take it. He pushed past the two changelings and continued his watch.

"Look, Sinopa, it's been a long day. We are all tired and probably have cabin fever. Maybe we should just go to bed," Sonia suggested.

I nodded.

You know it's been a bad day when Sonia has to be the voice of reason. She never woke me for my watch. She talked in the night, but I never saw with whom.

CHAPTER SEVENTEEN

C ome morning, we fixed breakfast. I kept my distance from Romero.
All night I had nightmares. Sonia, as my gruff guardian angel, stayed beside me throughout them. She always held this tone of, "I love you, but you're a pain in my ass." After saving each other twice, I guessed we really were sisters.

Most nightmares were of this High Wolf. His voice called me in the dead of night. "Come to me. Fight. Kill. Kill! Kill!"

Worse yet, I had more visions. I stood at the door again. The High Wolf pressed me, beckoned me, and pleaded with me to open the door. Large stone faces sang songs in harmony. My feet petrified themselves to the floor, and darkness rose all around me. It consumed me, muffling my screams. Creeping voices strangled my every waking thought.

Voices told me to fight, kill, and win.

I'd wake up sweating or with a scream, and Sonia threw a pillow to shut me up.

Myst ran thicker in underground mornings. It stuck to the ground like moist morning dew but obscured vision like fog. Not even my night vision could penetrate it. Romero offered me breakfast, calling me "Sleeping Beauty."

Being the teenage girl I was, the silent treatment was the only response he got. I stuck to my remaining plum tarts. For once, Sonia and I shared some. It was about time someone else came around.

As the morning pressed on, the myst only seemed to thicken. My migraine fizzled out from yesterday, but now it came back with a vengeance. I collapsed to my knees.

Sonia stopped beside me. A ting of metal struck as something fell against the cavern floor.

"Sinopa, are you okay?" she asked.

My throat burned. Myst suffocated me. I hyperventilated, trying to get air in my lungs. My scales rose prickly on end.

The Wolf crept into the back of my skull. "Kill. Why do you resist? Rise, my daughter. Fight. Come to me, my lost one. *Win*."

Romero called out to us. "Look alive. We have company."

There was howling in the fog. Our changeling companions fell on their knees as well. They were beating their heads into the ground, screaming. Their bodies shook, and their muscles bulged and grew. Their eyes glazed over. Tatters of clothes ripped in clots of fabric on the floor.

Two hulking behemoths towered over us. Veins bulged up and down their bodies. Their hearts squeezed their chests and pulsated through their skin. The cracking of bones and ligaments creaked across the walls.

The beasts snarled, and their jowls flickered, releasing spit and drool. Their snouts had grown as wide as cantaloupes. Their heads bulged larger than a bear's. Claws shot out as long as bayonets but a thousand times sharper. They charged.

"Sinopa, on your feet!" Sonia yelled. She raised her saber to defend me. I wheezed on the floor. She ran forward to meet him. The behemoth swiped. Her wings fluttered her back, and she plunged the sword into him. The thin blade snapped in the rippling chest of the beast. Sonia looked on in horror. The monster roared above her.

The beast smacked her in the air. Its claws pierced her shoulder and flung her against the cave wall. Her wings flapped weakly, breaking her fall.

"Guys, swords won't work against these!" she yelled.

The other behemoth barreled toward me. Sonia grabbed the sledgehammer off the floor. An echoing blast bellowed off the cave walls. Clattering rocks came down around us. My ears rang.

Romero tugged me to my feet. "Get your head in the game, kid."

I nodded.

I couldn't breathe. My lungs heaved. The myst suffocated me. Why didn't it have the same effect on the others? I felt strange—powerful even.

I raised my sword. Romero reloaded his pistol. Both beasts barreled toward us. Sonia struggled with the heavy hammer behind them. She flapped her freshly healed wings and charged. Her flight was shaky and unsteady. She zig-zagged after them. She raised the hammer, bowlegged and crashed it down on the beast's spine.

Clamoring roars and growls raised from the dropped beast, down but not out. The second behemoth was undeterred.

Romero fired another shot. The blast echoed once more, leaving my ears ringing. I attempted to fling the fallen stalagmites, but they only bounced off its face. Keeping happy thoughts was impossible. The beast stopped over me, raising its claws. An arm pushed me from behind.

Sideways, I could see blood spraying, material and skin ripping from Romero's chest. The beast loomed over him. Its massive paws held his legs to the floor. Dribble rained down from its smiling jaws. Its tongue scooped into his chest. Droplets of blood splattered as it shoveled into his rib cage. It slowly fed upon him, lick by lick, like an ice cream cone. "Yes, Feed. Kill. Eat."

I screamed at it to stop. I raised my glove at it and clenched my fist.

The beast shrieked and shook in place. Myst poured into my lungs. "That's it. Fight. That's how it starts. Ingest me."

My throat burned. Myst turned and wisped around me, raising my scales on end. Then, cracking. My knees clacked in fear. The beast shrieked louder. Its left heel buckled and splintered, then its right.

On its knees, it screamed louder. I gritted my teeth. My vision tinted red. I approached closer. My eyes watched as I broke him. Finger by finger, piece by piece—he cracked. The demon cowered before me, and bone by bone it bowed. I stood over the bleeding body of Romero. It had butterflied him open. He floundered on the ground, weakly plunging a needle into his thigh.

I parted my arms before me. The beast's arms tore from the sockets. The limp baby doll arms swung. Its body lay prostrate before me. Its head snapped at me, teeth gnashed, and eyes wet.

The High Wolf spoke. "Yes, finish him. Bathe in his blood."

My scales stood on end. Unbelievable strength took hold. I wrestled it by the snout and began to twist. Sonia ran forward and her hammer came down on its head. I pushed her aside and screamed at her for stealing it from me. My claws swiped and dug over and over into its lifeless eyes as I saddled its neck like a horse.

Sonia pulled me off and slapped me.

I stared at her. My vision cleared. Blood had stained her cheeks. I looked at the beast, then Romero, and then my hands. I wept.

What had I done? And how? Did I become like them?

Sonia and I surrounded Romero's bleeding body. The beast had torn his coat. His dress shirt lay in crimson tatters. Four long lacerations exposed his raw flesh. Glass shards fell from his coat as if vials of some fluid burned into his wounds. Even with these potions coursing through his veins, his consciousness wavered. I summoned all my strength to perform healing; I desperately wanted him to be okay.

"Save it," Romero said. "You're gonna need your strength."

I shook my head and, through my tears, did it anyway.

"Sonia, there's a vial in my pocket. Take it," he urged weakly.

She rummaged through and found it.

"Antiseptic. Treat yourself fast," he wheezed. "Saryx. They're called saryx. You'll become like them if you don't treat the wound." Romero coughed. "The mysts will change you."

She poured the bottle over her shoulder and winced. She poured the rest over his chest, and he cursed her. Can't say I blamed him.

"Kiera." He raised a hand to my face. "You lost control."

"No, I didn't," I lied.

He put both his hands on my glove as it pulsated white light.

"Yes, yes, you did."

"I saved you, didn't I? Just stay still, will you? You're going to make it through this."

He pushed my hands aside, "Don't lose yourself. I'm happy to have had an apprentice like you."

"Shut up! You will make it through this." I pressed my palms further into the lacerations. Sadly, the potions did more than I ever could.

Howling echoed through the cavern.

"Sounds like the Order heard our scrap. Sonia, you know what to do."

She nodded and picked up a small backpack that Romero had been wearing. Romero's cuts were sealing, but slowly.

"Sinopa, it's time to move," Sonia demanded.

"Not without Romero."

"Sinopa."

"Just give me five more minutes," I pleaded.

Romero fiddled with his pocket and handed me back my flintlock. "You've proved yourself today, my Kiera."

"I can't take that."

"It's yours. Take it."

"Kiera, we need to move!"

The howls came closer. I recognized them. Canine changelings, like the ones who chased me in Jasper's lair. Romero loaded another round in the chamber. "Don't worry about me. There can't be a performance without the lead. I guess that falls to you. The show must go on."

Sonia raised her hammer. Glowing eyes appeared through the myst.

"I'll hold them off," he said.

"You can't even walk, let alone fight," I said.

"Nonsense. I'm a magistrate, remember? I still have a few tricks up my sleeve."

He extended his hand out for me to help him get to his feet. Light trickles of blood still oozed from his chest. He staggered and fell to one knee.

"Guess I lost quite a few pints," he chuckled.

Glowing eyes lit up around us in the circle against the wall. I turned to Sonia and she to me.

"What are you doing? Leave!" Romero shouted at us.

"And miss your final performance? That would be in poor taste, don't you think?" I impersonated him as best I could.

"Guess we can't leave you behind, you dusty old fart," agreed Sonia.

Romero smirked and groaned to his feet. "Let's give them hell, then," he said.

One wolf charged, and Sonia sent him flying into the pile of dead companions on the sidelines. Romero popped off the one behind her. I hung back, hurling bits of rock with my magic as ranged fire. I refused to leave Romero. Wave after wave rushed, overwhelming Sonia. I drew my sword and dragged Romero after her.

We were surrounded. A large coal-colored wolf stood taller than the rest. Gold chains adorned his collar and a white tattered coat hung from his shoulders. Not an inch of the changeling's skin wasn't covered in fur.

"Release the pureblood," he growled. "The High Wolf commands it. Comply and your deaths shall be swift."

Sonia's white skin had been pasted with blood. Half of it was her own. Romero had slumped again to one knee, keeping the pressure on his wound.

I stepped forward. "I am she."

Sonia glared at me. She pulled a red stick from her bag and began fumbling with the pack.

The dark-furred changeling fixed his amber eyes on me. "Come," he said. "He's expecting you."

"Promise me they'll be safe. This doesn't concern them," I demanded.

The dark wolf growled. "You dare to think you can barter with me, lizard?"

Sparks flew. Sonia tossed me the bag and threw the red stick of dynamite against the wall.

"Take care, puddin'," she said.

She grabbed Romero's flintlock and blasted the explosives and the stalactites.

The walls shook and boulders caved in around us. I scrambled to a tiny crevice for safety. I could see Sonia tugging Romero. Walls and rocks came down. The wolves howled after them. Boulders stood between us. Dust kicked up in my face. I heard screaming and gunshots on the other side. I dug through the rubble and beat my fist, but it was no use. They were trapped.

I was all alone, cold and in the dark. Romero was right. I regretted ever getting them involved.

When the dust settled there was only silence. My night vision set in. Droplets of water trickled off the ceiling into puddles. I had to find a way around. I had to save my friends. I just had to. The cave was only a dead end. A few vents looked just small enough for me to crawl through, but the thought set my claustrophobia into overdrive.

Why did she do that? I could have saved them. We could have made a plan.

I guess she really felt how I did. I couldn't lose her, either, only now it was as though I had.

❧

MY MIGRAINE THUMPED my forehead over and over, drumming out any logic in my search. I resigned myself to being trapped.

I inventoried my supplies from our bags. It came out to several smashed plum tarts, half a canteen of water, a saber, Romero's journals, three sticks of dynamite, and a set of matches. I estimated it to last only a few days. Wendigos would find my body and suck on my bones. No one would save Sonia or Romero, and this High Wolf would never get what was coming to him.

I had to force down food to ease my nerves while I paced in circles. Most of the crumbs just trailed me on the floor. I listened closely and heard water. Ten feet up was a small ledge. I built a platform out of rocks and wreckage.

I hoisted myself, sweating heavily, onto the ledge. Through the tunnel, I could see a glowing green crystal overlooking a sparkling serene basin of water. I cautiously hiked my way through the dark. I had seen no signs of wendigos, but without a torch, they'd see me before I'd see them.

The light sparkled above in chandeliers of emerald glass. I bathed in the water. My reflection was hardly recognizable. Even after cleaning my hands and face, it wasn't enough. I left my soiled dress on the shore and stayed in the shallows. There was no need to drown alone while drowning my sorrows.

The thought of death didn't seem too bad—just to sink beneath the surface and let go. Just to end it painlessly. That would be a mercy. But I couldn't bring myself to do it. Whether that makes me a coward for thinking it, or by not acting upon it, I don't know. Staring into my campfire of fungus and dried hyssop, I cried, unsure of what to do next. I was all alone.

Howling sounded in the distance. I shook myself and fetched my clothes. My sword chinked from my waist. I was determined to save my friends. Nobody would stop me. The howling came closer. It was wimpy and deep.

"Stand back! I'm warning you," I called.

Two mismatched eyes stared at me from the shadows. "Kiera?"

A dog-faced changeling stood before me, covered in clay and mud. "Max?"

He charged, and I dropped my sword. He flung his arms around me and raised me off my feet, holding me tight.

I couldn't even return the hug, as he'd squeezed my arms to my side.

I began, "Max, I want to apolo—"

He held me tighter, nearly choking me. I felt like a tick ready to pop.

"It's good to see you," he said.

CHAPTER EIGHTEEN

M ax told me his story of how he had arrived underground. All the while, he talked with his mouth full of plum tarts. He explained how he hadn't eaten for days.

After returning to the banquet, he found all the sick Aerogapolian guards and some Northstrand navy as well. He made haste toward the gate and brought help. The doctor said if it had been any later, people could have died.

They regaled Max as a hero. But he had noticed not everyone had made it out. I never returned, and the assassin who had poisoned the banquet must still be out there. The consul could be in danger. Cobarde had no choice but to take Max, due to all the press. They led him into the mines.

Out of the public eye, Cobarde had planned to trap him and execute him like the others, but Max had escaped, catching a sweet scent. It was the smell of sweat, sweets, and gunpowder. My scent. He had stumbled blindly, avoiding their crossbow fire, into an underground stream, and it whisked him away—to here.

He set his leg up on a rock and showed me his splint. His leg had splintered on the rocks. The remains of his tux were wrapped around his ankle and tied to a torch. Seeing how he had better vision in the dark, the torch was no use to him. He'd wandered this cave for days. Finding my crumbs, he howled out for help . . . and here he was.

He immediately hobbled over and barked at the bats because they had kept "interrupting" him tell his story.

"Who do you think you are? Arf-arf, arf-arf-arf! How did you even get down here? Arf-arf, arf-arf, arf!" he barked.

The bats stared at him placidly.

"Wait a minute. Max, you're a genius!" I cried.

"I am? I mean, yes, I am. And to the bats, as a genius I say, Arf-arf, arf-arf, arf!"

I pulled him back to the fireside.

"Max, don't you see?"

"See what?"

"The bats."

"Yes, that blind scoundrel is giving me the evil eye."

I laughed.

"No, Max. If there are bats, they need food, and food means . . . ?"

"Freedom."

"Good boy."

Max's tail wagged. "I've missed you," he said. "You're not mad I didn't stay, are you?"

I shook my head, smiling.

His tail wagged harder. He stood up and tried to come over beside me and tripped.

"You okay?"

He nodded with a whimper.

I went over and dragged him back beside me. He seemed to enjoy it too much, like a child scooting across the kitchen floor.

"Now, let's take a look at that ankle."

He growled and pulled it away.

"How am I supposed to help if you won't let me look at it?" I asked.

"It's fine."

"Max, you're hobbling like a peg-legged idiot. Just let me see the—"

He withdrew from my reach.

"Fine, be that way. Suffer for all I care," I said, crossing my arms.

"My sister's a doctor, I think," he replied. "I may be a bit shaky on the whole memory thing, but I'm fine."

"I'm just trying to help. You don't trust me?"

Max huffed and propped up his leg on a rock.

"That a boy," I said.

I unwrapped the bandages. The idiot had stuck the pitch in the meat. While it preserved the torch, it meant the wound was dirty. I cleaned it thoroughly, sufficiently getting wet from him shaking the water off. Interestingly enough, his body appeared human, not changeling, from the waist down. He had shaved his legs smooth as a baby's behind.

"What's the call, doc?" he asked.

Now, I was no doctor, but even I could tell the bone was broken.

"It's not looking good. I'll see what I can do."

To be honest, I wasn't sure what I could do. I took deep breaths.

Think soothing thoughts. Gentle ocean breezes. The hot springs at the Starshell fortress. The soft enveloping way Max held me tight. I mean, no. Not that last one.

Max was sweet. Blunt, clingy, and stupid, but sweet. I don't know. I enjoyed being around him, but he could be annoying, and well, I still had infatuations over Rudolph. Not that I could ever admit my feelings about him out loud, though.

I took a deep breath and tried to shake out my nerves. Part of me doubted whether this would even work. I had never healed bone before, and my migraine held a scalpel to my brain, ready to lobotomize me.

Here goes nothing.

A dull glow emanated around my fingertips. His fur burned hot. When I massaged it, it grew cold. He whimpered and whined as I pushed him back from picking at the wound. *Heavens, how I wished I had a cone!* My fingers sank through his skin like water. His ankle glowed. In my vision, it appeared that my hand phased through his leg. My claw snagged on something sharp and jagged.

Max yelped and squirmed away.

"What are you doing?"

"Healing your leg. What else? Now hold still."

He continued to crawl away, kicking and crying for me to let him go. I held tight to his leg and flipped him over to his back. I dropped my knee on his chest and clamped on his snout.

"Max, look at me. Max," I said, snapping my fingers.

His breathing was heavy. I could feel his chest rise and fall like a ship on the ocean. He whined, but I held his snout shut.

"Look, Max. I'm gonna help you, okay? But that means you gotta hold still."

Max, muffled, tried to say something.

"Listen to me. I'm gonna let go of your lips, but I've gotta trust that you're gonna be a big boy, okay? No more whining. Otherwise, I will get my belt and you will have a fancy new muzzle. You don't want that, do you?"

He shook his head.

I love-tapped his cheek. "Good boy. Now, what is it?"

"But Kiera, that really hurt!" he burst. "And I don't know what you're doing. One moment your hands were there, and the next . . . the rest of you won't disappear, will it?"

I shook my head and held back my laugh as best I could. I couldn't believe he was serious. The poor sap must have never seen magic before.

"Are you ready to try again?"

Max shook his head. His bottom lip puckered below his big sad dog eyes.

"Oh, come on, buddy. I really need your help down here. What will it take for you to help me? I got some plum tarts. I got this sword—a little bent, though. What do you want? What would you like?"

"How about a date?"

It took me aback for a moment. Me and my big mouth.

"Didn't we just have a . . . ?" I started.

"But you kind of . . ." Max trailed off.

"Yeah, that," I scratched my head. "Sorry. I'll tell you what: if we get out of here, I owe you one, okay?"

He nodded.

"But you gotta help me get outta here, all right?"

He nodded.

"All right. Deep breaths, okay, buddy?"

Max gulped. He nodded and tucked back his ears.

Here goes nothing, again.

My hand pulsated and glowed brightly. Max's eyes widened with fear and astonishment. My arms rubbed up and down his leg, petting and massaging through his brown field of fur. It turned hot, then cold, then back again, until finally, my hand sunk beneath his skin.

Max whimpered and whined. "How did you—"

I put my finger to his lips and shushed him. "Shh. All right, Max, this may hurt, okay?"

He shook his head, and I held his snout.

"I can't have you biting your tongue, so I want you to look at me, okay?"

His head cocked in confusion.

"Just look at me. Look into my eyes. Think about our date. Everything will be okay."

He nodded. His jaw clenched, and he licked his lips to brace himself. I had to reposition myself now to reach for his leg blindly and hope I could splice both ends together. I eased down on my side and turned him to match me.

I dipped my hand through his fur, and his eyes widened.

"Don't look at it. Trust me. Eyes on me," I crooned.

His pupils darted back toward mine. They were soft, scared, and confused. Two mismatched gems shone before me. I fished for the leg bone, doing my best to calm him.

"You're doing great now. Keep it up."

I caught the end of the bone and he winced. His eyes closed and his body squirmed.

"Look at me, Max. Max! Look at me."

I caught the other end of the bone with my pinky and pulled them together. I had to twist the bones and lock them together like a jigsaw puzzle. His teeth bared and he growled.

He rolled over onto his back. I held on tight with both hands and placed my knee on his abdomen to hold him down. It did no good with his dented breastplate. I felt every breath he took. The warm air blew past his wet nose and hit my face.

Max continued to struggle. If he kept moving, he may break another bone. I began sealing them together. My fingers wielded hot, then cold.

"Look at me, Max."

He thrashed, with tears in his eyes, staring up at me.

"It's all right. I got you," I said.

He nodded and licked my fingers.

I ran my hand up and down the bone, smoothing it out. His eyes stared deeply into mine. I let go of his snout and petted his ears back. His chest rocked me up and down.

"There you go. That wasn't so hard, was it?"

"Easy for you to say," he groaned.

He licked my face once before I pushed his snout away. Who knew where that tongue had been? I couldn't believe I had kissed him.

He began inspecting his leg. Then he looked solemnly at me. "You're a sorceress?"

"That's not a problem, is it?"

He bent his ankle back and forth. His paws ran through his fur. He looked up at me, overjoyed. "No, not a problem at all, packmate."

CHAPTER NINETEEN

W e investigated the bats in the cave. At dusk, they took flight and flew out of sight across the basin. The direction I was hoping not to go—toward the water. Great.

Max plunged in with a cannonball.

"*Water* you waiting for?" he teased.

There was no way anyone would have known Max had a broken leg. He doggy paddled all over the pool. I told him to take it easy and he splashed me from the shallows.

"Stop it! You're getting me wet."

"That's the idea," he laughed. "Hop in; it's not too cold. Let's go."

He was lucky I didn't break his other leg. Now I was no doctor, but I thought he needed rest.

I dipped my toe into the water and pulled it back out with a shiver.

"It's freezing!"

Max laughed. "I know. It's exhilarating. Let's go!"

I scanned the vast basin. I couldn't do it. "Max, I have a confession to make."

"You're a vegan?" he guessed.

"What? No. Where did that come from?"

"I was thinking of food. I've never seen you eat anything but sweets. Wait, let me guess. You're a sorceress?"

"Yes. But—"

"I knew it."

"This isn't about—"

"Nothing escapes my keen canine eye."

I snapped, "Well, if that were true, you'd know I was trying to speak now, wouldn't you?"

Max's ears tucked back. "Sorry," he mumbled.

"It's all right, Max. It's just . . . I can't swim."

He looked at me, confused. "What do you mean? Everyone can swim."

"Not me."

"Not even a little doggy paddle?"

"Nope. Never."

Max frowned. He scratched his chin for a moment, and then his eyes lit up.

"That's okay. I can teach you."

"Thank you, but that's really not necessary."

He raced out of the water and sprayed me everywhere as he shook himself dry.

"Watch it! Let's look for another way around."

Max cracked a mischievous grin. He grabbed me off my feet and carried me over to the edge.

"Hey, what are you doing?" I shrieked. "Hey!"

"In you go," he laughed.

"This is not funny. Put me down. Put me down now!"

My tail pounded him in the face. He swung me by the edge and wound up for the toss.

"But there *is* no way around," he explained.

"Stop. Don't you dare. Let me go."

His face had that terrifying dog teeth grin. "Okay."

"No. Please. No!"

"Cannonball!" he shouted.

I screamed, flying in a mass of flailing limbs, and sputtered insults. The water smacked the back of my head. The world muffled. The ice bath froze me to my core. My arms attacked the water, desperate to stay afloat, but my body only continued to sink.

I screamed for Max. My eyes burned in the salty brew. The lights grew more distant. Something plunged beside me. Two dark arms strangled my waist.

I rose to the surface, choking. I blinked, trying to stop the burning. Max held me close and looked me over. His fur grew two shades darker when wet.

"It's okay," he said. "Breathe."

"What the hell was that for?"

"I thought it would be funny. I didn't expect you to sink to the bottom."

"Don't. Do. That." I backhanded him on each syllable for emphasis.

"Bring me back to shore, please," I begged.

My dress absorbed all the water like a sponge and stuck to my thighs.

"Look, you're already out here. You don't want to give it a go?" asked Max.

I shook my head and shivered.

"Why not? You have nothing to be afraid of. I'm right here."

And that's supposed to be reassuring? You already tried to drown me once.

"I've already tried," I answered. "It's no use. It's a lost cause. There has to be another way around." I began sinking again, and he pulled me up by the horns.

"Kick your legs. It will help you stay afloat. That bad attitude is what's weighing you down. It sounds to me like you have already given up. There is no other way around, Kiera. I've looked. I can help you, but you can't quit on me. I'm not giving up on you if you won't. Deal?"

I cracked a weak smile. He was a persistent pooch. I'll give him that. No matter how much I pushed him away, he kept crawling back. It didn't help that he was dumb as rocks and built like them, too. The idiot had thrown me in with all our supplies. No doubt the food was wet.

"Deal. But only for a bit. I'm freezing."

"I know. It's refreshing, isn't it?"

"Easy for you to say. You look like a cheap throw rug. You have all that fur. Give me some of that."

Max tugged at his loose clumps of fur and handed them to me in soggy wads. Apparently, sarcasm was a foreign language to him. I dropped the wad and wiped my hands in disgust.

"All right," he said, "first off, I'm gonna let go."

"Don't let go!"

"How are you going to learn how to float?"

"Please don't let go."

"All right, we'll start with something easier for a warm-up."

"Can't we practice some place shallow?"

"I'd have to toss you in again. No retreat, Kiera. Besides, fear can be a great motivator."

I mumbled to myself, "This dog will be the end of me."

"That's right. Tell them fears who's boss."

"Please kill me."

Max showed me many techniques and helped me practice them—emphasis on the showing, though. His accent took some getting used to, and he wasn't good at explaining things. At all. Every time I did something wrong, he nipped at me.

"All right, hop on my back. We'll practice kicking."

I draped my arms over his shoulders, and he nipped at my fingers. Not hard, but just enough to force his point across.

"Please don't choke me," he said.

I slid my hands down his slick metal breastplate and couldn't get a hold. He snapped at my shoulder.

"Just tell me what you want me to do. You have words, you know," I scolded.

"Loosen the straps. Hold on from under the armor."

I began frustratedly fiddling with the wet leather. Only a few minutes in, and I was ready to quit. My hands slipped between the cracks and ran through his fur. My fingers rested on his chest. Warm, hard muscle stood beneath all that cushion.

"Ready?" he said.

I nodded.

He interrupted my fantasies only briefly. Surely he couldn't be all bad, with such a physique.

We practiced kicking, swimming in a circle. He was a better friend than a teacher. His every movement paid consideration to me. He never lost patience. He slowed down so I could catch up. He made sure I wasn't too cold.

And any moment the sweetheart saw me slipping, any time I was falling, he was there. He'd pull me up. With those cute, mismatched eyes, bright whiskered smiles, and that goofy twitching ear, he'd hold me close.

"It's okay. I've got you," he'd say, and then he'd ask me if I wanted to continue.

My heart fluttered. Although it may have been an ice bath, he warmed me from the inside out. We kept going. My heart remained determined to let this feeling last forever.

When we ended up staying an hour in the water, I was ready to call it quits.

"Wait for one last test," Max insisted. "Swim to that rock by yourself, then I'll help you to shore."

I bit my bottom lip. "By myself?" "I believe in you. Remember the doggy paddle?"

I sighed, "Yes, I remember the doggy paddle."

"Good," he said, "I should get a patent. I'll be with you every step of the way."

I stared at the spire of rock. It was so close, yet so far away.

"You mind giving me a push?"

He gently guided me in front of him. I straightened my dress around me. Gotta watch those wandering eyes. I might as well have been swimming in a mop head. I curled my tail around him. My legs bent like a loaded spring, ready to pop off his chest.

"Ready?"

"As I'll ever be, I suppose."

"That's the spirit."

He counted, and I kicked off his chest. I heard a yelp behind me. My heel had hit his face. Over my shoulder, I saw him wave me on, rubbing his nose. My feet paddled. My arms scooped at the water before me. Not the most elegant first swim, but it worked. Not much was elegant about me. Breathing and rhythm were the hardest part.

As I neared the pillar, small schools of cavefish glowed around me. Their bodies shimmered, oddly translucent. I lost stamina.

Come on, Sinopa. Almost there.

I paddled harder. Max cheered behind me.

Just a few more yards.

I scooped with my arms like an idiot. My lungs were on fire. I swear I didn't have the stamina God blessed a third-grader.

Just a few more feet.

I felt myself sinking. Fish darted all around me. Sharp needles stabbed my leg. I screamed. Water shot into my lungs, and something pulled me under.

My eyes burned. Bubbles escaped my throat. My cries only gurgled in an endless blue. All I could do was watch as they warbled further away. The world got darker and darker. I tugged at my leg. Small, searing suction cups slithered up my foot.

A dark tendril weaved its way around my ankle. It squeezed and twisted my skin. Salt seeped and rubbed into my burn. Blood sprayed in a blotchy, dark mist. As water drained and siphoned my blood, a blooming maw opened.

Several shadowy petals flicked about like sea kelp, masking the entity. My exhausted muscles tugged harder. A second sweeping arm with bristling black barbs clenched on my calf. I bit my lip. The water swayed around me. The arm rocked me back and forth. My last breath's bubbles twinkled in a long trail.

A shadow broke through the light. Lightheadedness set in. Max paddled into my peripheral vision. His fist pounded on the tendril. His eyes turned to me. I felt faint. His jaw snapped down on the tentacle. A shrieking blast echoed in the water.

My body was flung out of the water. I skipped and smacked into the pillar. My horns cracked the rock. I hugged the side of it, gasping for air. My nostrils burned. I caught my breath.

Where's Max?

My head pivoted. The waters churned.

"Max? Max, where are you?"

Numbness replaced the burning sensation in my leg. I couldn't feel my toes. My arms slid down the pillar. I drifted into open water. My head hardly kept afloat. Ripples stopped, and the water grew still.

"Max!" I called out frantically.

How long can dogs hold their breath?

Ripples formed, and a head burst from the surface, gasping for air.

"Max!"

He swam over and I held on to him like before. He attacked the water for dear life. Hand over hand, arm over arm. I squeezed tight and kicked with my good leg. I hoped it would help somehow, if only a little.

Arms lashed out around us. Max tunneled in and out of the stonework. Rocks crumbled, injuring the eldritch arms.

"Get ready to dive," Max warned me.

"You're crazy!"

He paddled around a corner, and we caught our breaths. Screeches followed. My thoughts turned to the wendigo. Echolocation. It was blind.

"You all right?" he asked.

Our chests heaved. "I can't feel my leg."

"Sorry. So, over there?"

The salt strained my eyes. My dark vision couldn't pick up anything.

"There's an underwater cave that's lit from the other side," Max said. "We can make a break for it if we're quick enough."

"I can't go underwater. That's when it's the scariest."

The screeches came closer in sadistic dolphin-like clicks.

"Kiera, you've ventured down here bravely, in darkness, for days. Are you really going to quit now?"

A pillar crashed into the water. Hard green emerald bits fell from the ceiling. It was getting closer.

"What do you want me to do?" I asked.

"Count to a hundred. You don't have to look at it. Just count to a hundred, and when you open your eyes, we'll be there."

I grabbed onto his back and snuggled my head against him. *Don't lie to me, Max.*

"Deep breath now," he called.

"You ready?"

Max sighed. "As I'll ever be."

I grinned. With one last breath, our feet pushed into open water.

CHAPTER TWENTY

A deep whooshing sound besieged us. I held on tight with my eyes shut. That sinking feeling, where one can see the light hitting the water's surface always terrified me.

I squeezed harder. Max's armor slipped, and I rested my head on a cushion of fur. Hearing his heartbeat was the only comfort to my nerves. It was steady but articulated. I started counting the beats. *One one-thousand, two one-thousand, three one-thousand, four one-thousand . . .*

Screeching surrounded us. I squeezed, and he paddled faster. His heart raced. *Fifteen, sixteen, seventeen, eighteen.* Wet smacks and crumbling came from our right. Max rose to the surface. *Breathe.*

Back down. *Thirty, thirty-one, thirty-two, thirty-three.* Max turned and snaked. We leaned left. Leaned right. Hard impacts rumbled behind us, followed by a sadistic squeal. My head hurt. The creature was close. *Forty-six, forty-seven, forty-eight.*

I could feel the water jet behind us. A rhythmic swoosh chugged like an underwater freight train. Max's tail bobbed between my knees like a tiny propeller. *Sixty-seven, sixty-eight, sixty-nine.* It was getting harder to count. My heart pumped faster than Max's.

The water pushed up on my hair. We dove deeper. Almost there. *Seventy-*

four, seventy-five, seventy-six. Something squeezed. Lightheadedness swept in. *Eighty-seven, eighty-eight, eight-nine.* It yanked my leg out from under me. My arms slipped from Max. My eyes opened. Pain shot up to my thigh. I tried to scream and bubbles poured from my throat.

Max raced back several feet away from the exit tunnel.

The world went black. My head bobbed. The rest was all a blur. A piercing cry. A warm patch of water. Black clouds. The world echoed as in a barrel.

"Kiera!"

Hard pounding pressed on my ribs.

"Kiera!"

Yes, I hear you. What happened?

Air entered my lungs. My body felt limp and heavy. More pressing on my chest. Moisture and pressure, like a washcloth, wrapped around my face. More air. Hard smacks hit my cheeks and made my eyes rattle. I couldn't move. A brown figure muttered over me.

Ninety-seven, ninety-eight, ninety-nine, one hundred.

My eyes flicked as the shadow blew into my mouth.

I choked. Water and sludge trickled from the corners of my lips.

"Kiera!"

I opened my eyes. The first thing I saw was the frightened figure of Max straddling over me. His arms lifted me up and held me close. One hundred. We were safe, just like he said.

The silver silhouette of my savior hovered over me. Darkness enveloped us. Impregnable darkness.

"Thank goodness you're all right! You're all right, aren't you? How many fingers am I holding up?"

He shoved his paw in my face and covered my eyes. I panted and pushed him away.

"None."

"Oh my gosh, you're blind!"

"No, that only works with your—"

He was too busy blubbering in the dark, tossing supplies from the soaked bags, looking for anything that might help.

"This is all my fault," he said.

"Max, heel. I'm not blind. It's just dark, that's all."

"Oh, thank heavens."

I shivered.

"It's cold. Let's get a fire going."

My eyes adjusted to the sea of endless black. It wasn't much help, though. My left leg felt numb.

I taught Max how to build a fire. Campfires became life, underground. They meant protection, food, and shelter.

Starting them proved no simple task. It's not like a tree was right around the corner. We used a few dry journal pages as kindling. I smoothed them out while Max, being the seeing-eye dog, fetched some fungi to keep it going.

Water soaked all our matches. After the third match, we felt we'd need to try rubbing things together and hope for the best. It took seven matches to find one that would ignite.

The fire glowed, and for the first time, we could clearly see each other. A scratch ran across his left eye, the blue one. Dried red clumps matted on his arm.

Looking down at my legs, several black barbs stood like porcupine quills from my calf. Black ichor trickled down my ankle. A similar faint ink smudged over both our faces. The entire cave reeked of wet dog and raw fish.

"Max, do you mind?" I said, gesturing to my leg.

"What?"

"I can't feel my leg. Can you, like . . . ?"

He squatted down and began poking the barbs.

"Don't touch it."

"What are those?"

"Don't know. Something from the fish, I guess."

He lifted my ankle up and pulled one out with his teeth.

"Max, what are you doing?"

"Getting it out," he grumbled with it in his mouth.

"Those could be poisonous for all you know."

He spat the quill out on the ground.

"Tastes fishy," he said.

I rolled my eyes. I still couldn't believe I'd kissed him. "Be more careful. We don't need more injuries."

He sat down and propped my foot in his lap. He began twisting the quills. I winced as my nerves suddenly came to life.

"They're in deep," said Max.

"I don't care how you do it but make it quick."

"Right. Hold still."

"Wiseass."

He yanked on the barbs with both paws.

I squealed and bit my lip. I gripped under my knee. He held my hand and yanked with the other.

Blood trickled, mixing with the black substance. It was no use.

"Screw it," he said.

He chomped down and bit at the barb and pulled it out in one clean motion. My head jerked back in pain.

"Max! What are you—"

Before I could finish, he pulled each one like a band-aid and smiled at me with the bundle of barbs in his mouth. Like a puppy with a new toy.

His jaw dropped the slobbery mass beside the fire.

"Ta-da!"

I could now lift my leg. The blood trickled down my calf. My ankle was sore, but I could flex it.

"Thank you," I said.

"Does this mean I still get that date?"

I laughed. "We'll see."

"I guess you could say now the shoe's on the other foot."

"I take it back," I teased.

Again, there was no telling where that mouth had been. He tore off a piece of his pant leg and wrapped it like a bandage.

"What's this black stuff?" I asked.

"Not sure. The thing shot ink everywhere after I hit it."

I began thinking of the saryx. I quickly searched for a bottle of antiseptic, then I remembered we had already finished it.

"It didn't bite you, did it?" I sat up and reached for his arm.

· · ·

"Scratched me, maybe," he replied.

"This is bad, Max."

"What are you talking about? We're safe."

"I heard if some of these creatures get you, you'll become like them. Saryx."

"You mean I will become a fish?"

I stared into the fire. "I don't know," I sighed.

The fire crackled between us. Crickets chirped in the underground cave's silence. Only Max's stomach dared to disturb it.

"Can I at least not be a hungry fish?"

I fished—pardon my pun—through the bag for any unsoiled crumbs of food. All of it slipped out of the bag in a wet smack against the stone floor. Only one tin of custard had remarkably held its form.

"I feel it's only fair that you have it," I said, handing it to him.

"What are you going to eat?"

"You saved my life; take it."

Max looked at the brown, watery custard that fit in the palm of his hand and opened it. He took his claw and drew a line down the middle. There were no spoons in the bag. He insisted I take my share, "You need to keep up your strength."

"All right, I think the only fair way to divide this is—" We devoured the tiny portion of food in seconds.

The dissolved frosting and pumpkin had lost most of its flavor, but we needed some form of nourishment. Our eyes met, grinning. Frosting covered our faces. Max licked the tin, then his nose. He leaned in and licked my cheek clean. I shuddered with a groan. "We need to work on personal space."

"Sorry."

I sighed. The flintlock lay between us. I shivered and told him that whoever turns into a saryx first, the other vows to shoot them. Max, being the goody-two-shoes he is, said he could never do it. I couldn't argue with him for how cold I was. My bones had frozen solid. My dress stuck to my body, clinging to my skin.

"You okay?" Max said with worried eyes.

"I'm fine. Just cold. We need a bigger fire."

"Take off your wet clothes," he said.

"What?"

I guess I hadn't noticed, but when Max removed his pants, bare skin rose to his pink hearted boxers. Again, his legs were human, not dog.

"I said maybe you should—"

"No, I see where this is going. 'Take off your clothes, Kiera,'" I mocked. "'Then we'll huddle for warmth.' What do you take me for? You just want my body, don't you? Nice try, but no."

"What kind of dog do you take me for?"

I chuckled, "A dog, I guess."

"That's an unfair stereotype, and I won't have it propagated any further."

"You don't even know what 'propagated' means," I said and sneezed.

"See, you're catching a cold," he chided.

"No, I'm not."

"Kiera."

"I'm not taking off my dress!"

"Why not? Scared?"

"I'm not scared," I snapped. "Just maybe a little shy, that's all."

"Sound scared to me. You're hiding something. Just let it out. You'll feel better."

"You just want to see me in my underwear."

Max's eyes darted and I realized it hadn't crossed his mind. "I just don't want you freezing to death after I hauled your body to shore and pumped the water out of your lungs."

"Fine, turn around," I relented.

"What?"

"I'm taking off my dress, you big baby, now turn around."

"This is ridiculous."

"Turn around *now.*"

"You don't trust me?"

"Can I? I'm alone, trapped thousands of feet underground with a man I hardly know who could easily overpower me, and no one would hear my screams."

"You're insane," he said flatly.

"Turn around. Now."

He grumbled a low growl and scooted his back to me. I ran my fingers over my midriff and glanced at his back.

"No peeking," I warned.

"I told you, I'm not that type of dog."

I pulled my dress off and revealed all the scars that had been hidden from view. Seared burns straddled my thighs. A pale patch of skin, where my belly had been forcibly descaled. Brands, sears—all the marks showed I'd been beaten, abused, and raped. My shame was on full display. I hunched down beside the fire in a ball. My knees covered my stomach.

"Better?" he asked.

"Yes."

"Now can I turn around?"

"No. I'd rather you didn't."

Max exhaled. Silence dominated the camp again. He couldn't just sit with his back to me all night. I shivered again, letting out another sneeze.

"Bless you," he said.

"Thanks."

"You know, Kiera, we have a saying among dogs that's applicable to this —you know, now that we're packmates. One dog will view the other as equal or above and surrender himself to the other."

"Surrender?"

"Sorry, *humble* himself before the other. He'll drop all his weapons and bow before them. The greater places himself in the feeblest position and flings himself in service or death of the other. They're our equal or superior. We call it 'showing our underbelly.'"

It sounded appropriate somehow.

"I'll show you mine if you show me yours. But, if not, in case this disease turns me . . . you know . . . I just want you to know that you've fed me, and you're the alpha, and I . . . I . . . ."

"Turn around," I ordered.

He gulped.

Max turned and left his legs crossed. I kept mine raised, hiding my abdomen. My breasts sat, tucked behind my bra, on my knees like juicy ripe tomatoes. The sack of forget-me-knots peered out of one cup.

"Pinky swear not to tell anyone?"

He scooted across from me and swore. I took a deep breath, closed my eyes, and dropped my knees.

Pink and shriveled skin stretched over my stomach. Where other girls are peach-skin-soft and tight in their pathways, I was wrinkled, mangled, and squished.

My skin—yes, skin not scales—crinkled like a wet sun-beaten raisin. Brands stenciled in goblin crested my seared thigh meat.

"Oh, Kiera . . ."

"Go on, say it. I'm disgusting. I'm ugly, weak, and I'm a monster." Tears welled up in my eyes.

"Kiera, I'm sorry. People don't treat us very well."

"It's not just people. I deserve this."

"No, no, you don't. You can't blame yourself. It's not your fault," Max tried to reassure me.

"I'm a monster," I repeated.

I pulled my knees up and cried into my hands.

Two warm paws grabbed my fingers and pulled them away from my face. His arm scooped around me.

"I don't think you're a monster," he whispered. "You're very brave and sweet—"

"What does it matter? It's not just this. You weren't there. I lost control of my temper and hurt my friends. I lost my restraint. Impulse surmounted me. I became a beast. Like everyone says I am."

"You don't look big and scary to me. Small and round, and maybe chubby—"

"Easy."

"You are who you choose to be, Kiera. You're only a monster if you choose to be."

I scoffed at the idea. "How could I possibly have a choice in all this? They threw this at me. I didn't choose to look like this. I didn't choose these scars."

"Yes, but you can choose how you react. The past is gone, and most things are out of our control, but you do have a choice. You can choose to let them define you or not. Who are they to tell you who to be? You live your life. Don't let them win."

He began undoing the dangling straps at his side.

"What are you doing?"

"Showing you mine. You're my packmate, and a deal's a deal."

He closed his eyes and exhaled, just like I had. He was just as uncomfortable as I was. Chocolate fur glistened, slick and moist. His chest exposed an oily sheen. His waist curved white and lightly fluffed, exposing a long scar. Beneath his fur, a second long scar ran where his dented breastplate sat.

I reached out to examine it and drew my hand back. He nodded the go-ahead. I ran my fingers down the raw gash in his chest.

"People treat us differently. But it doesn't mean we have to be different. I got this one during my training, the first week of basic."

"So you do remember?"

"It's foggy, but yes. Some things you never forget. They told me I'd never become a good guard dog. But I picked myself up and kept going. I will show my chief and my masters I am a good guard, that I am a good dog."

The rosy gulch ran a good foot long, diagonally. My fingers traced it down to a firm cotton abdomen. The second stretched just a few inches from his belly button.

"The other one?" I asked.

"It's more personal."

"You don't have to tell me if you don't want to."

"No, maybe it's best I save it," he agreed.

A man with secrets. Ooh-la-la.

I pulled out the small sack from my bra and handed it to him.

"What's this?

"Open it."

He pulled out one of the cracked spheres and it bit him. Images of young pups flashed and called for their Uncle Max.

He fumbled over his words in astonishment.

"My memories! How did you—? How could it—?"

He threw his arms around me and wept.

"I have a family. I have a brother and a sister. Everything is so clear," he cried happily.

He pulled away and attempted to lick my face. I pushed his snout away.

"Right. Sorry." He scratched the back of his head.

I sighed. "It's all right."

"You know this only proves my point," he said. "You're a good person."

"Stop, please."

"Regardless, Kiera, you're beautiful to me."

I shook my head. "No, stop. I'm not. But what does it matter? We're probably infected."

"You don't know that."

"There's still that chance that we will turn on each other. You weren't there. We could hardly take them on with three of us. I will become a monster even more."

"You're not. I'm here; I won't let that happen."

"Yeah, right. What are you going to do?" I challenged him.

"You see the second scar? This one I'm proud to bear. I was willing to lay down my life for my pack, and I'm willing to do the same for you if need be."

I winced. "Oh, stop. Max, you don't even know me."

"Of course I do. We're packmates."

The poor idiot doesn't even know my name.

"Even if I don't, I want to. Let me in. You don't like me?" he asked.

"I do, but—"

"What's the matter, then?"

"I can't be with you," I snapped.

His ears tucked back after I yelled at him. "What?"

"There's somebody else. I'm down here for him, and for all I know, he's dead."

Max's eyes glowed as they stared at me. "I'm sorry," he said.

"Quit apologizing. Stop it."

"I'm sor—yeah, right."

"Look, this is all happening so fast, and I'm tired and confused and hungry, and you make me feel special and my heart flutter, but I don't want to hurt you because you were so nice, and—and—*I* should apologize, not you. I'm the reason you're in danger. I'm the reason we'll probably die down here."

Tears returned with a vengeance. *Gosh, I'm such a drama queen.*

Max held me tight. "Shush. It's okay. I've got you. Even if you do turn, I'm not going anywhere. I meant what I said. I—I love you."

My lips touched his in one shaky smooch. I pulled away and sniffled as he held me close. Max rocked me as I wept myself to sleep. He thought I was crying over Rudolph. In reality, it was because I had just stolen a second kiss and he deserved much better.

CHAPTER TWENTY-ONE

W e snuggled together for warmth. I gave him a firm warning.

"I feel anything solid, it better be your keys in your pocket or I'll fix you right quick. Emphasis on 'fix,' capiche?"

Max gulped with a nod.

I made it clear it was only because I was cold. He let me have my space after my spell, which was perfectly fine with me. I felt so awkward around him. Sure, he was sweet, but I still held hope that Rudolph was out there. He was a master, after all. Max deserved better. I had used him, wrapped him around my finger, and spun him loose. Yet he refused to let go.

How could he keep forgiving me after all I have put him through? Did he even forgive me? Maybe he's just too stupid to realize it. He sure seems blind to the fact that I'm not interested.

That's the thing with dogs—they're loyal. He was certainly more loyal than any *man* I'd met.

His body enveloped mine. I snuggled up in his lap and lay back against his chest. My flintlock rested in my panties in case Whiskers got smart. Max wasn't like that, though. His touch gently jostled me, side to side. His fur clicked, with the static of a warm blanket while his firm arms slowly rocked me to sleep.

You couldn't really call it sleep, though. I had that same dream again: I was wandering down a brick road. Gold bars lined my path. A hefty metallic door stood before me. Carved faces sang. Myst billowed around me.

The grizzly voice whispered in my ear. "Yes, kill. Feed. Feed it. The way will be open to you. Kill. Kill. Kill!"

"No! I'm not a monster!" I shouted back at it.

A row of teeth unhinged and sneered at me. They split into fours and swallowed me in a cloud of smoke.

I awoke alone on a wooden floor. My back stung. "Bitch needs to be taught her place," said a voice behind me. It was Big Papa—sorry, Pater. He's no father of mine.

"She didn't mean it," cried Al.

There was the sound of pummeling flesh.

My hands grew stiff. I could only make out faint shapes. I was blindfolded. Ropes hog-tied me on my knees in front of a bucket.

Not this dream again.

The door flew open behind me. I struggled to break free.

"Now, do the job right. The snake deserves to die. Luckily, we can be very forgiving," snickered Pater.

Al undid my blindfold. Blood dripped from his nose and bruised forehead. One of his teeth was missing. He truly was my brother in suffering. A bucket full of ice and water hung above my head.

"Now, half-pint, how do you break up a broody hen?"

Al's eyes stared at the floor. "You dip it in a bucket of water," he murmured.

"Demonstrate," Pater commanded.

Al's lip quivered, looking down at me. Blood and snot poured from his nose. He shook his head.

"Need I remind you, she said no, and this is her punishment."

Al looked me in the eye, and I nodded.

His sickly fingers held my cheeks. My head hovered over the bucket of water. Ice clicked and popped, melting under my breath. He plunged my head into the bath, and I held my breath. Every nerve in my face froze. He pulled me out, then he grabbed me by the hair. If it was any consolation, he held my hair back. They dipped me again before I caught my breath. The bucket bubbled. The world muffled itself. Voices roared over me. The bucket turned over and my nose pounded into the floor. I coughed and gasped for air.

Pater roared at Al, "What do you think you are doing?"

"I just thought . . . we did a lot of work and she might—"

They dragged me and threw me in a bathtub. My chin rested on the lip.

Al had shown me kindness in holding my hair back. To Pater, he had shown weakness. He made me watch as the waters rose higher and higher. They gathered bucketful after bucketful. Even if it took all day, Pater was determined to drown me.

When the water touched the tip of my nose, Pater shoved my face into it. Water thrust down my lungs. I squirmed, and he pulled my head out. He flipped my legs over the lip and submerged me face down. He pulled me out, and I gasped. The air was short-lived. He flipped me over and shoved me under. My arms now lay in front of me in a satanic baptism.

"Gotta make sure the hair gets wet," he instructed Al.

The demon dunked me slowly. As I begged, water choked my cries. Light flickered over the surface of the water. Pater's face turned into a charcoal wolf. I didn't remember that part of the dream. He yanked me out of the water and rested my chin on the broken faucet as I choked.

"Now are you going tell me no?"

I shook my head.

"When a man tells you he loves you, you say it back, you got that? It's bad for business. What's the matter with you? Saving yourself, she says. I'm the best man you'll ever have; you got that?"

I nodded.

"Next time, I'll hold you under 'til you stop kicking."

Al cowered around the doorframe of the bathroom.

"You!" Pater snarled at him. "Clean this snake up. She's unfit for the air she breathes. Monster's weak, stupid, and worthless."

His words stung more than the water in my lungs. I quailed, drenched in my failure.

Pater left the room without looking back. Al untied my binds. He washed his face in my bathwater, and the entire tub turned red. I saw Jasper's face grinning from the drain. *What's going on?*

Al held me close. I heard him speak, but it wasn't his voice—or, at least, it wasn't *just* his voice. A chorus spoke with soothing doublespeak, "It's okay. I'm here. I've got you. It'll all be over soon."

I recognized the second voice as Max. My thoughts drifted to him, and I heard the cork pop. The tub drained. And sucked me down with it. The four-fold jaws swallowed me again.

I awoke underwater again in a sea of black. Max spoke to me. "It's all right, Kiera. I got you."

The funny thing was, I could breathe. I began rattling off my list of apologies when I saw Max appear across the way. In the deep of black ichor, a tendril curled around his ankle. I begged him to fight it, run away, anything. He stared at me and spoke empty comforts, then his body shot straight down into the darkness. There was no trace of him. I seethed. Myst churned around me.

"Yes. Yes, feed. Feed your passions. Feed your anger, my child."

My vision tinted red. My body took flight, clawing at the water after Max. Every muscle pulsed. My heart rate accelerated. The tentacles choked his body, and one arm reached for me. I swiped at it and tore through a screen-like fabric. White light flashed through a slit and the fluid vomited me through the holes. Max lay before me, holding his throat. The air whiffed of sweet beet juice. My lips smacked at the possibility of food.

"Kill. Kill. Eat. Feed. Win. Open the door."

Max's snout and chest were covered in open gashes. The sweet nectar poured from his neck.

"Max?"

I looked at my hands. My fingers had grown to six inches; knives extended from them where my weak kitten claws had once been. I don't think I need to explain they weren't covered in nail polish.

Max heaved before me. His eyes cowered before me in disbelief.

"Kiera? Kiera . . ."

"Kill. Feed. Eat. Win. Come to me. Fulfill your destiny. Affirm your birthright."

"Kiera, wake up."

"Who are you? What do you want from me? Fix my friend!" I shouted, but all my words came out as screeches and lioness growls.

I moved after Max, and he crawled away from me. A red carpet of blood trailed after him. His head shook. His neck peeled at the cut like a mask, and a black wolf lunged at me.

I jumped awake, smacking Max in the jaw. I'd been sleeping in his lap. I scuttled away from him and studied him across the fire. My chest heaved.

"Are you all ri—"

"Stay away from me," I snapped at him.

I felt wet. Looking down, I realized I had drenched my drawers. I crossed my legs in shame. I pulled the flintlock and cocked it.

"It's all right. It was only a bad dream," said Max.

"How can I be sure? Everything felt so real."

Max stood up. "You're crazy."

"I said stay back."

"Relax. I'm going to wash myself off. You might do the same. Just take it easy. These caves must be getting to you."

I didn't know what to believe anymore. Who knew how long it had been since I had seen the sun? A week? Three days? Two days?

A voice whispered to me. It whispered in *my* voice. "Come to me, my daughter. You'll be safe soon."

The dreams were getting worse. I checked my ring. My moonstone had cracked.

CHAPTER TWENTY-TWO

Y ou can imagine how embarrassed I was at having wet myself. My first time sleeping with a man in eight years, and I pissed the bed. Go figure.

Max's patience and forgiveness continued to astonish me. *I'm so sorry, Max. Wherever you are now, I'm sorry.*

I fell asleep again, holding the saber and my flintlock in my lap in a standoff with the cock-eared bastard I was sure was an imposter. Cleaning up was out of the question. I demanded to know what had happened to my Max.

More nightmares followed the moment I closed my eyes. Each time, I awoke in the arms of my faithful watchdog. Sometimes I dozed off, others he'd lick my cheek and tell me to go back to sleep. This was my Max. I slept more than he did, keeping watch over me.

When I couldn't sleep anymore, I kept watch while he slept. The teddy bear was a good snuggler, I'll give him that. I gingerly lifted the big lug off me and I washed by the edge of the pool. I wasn't going in past my knees, though. Nothing, I repeat, *nothing* was worth going back in that water.

Undoing the wrap, I washed my ankle. I nicked my scab, and it began to bleed. I blotted it dry and black ink ran from the cut. I continued to blot it and returned to the fire, thinking it may have been a trick of the light. Nope. Ebony fluid trickled before the cut reformed.

What's happening to me? First the voices and the dreams, then anger, now black blood. Could I already be turning into a wendigo?

I felt sick to my stomach, and it didn't help that we were out of food. I cuddled beside the peacefully sleeping lump of fur. His ear twitched while he slept. I flicked and played with it with my finger. He was much less annoying while he slept. Even kind of cute.

He yawned, releasing a gust of fishy breath.

Yeewck. Never mind.

"Morning," he sighed.

If it even is morning.

He rubbed his dreamy eyes. Flames of light flicked his irises, illuminating a stunning spectrum of vibrant hues: inviting robin's egg, the hard aqua protecting shell of sea turtle, and in his right eye the feathers of an eagle, iron clay of a blazed trail, wild, strong, and untamed.

"Everything all right?" he asked.

I returned to earth and blushed. "Yes, everything is just fine," I said.

Max's stomach growled. Mine echoed in agreement. "You wouldn't have any more food on you?" Max asked.

"Fresh out. We could try to go fishing. There were plenty of cave fish."

"Blech. Sushi?" said Max in disgust.

"Yeah, I don't like sushi, either." *Maybe we do have something in common.*

"The cave collapsed anyway," Max pointed out. "We probably wouldn't even get a nibble."

I sighed. "Best keep walking, then."

"Uh, Kiera?"

I began re-wrapping my ankle. "Yes? Max, if you have to go to the bathroom, just go. We've been over this. You don't have to ask permission but give me a heads up so I can look the other way this time. So I don't need to bleach my eyeballs again."

Max pouted. "I was nervous, okay? But I, uh . . . it's not that. Those dreams last night . . . are you okay?"

I bit my lip. My fingers pulled and fidgeted with my dress as I shook the dust off it, now dry by the fire. *Could I tell him? No, trust no one. For all I knew, he could be a spy or some secret bigwig, like Romero.*

I slipped my dress over me, covering my scars and hiding my underbelly. "Peachy as a poodle, Max. Now let's pack up and get going, hero," I said, feigning a laugh.

"Good. You had me worried," he said.

I felt bad lying to the little sweetheart, but I couldn't tell him the truth.

Max packed the bags and stamped out the fire. Before putting it out, he scrounged out a makeshift torch for me. We followed the path, finding a glimmer of light.

I insisted on him treading lightly, and he agreed to keep pace with me. Migraines kept me from attempting to heal my ankle. There was no way I could fix another broken bone.

Another rope bridge led to the other side of the chasm. I backtracked, searching for another way forward. Sadly, the only way forward was into wendigo country.

Max never seemed to understand, which was typical for him, what a wendigo was. I relayed as much as I knew. My stories were met with blank stares and delayed, "Wait, what?" I could explain the same thing three times and he'd hear it but not comprehend it. It was probably a dog thing—or a guy thing.

The sun brought life back into my bones. My spirits rose in the heat like a biscuit. Sea spray dashed at the rocks beneath us. Brackish smells blasted our nostrils. The seagulls squealed overhead. It was like waking up from one of my dreams—walking unsteadily across the bridge in daylight, only to reenter the nightmarish hell that awaited us.

I broke a branch off a dried shrub and gave him a torch. Under no circumstances were our torches to go out. Water trickled from the ceiling, pinging into the puddles below. Sulfur replaced the salty brine fumes. Max sneezed several times. I guess the smell was a hundred times stronger for his nose.

The hardest part of this stretch was reminding the pea brain to shut up. You wouldn't think it would be that hard, but he was happy to admire the cave formations. Loudly, too, I might add.

Meanwhile, I panicked that, at any moment, some serpentine spider beast would whisk him away and spit out his bones.

Good times.

The cavern widened as we went along. The room expanded into a vast lair of pillars and spider webs like before.

Nope. I'll not be breakfast today.

I grabbed Max by the snout and pulled him along, taking another way around.

"Keep quiet," I shushed him.

Not looking where I was going, my horn smacked into the rock wall. I cursed, my voice echoing down the halls. Max snickered.

Clicking and pops responded through the halls ahead.

Guess I pat myself on the back, huh?

I pulled his arm to run. The road forked. The lair or the bridge. My tail flicked with anger as we charged into the lair in hopes of an escape. We darted between the pillars. Thick wool-like strands of web encompassed many of them. Bones of bear and human skeletons scuffled across the stone. Our breathing hurried. Our sounds alerted them to our presence.

A single wendigo swung from a greasy white cord, from the ceiling, behind Max.

"Look out!" I cried. I tossed my torches, bouncing them off its scaly face.

Max froze, staring up at the screaming behemoth over him. He was defenseless.

I pulled him by the hand and ran.

"What was that?" I shouted.

"Not sure; it caught me off guard," he panted.

There was a wall of web blocking our path. Max tested it with his foot and whined when it stuck fast, desperately trying to remove it.

"What did you expect to happen?" I complained. I grabbed him by the waist and heaved, falling on my tail.

Standing back up, the creature hissed, blocking all escape. It was blind, but still lethal.

Max drew the saber from my waist. I fished out the waterlogged flint-lock. Gray slime poured from the barrel. I tucked it away. I didn't have any bullets anyhow. *Magic it is, then.*

The wendigo's legs drummed against the walls. It searched and listened for movement. Max charged at it with a howling war cry. Reptilian arms batted him away in blind swings.

Max rocketed through the air, caught in a sail of cotton. He struggled, trying to saw through the webs.

I desperately hatched a plan. Breaths rose in and out. Myst condensed on my palms. I only know levitation and healing. I'd learned nothing else.

Think, Sinopa. Think.

The sinewy fingers of the wendigo struck the ground, pattering closer and closer.

"Hey, over here!" Max shouted.

The beast turned. It started back toward him.

"What are you doing?" I fussed at Max.

"Improvising. Get me out. Quick!" He struggled and whimpered in the web. His every movement remained feeble. The hope left his eyes.

I scanned the room. My eyes caught his torch on the ground. I pulled it toward me. The torch twitched and rolled before jolting end over end to me. I flung it into the wendigo. The light bounced off the beast's face again and into the dried webs, setting them ablaze. The flames licked the webs and rose toward Max.

Well, perfect.

"Kiera, I need some help here," he said, blowing at the blaze futilely.

I tried to pull him off the web. He ended up rolling into a silk cocoon. He thumped on the floor with a yelp.

The wendigo's eyes widened in the piercing dark. Its prey was helpless. It drooled.

A voice called me from the Myst, "Kill. Kill. Must feed."

My throat burned. I began coughing and convulsing on the ground.

Let go of my friend. Get out of my head.

Anger flowed through my veins. My vision tinted scarlet. I charged. The wendigo rammed the web sack into the pillar. My muscles bulged. My claws sharpened. Everything blurred as if the world were spinning, or maybe I moved faster.

I peeled the sticky sack, snapping it like a clammy shell. My neck cracked as I glared at the beast, roaring with a charge. I locked arms with it, stopping it dead in its tracks. My bones popped. I stood taller, eye-level with the cedar-like creature.

CHAPTER TWENTY-THREE

The wendigo snapped at my face. I butted its jaw with my ram horns. His bottom lip popped. I pushed him reeling to the ground. The beast squealed like a slaughterhouse swine. I leaped and pounced, dropping on its throat. My claws drilled into its tongue and the roof of its mouth. All the while, I sensed I was trapped, observing from my body from a distance, yet choosing to go on.

The wendigo cried out in agony. My muscles throbbed. I had never exerted myself like this. Like a pistachio, its serpent head butterflied open. Its neck flopped open in a flowering bowl of teeth. I ripped its tongue out with my fangs and swallowed the tip. I towered over my kill, raising my own Amazonian scream. Max cowered beneath me with his tail between his legs. He fumbled for my saber on the ground.

"Kiera?"

I growled at him.

Stupid mutt doesn't even know my name. Stupid mutt almost spoiled my kill. Must kill. Must eat.

"Kiera, listen to me!"

My shadow cast over the fidgety pup.

"I don't want to hurt you," he warned, raising the sword.

I dropped to all fours and roared in his face. His saber sliced my cheek. I winced. The blotches of red smeared. I blinked and shrank with painful pops at my joints. My balance was off. I fell into Max's arms and trembled. My cheek bled. My dress hung in tatters, coated in wendigo flesh and blood.

Max shook, too.

"I didn't mean to—I—" I stuttered.

I had snuffed out our last torch. More clicking echoed in the cavern. We weren't out of the woods yet. Silver thread-like strands descended from the ceiling. It was time to move. Max hoisted me over his shoulder and ran. His toenails clicked across the cave floor. He stopped at a wall. Dead end.

I caught faint impression in the stone. "I found a door here," I said.

Max set me down. An iron door was built into the stone. I tested the knob. Locked. Max rammed it several times with his elbow. I pulled out a hairpin.

Two screeches approached both sides of the door.

"Keep them busy," I told Max.

"Easy for you to say," he replied, drawing the saber again.

"Just do it."

"Okay, okay, no need to get bossy."

Time to put those lessons to good use. Three locks reinforced the door. I removed the rubber knob with my teeth and got a-picking.

Max raised a howl and ran between two sets of galloping legs. They gave chase with a roar into the dark. *Please be safe.* I jammed and jiggled until the top lock released with a satisfying click. Lightheaded and sweating bullets, I approached the next lock.

A torch glowed in the distance as Max raced and skirted past the door. "Bad idea, bad idea."

One wendigo skidded, crashing into the pillar and bringing it down on itself.

The second lock was rusty. *Where's a can of oil when you need it?* My pin snapped. I patted my hair.

Where are all my pins?

I only found one.

Need to make this count.

I steadily eased it inside the worn crevice. You could hear a snap. At first,

I thought it was the pin, but it was a tumbler sticking up out of the way. Each tumbler was more difficult than the last.

Max sprinted straight for the door. He held his knees, panting.

"What's taking so long?" he heaved.

"Patience is a virtue," I reminded him.

Three wendigos circled, like moths drawn to a flame, around the door. Max stood up to face them, gassed. He held the torch up and backed to the door just as the second lock clicked open.

I pulled on the door. "No good. Still one more."

"Hurry, will you?"

He pulled his sword out in front of him. Hissing surrounded the door. Max charged again. He howled, echoing over the cavern walls. He jogged forward and weaved around the center wendigo. His ankle caught one of its many legs. He stumbled and fell flat on his face. The torch rolled behind the creature.

Two of the tumblers clicked with ease. A small metallic *tink* came from the bolt. My last pin had snapped. The wendigos surrounded Max in the darkness. I poked at the lock and patted myself for anything I could use.

"Kiera, help! Please!" He cried.

I lobbed the torch, scattering the wendigos. Max crawled to it and waved the torch in their faces. They leaped back in the blinding light.

I had no bobby pins. What was I supposed to do? felt useless, staring at my hands covered in wendigo juice.

That was it! My hands! I protracted my claws and began fingering the lock. The reptile arms behind Max swiped at him. He swung his torch with one hand and saber with the other. Max shook and turned to me.

Clink. I stared at my palms in disbelief.

"Run!" I yelled.

Three heads turned my way with a deafening bat screech. Max's torch cleaved one in the arm, and then he mad-dashed the iron door.

His toes clacked. Our hearts drummed. Their spider legs glided end over end. Soulless onyx-colored pupils stared me down. Drool and spittle splattered.

Max dove inside, and I pushed the heavy door shut with a creak. Cries echoed in the doorframe as if they roared into a tin can. Max rose to his feet to help me with the door. Sweat poured into my eyes and mouth.

Max reeked of it, too, as he huffed beside me. Inches from closing, a wendigo pounded the door. We leaned against it with all our might.

Again, it inched closer. This was do or die. Push. The door groaned tightly into place. The metal creaked from the other side. I latched all three locks on our side for good measure.

One final, desperate ram from the wendigos caved in part of the door. Hissing and growling hovered around the other side and then slowly faded away.

Max pressed his back to the wall and slid to the floor, exhausted. I leaned back and held my chest. We turned to each other, out of breath.

I couldn't help but laugh. We had done it. He laughed, too. He let loose the awkward dog laugh without fear. I glided down the wall to the floor and made snow angels in the dirt, sort of an impromptu happy dance.

"You couldn't pay me to go back there," I joked.

CHAPTER TWENTY-FOUR

We caught our breath and made camp in this strange new place. Metal lined the paths in the cavern. Red glowing lanterns hung from the ceiling from where we came. Glowing chandeliers of emerald hung like twinkling starlight above our camp.

Max's stomach growled. "Oh, so hungry," he groaned.

"Me, too," I said, hunched by the tiny fire.

"I need to eat something. I'm dying here."

"Yeah, buddy, I know, but—what are you doing?"

Max had hunched over and taken a bite out of a mushroom that grew out of the floor.

"You can't just eat that. It could be poisonous," I said.

He swallowed.

"Those better not be hallucinogenic, either. I'm not carrying your tripping corpse foaming at the mouth."

"Tasted fine to me," he shrugged.

"Still, you gotta be more careful. You can't just wander about putting anything in your mouth and hoping it's edible."

"It worked for my brother, Manni. Do you want some?"

I inspected the foam mushroom head. "I think I'll pass," I said.

"You need to try more things. See the world; live a little."

"Ha. That's what got me here in the first place. I just hope to live another day. If we're lucky, we'll get out alive."

"What's your favorite food?" Max asked.

"What? Where'd that come from?"

"You said I don't know you, and I'd like to. Go on. If you've traveled, what's your favorite food?"

I sat and thought for a moment. My legs swelled like loose gelatin, or like a baked potato ready to burst. I couldn't sit still. "Well, I love blackberries. That's the one food I really enjoyed growing up."

"No, you're not getting off that easy. That's a dessert. I mean a meal. Your favorite meat, or a side dish."

I massaged my thighs in thought. "How about string beans?"

"There you go. That sounds so good right now."

"Serve them up in some fatback off a ham hock."

"Oh, my gosh, stop!" Max drooled.

"Side it with some spiral ham," I continued. I held my stomach and laughed.

"You're despicable," said Max miserably. "Baked with pineapple glaze . . ."

I stopped. "You know, I've never had a pineapple."

"You must try it sometime, considering you are one," Max teased.

"Still not going to tell me what that means, are you?"

He twisted an invisible key at his lips and threw it away.

"I'll pry it out of you eventually," I said.

I scooted beside him and rested my head on his shoulder. My eyelashes flicked up at him in butterfly kisses.

"I have my ways," I giggled.

His eyes locked with mine, unblinking.

"Maybe, when this is all over . . . my sister has a farm with rows and rows of green beans. I used to sit down and eat, following down the path. You could have all the green beans you wanted."

"I'd like that," I said.

The fire crackled faintly. There wasn't much fuel to keep it going. I tore a few more pages from the journals and tossed them in. It wasn't like I could read them much, anyway.

"All right, my turn," I said. "Favorite color?"

Max licked his lips with a yawn.

"Cherry. Like wild Bing cherries, or a dark red rose."

I blushed a deeper pink. My fingers reached up and rubbed the nick by his nose.

"Mine's blue," I replied.

Max swallowed. I stopped short of his lips. I pulled back.

"Maxy, boy, you've saved me twice now."

"Like you have me."

I stopped. I guess I had, come to think of it. Once with the leg, the other in the cocoon.

"I feel I need to apologize," I said unsteadily.

"What is it this time?"

"I stole two kisses from you.

"It was only my first kiss. No biggie."

I shook my head. "Way to make me feel better," I muttered. "I'm sorry. I should have asked, and you deserve better." I cringed, admitting it out loud.

Max flicked my nose. My eyes were closed so I wouldn't see his conde-scending glare. When I opened them, he gazed at me with quizzical devotion. His head was cocked sideways and his crooked ear twitched.

"What do you mean, 'stolen'?" he asked.

"I took them without permission, I guess."

I had never thought about the expression much myself. I just knew it was wrong. Again, it was much worse admitting it out loud.

"Can't you just give them back?"

I laughed. I couldn't believe he was serious. "No, I don't think it works like that."

"Says who?"

I shrugged.

"Well, as a guard of Changeling Aquatic Police Patrol, I order you not to steal any more. This is your final warning."

I smiled and gave him a salute. "Yes, sir."

"As you were, citizen."

We both laughed. It hurt to smile. I rubbed my cheek.

"Let me see," he said, tapping my fingers out of the way.

I turned and faced him.

"Are you sure you're all right?" he asked, examining my face.

I shook my head. "I don't know. Maybe it's the wound from the monster. I've had a fit like this before."

"You had me scared."

I nodded. I was unwilling to admit that I was also scared.

"You don't know anything about this? Any way to control it?"

I shook my head again, feeling helpless.

"No, I have little control. The adrenaline pours in and I'm weak to stop it, but I feel . . . exhilarated. I'm powerful. Nothing can stop me. I'm invincible." My eyes darted to the floor. "If I turn on you, Max—"

"That will never happen."

"It just did."

"It did, but I brought you back."

"This time. What about next time? I—I don't want to hurt you."

"That will never happen. I won't let you."

"I told you I was a monster."

"You saved my life, Kiera. Does that sound like a monster to you?"

"Yeah, only to eat you next."

He held up my chin with his cottony mitt. "Look at me. You are not a monster."

I leaned in. His finger stopped my lips.

"Slow down, thief. Caught you in the act this time."

It hurt to smile. "Suppose you'll put me under arrest, then," I teased, running my claw in a circle around his ear.

"True. I'm going to have to ask you to give back the stolen property."

"And what if I don't?"

His eyes searched mine for an answer.

I helped him with one. "You could always try to take them back," I suggested.

His fingers curled in my hair. His breath blew warm on my face. My tail flicked like a pussycat.

"Is that so?"

"May not work, though."

"Worth a shot."

His wet lips combed over mine. Every moment revealed a thousand more, droning on and on in continuous nerves, as it'd never stop. His head tilted with a soft smooch, and I pressed harder. I wasn't afraid to get rough. His nose rubbed onto mine. His whiskers bristled, stiffly skirting my cheeks in circles. I pushed him forward and stroked his ears back. My claws pricked his skin, tracing their way down his warm blanket. Each strap of his armor unwound with soft smacks.

His tongue traced my fangs, finding every crevice. No place was safe. I pulled my lips away. Max panted, and I played with his scars.

"How was that?" he asked.

"You might have returned one," I admitted. "The other I've lost track of."

"You lost my kiss?" he said, offended.

I thought for a moment. "It's around here somewhere." I let my dress fall off my shoulders. "You're going to have to find it."

Max frowned. "Kiera, I—"

I kissed him again. My fingers caressed his snout. I was ready to suck him dry. He looked at me, unsteady and shaken. I traced my claws down to his waist. He pushed me away.

"Kiera, stop."

"Why? What's the matter?"

I began picking at his belt buckle.

He shoved me this time. "Kiera, please." His face flushed, and he panted. "You're my first and—"

"Well, you got nothing to worry about, li'l pup. Momma's got you." I grabbed his hands and ran them down my midriff. "She's experienced and ready to turn you into a man. All the way."

He gulped. I tugged at his buckle and he snatched my hands away. "Please I—I'm not ready," His eyes scanned me, unsure for himself whether he was making the right decision.

"You're rejecting me?" I asked, incredulous.

"No, no."

I crossed my arms and turned my back to him. My tail backhanded him across the face.

"Kiera, I love you, but—"

"Save it. I put myself out for you, and you blew it, kid."

"Kiera, if you'd just let me—"

"My name's not Kiera! Gosh. How long will it take you to grasp that through your thick skull?"

He whimpered. "You lied to me?"

"Newsflash, genius—I've been lying to everyone. So what's your excuse? Balls haven't dropped yet? I'm not your type? I hear that one a lot. Gay, perhaps?"

"No, Ki—I mean, packmate. I love you. I want you; I really do."

"Not in the right place right now, then?" I sneered. "Oh, I'll do you one better. You're a bitch, not a man."

"I can't go down that road with you, Kiera!" he shouted.

"Then be a man and prove it."

I had finally pushed him to his breaking point. His teeth bared and his ears tucked back. He growled and stood up over me.

"I am not that kind of dog. Do those scars mean nothing to you?"

I squirmed, trying to escape.

He continued, "I've seen what that path will do. If I did that, I'd be no better than them. You'd be no better than them."

I looked at my stomach and stopped resisting. He let go and helped me up.

"Kiera, it's not that I don't like you. You're worth the world to me, pack-mate. I just . . . can't disrespect you like that. I'd be taking advantage of you. That'd make me a bad dog."

Poor idiot still didn't seem to realize I had taken advantage of him. That's what I was apologizing for.

"Oh, great, you're back to that again."

"If it were up to me," he continued, "we'd be wed this evening."

I rolled my eyes.

"Honest. Don't think I wouldn't. I want to spend the rest of my life with you."

"You are drunk on infatuation, my friend."

"You're not thinking clearly either. You almost stole my virginity. It may be a wait, but you're worth every second. Every heartbeat is worth the wait."

I wasn't buying it. I wiped his disgusting dog drool from my lips. The mutt deserved for me to rage and pound his face in. I hadn't been rejected like this in years. Mostly because I hadn't dated in years, but that's beside the point.

Still, that pooch knew what heartstrings to pluck. The virginity line reverberated. But how could he just arpeggio over my feelings like that?

My fist clenched, ready to fix him good.

"I understand if you're upset. You have every right to slap me. I won't stop you. Go ahead, do your worst."

Slapping was the least of his worries. My saber could easily neuter him right now. He'd never love again. Problem solved. I clenched my teeth. His ears braced for a beating. His crooked ear flicked in its cutesy little tick. I lowered my fist and looked him dead in the eye.

"You will never be with me," I said, and walked away into the darkness of the cave.

CHAPTER TWENTY-FIVE

I pressed on, without Max, in the dark. I could hear him howling back at the camp. Somber cries, but he wasn't following me. I wished he had.

My words had been harsh, but I meant them, as foolish as they were. The nagging temptation to return to camp never stopped bugging me. It was much colder without my dress. Served him right, in my mind, if I'd died of hypothermia.

Nothing would have made me happier than to prove him wrong. Any way to slight him, it didn't matter. I pressed on out of spite. My vision was stunted. Dull red lanterns lit my way. I figured someone had to be down here to have lit them.

The lanterns didn't flicker or burn like oil or candles. They rotated and spun with two beady bulb-like eyes. They must have run on windmill-like power, that magic, zappy stuff.

The sound of water met my ears. Another basin flowed with waterfalls pooling into it.

I bathed under the falls where no one could hear me cry. I was too tired, though. Instead, I plopped down in the dark on the bank. Wendigo or not, I gave up. I was too exhausted to go on. Sleep overtook me.

Nightmarish calls haunted my slumber. Being alone made it worse. No comforting words came from beyond the veil. No arms held me close when I awoke.

The dream got worse. The dark wolf figure became more pronounced; a crown of antlers adorned his head as if he were a king. One elk horn splintered as devil horns reaching toward the heavens. The other glistened as ivory milk tinted with a hint of gold flakes. A large bat wing beat in the shadows, pursuing me. He was my hound of hell.

"Almost there. Yes, just a little closer. Come, my spawn." His voice changed and spoke to me in my own voice. "I will protect you, my daughter. You will be safe. I'll prepare a feast and come out to meet you."

The two voices shouted over each other in a sphere of spiraling scale and feather beams. The ball caged me inside and jolted me awake.

I wiped the sweat from my face. The grizzly voice whispered in my ear, "Come. Eat. Kill. Win." It's words echoed. *But I'm awake. How?*

I pieced together the dreams. The dark voice must have won over my thoughts.

"Win what?" I asked into the shadows.

The voice cackled and drifted into silence. *Okay demon, good talk. Keep your secrets. I'll end you soon enough.*

I followed the red lit road. The walls were sweating myst. Metal bars lined the pathway, and the floor held together with rusted grates over water. A dark canine stood under the crimson light at the end of the corridor.

I stood still. My captor stood before me as he promised. I stepped forward.

"Are you the High Wolf?"

The beast's ears perked. Its head turned. Two glowing eyes beckoned in the distance.

"What did you mean 'win'?"

He didn't speak. The beast stepped closer. A sword glistened in his paw.

There was no backing down. "Where are my friends, you coward? Face me like a man."

The beast charged. I breathed in deep. Myst siphoned around me. Every footstep clang after me. I held up my hands, ready to blast. Two arms swung around me. Dented plate held me close, almost taking me to the ground.

"Max?"

"Thank goodness you are all right," he said, licking my face.

I pushed him away.

"Why wouldn't I be? I can take care of myself. Sexist much?"

Max frowned and helped me up. "I never said you couldn't." He held out my dress and sword.

"Give me that," I said, snatching it away from him. I got dressed and glared at him.

"What are you doing here?"

"Looking for you," he said.

I crossed my arms. "I said I'm fine, thank you very much."

Pressing on, I began swaying down the hall. My migraine almost floored me.

He helped me to my feet, and I pushed him away. He followed me like a sad puppy.

Max whined. "Can you at least talk to me?"

"What's there to talk about?" I sulked. "You made yourself clear enough."

Max remained silent the rest of the way down the corridor. Lights beneath the catwalk made the water appear green. The metal bent unsteadily beneath us, but it held.

As we neared the end, a camp appeared in the distance. Red lanterns lit up the ceiling. Yellow ones, like the Aerogapolis city lights, hung on poles. Water wheels turned. Hamster wheels held more changelings jogging in place. Changelings flocked everywhere. They were armed. Some with leather. Others wore rusty plates, like Max.

Two jackals appeared around the corner with lances. "We've been expecting you. Come daughter of the High Wolf, princess of pureblood."

"Daughter?" I asked.

Max stepped forward with my saber still drawn.

"Put it away," I shot coldly.

"But," he whimpered.

"Now."

He pouted and sheathed my sword at my waist. As we passed the jackals, Max growled. The two lances crossed our exit.

"He expects you in the vault and extends his apologies for not being able to welcome you personally."

I thanked him and walked on. Max raced to my side. The annoying squirt never left my side. Changelings of all kinds had gathered. Birds, otters, mice, bears, wolves, lynx— you name it. Murmurs rose. Many stopped and stared. Some dropped to their knees. They tossed their cloaks before us as in a triumphant parade. In their eyes, royalty had arrived. I couldn't believe these had been the same people Jasper had sent to kill me.

The procession led us to a steel wall guarded by jackals in full-plate armor.

They nodded at me and began turned a large metal wheel. Steel beams slid in a "z" shape as it spun. Exhaust of steam hissed as the large door cracked ajar. I stepped forward. Max did the same, and lances barred his path.

"Halt," they shouted.

"It's all right, he's with me," I said.

"He ordered for you to come alone."

Max growled. He was ready to engage.

"Max, stay."

His tail drooped. "But, what if something happens?"

"I'll be okay. You're the one I need to worry about." *I sound like Romero.*

"Close the gates," the jackals shouted.

Max whined beyond their lances. The door slowly slid shut. He followed the gap of light. It was hard not to run through it. *What am I saying? He hurt me. He deserves a little silent treatment.*

CHAPTER TWENTY-SIX

E verything appeared red. The faint red lit the corridor. I gripped my saber, ready to draw it at the first sign of trouble.

This monster has haunted me long enough. It was time for answers. Who was this creep? What did he want with me? And the sorcerers? Most importantly, where were my friends?

Sonia and Romero better be alive. Or he won't be.

A cracked oak door stood at the end of the tunnel. Light bled through shredded claw marks.

I pushed it open gingerly. I scanned the area for saryx and wendigos. The room was well lit. Lanterns were everywhere. I walked into a kitchen with pristine hardwood floors, cherry cabinets, and marble countertops.

Not the demonic lair I expected. This thing had already jacked up my brain once, and it wouldn't happen again. This could be a trap. I drew my blade. He wouldn't get the drop on me. I would not be a victim. Not this time.

The next room was an empty dining room. Portraits hung on the wall, some ancient and yellowed, others more recent and in full color. A fire crackled in the next room over.

The floor creaked as I entered. A library of books lined the walls. Papers lay scattered in a trail across the room. Hardwood desks sat on both ends of the room.

A figure sat in a swivel chair with his back to me. His head bowed over something in his lap. Two horns, like those in my dreams, rose from its head. Its ears perked.

"You wanted to see me?" I asked.

"So you've finally come," he said. His voice was calm and soft, almost hoarse or choked.

I readied my sword. The figure turned. A worn leather-bound book fell from his lap as he stood up. He was short—just a tad taller than me. His eyes fixated on me. They were glazed white with cataracts. Strips of a soiled white coat hung from his shoulders. It covered little. His fur glistened the darkest black. Patches of white at the whiskers gave an impression of age.

"Come closer," he said. "Let me look at you. It's been far too long."

I slowly tiptoed forward and extended the end of my sword out in front of me.

"My, you're skittish. Come, my child, you're safe here. Come. Relax. Come."

I stood a few feet from him and he tapped the sword's tip downward.

"There's no need, love. You're safe. Trust me."

"Where are my friends?" I demanded.

"They're here. Everybody's safe and sound. Relax."

He stepped toward me and I put the sword under his chin.

He smiled.

"Just like your mother—always the tease."

"Stop talking. I want answers. Who are you? Why are you talking like that?"

"Whatever do you mean?" he replied.

"Don't play dumb with me. The voices . . . the visions . . . I know it was you."

The wolf-changeling sighed. "Sit down. This may be hard to take in."

"I'LL STAND, THANK YOU," I growled. "I've fought two abominations of nature. I've been violated and hunted by your cronies, and I've trekked countless miles for I don't know how long underground. And I've withstood it all. What could you possibly say that would be hard to take in?"

"You poor thing. You must be famished. Would you like some tea?"

He poured me a cup of tea and one for himself on a tray.

"Have some tea?" I said, frustrated.

"Of course. Jasmine eases the nerves. It was your mother's fancy."

He stuck the cup in my free hand and folded my fingers around it with a love tap.

I squinted at him. *This better not be a trap.*

I sipped it. It tasted funny, and I spat it out in his face. My thoughts immediately turned to poison.

"What did you give me?" I asked in alarm.

The old wolf wiped his whiskers. He lapped a little off the top. "Hmm, you're absolutely right. This is cold. This certainly won't do. You deserve only the best. I'll brew a fresh pot. It'll only take a—"

"Sit down," I barked.

The wolf blinked, drew his ears back, and swallowed. He walked over to his chair and sat back down. "Okay . . . you're right to have questions. We all have questions. You have every right to blame me. Before we get too far, do you see that vial across the way?"

My gaze turned to a green pasty test tube.

"You should know that I am fairly ill," he explained. "Should things go awry with my health, I may need you to revive me."

I'm not losing him now. I walked over, grabbing the corked tube and eyeing this crusty old freak. He loaded the tube into a syringe he dug out of his tattered pockets.

"It is truly a pleasure knowing I have seen my firstborn before I die. You look so much like your mother."

I sheathed my blade and handed him the vial.

"Who is she?" I asked.

"The more accurate question is, 'Who *was* she?' We have been through many changes, my dear—beg your pardon, but I don't even know my own child's name."

I crossed my arms. "But you seem pretty sure I'm yours, how so?"

"I've watched and searched. It's been years and I've never stopped looking for the one I lost. Your markings. Your scales. Your eyes. That determination." The changeling smiled, "All of which is so much like her. Your mother left us so long ago."

"I'm sorry." *What am I saying? This must be some kind of trick. I can't let him in my head.*

"It's quite all right. It was her choice. I just wish I could have stopped her, that's all. Your name, my precious—I must know your name."

What name do I tell him? Am I really okay with telling him my real name? Screw it. I'm not afraid of him. "Sinopa," I said.

The wolf breathed in as if smelling a flower. "Funny. Your mother and I fought so hard over what to name you, yet neither of us won, did we? Age is a funny thing for us, Sinopa. Time comes and goes and we stay the same, and yet we're so different."

He had trouble with the '*s*' sound, just like Max. It must be a dog thing.

"All right, 'Dad,'" I mocked. "What are we? Riddle me that. We're changelings, right?"

The wolf frowned, wounded. "Half right. You and your siblings were the first of your kind. You've met Jasper already, haven't you?"

"How did you know?"

"My hounds told me."

I cast out the thought of that parasite. "You should know what he did, then," I growled, "and that's nothing compared to what I have in store for you."

The wolf hung his head low. It seemed like a hard pill for him to swallow.

"I'm sorry," he rasped.

"You're sorry? I didn't come all this way for an 'I'm sorry,'"

"You have every right to hate me, but I had nothing to do with that. Had I known what he was doing, I would have executed him immediately. Why did you hide from me?"

"A big scary voice shouts at me in my sleep and I'm not supposed to wet myself?"

He raised an eyebrow. "Pardon? I would do no such thing."

"The voice claimed to be you!"

The wolf sighed. "Then I am getting worse. The decay has already set in.

It may overtake me as it did the others. Fenrir will be the last survivor of the Alpha Project. The lone wolf. I must take precautions."

He stood up, and I grabbed him by the shoulders.

"Where do you think you're going?"

His eyes widened, staring at me. "No . . . you're right. You're absolutely right. We must instate the new alpha from one of our own. Someone who has proven worthy. Sinopa, you must bear this crown."

"What?"

"You must claim your birthright," he said.

I shook my head. "I don't understand how this is even possible. I don't look like you. Speak plainly."

"You must be the new high bearer, take my title, and live on."

"You are not my father, and I will never become a monster like you," I snarled.

The changeling High Wolf dropped to his knees, holding his chest in pain. I began shaking him for answers. He reached for the needle, sticking it in his thigh. He inhaled with a choke.

"Ol' ticker's about had it. 'Heart of a lion,' they'd said." He chuckled.

I gingerly helped the old man back into his seat.

I hope this fool doesn't croak before I get what I need out of him. I sighed and decided to take it easier on him. "Back up for a second," I said. "You're a . . .?" I was at a loss, looking at his hodgepodge anatomy.

The beast's breathing settled. "I'm a man—or was one. Many within the Order have forgotten our past lives, some out of choice and others due to drugs, as they are the primary means of dealing with our condition."

I almost found pity for him. Almost. I crossed my arms and sat across from him. "Start at the beginning, please."

The High Wolf nodded, clearing his throat. "There were seven of us once your mother joined," he began. "I can't imagine it without her. We called her Cerra. Cerridwen, really, for she was the mother of our project. I had known her since the academy, I think. It's hard to know what the decay hasn't falsified. Who knows when it will take me completely?

"But I am getting ahead of myself. We scholars had accepted a tremendous opportunity to learn about the sciences, magic, and ancient cultures.

Funding came from the crown itself. We were to investigate the subjects known as purebloods. That's where everything started.

"The founders of these nations had entrusted purebloods with the knowledge and protection of artifacts known as 'Vestiges of power' or 'the seven evils' to some. We found proof for a few claims. Sadly, most only led to dead ends.

"Then I showed the research to your mother. She was a changeling much like yourself: young, smart, cunning, and stubborn as a mule."

I laughed despite myself.

"Cerra saw things with fresh eyes. Research led us to the city of Aerogapolis. We believed there were more ruins beneath the city, similar to Temple 42, belonging to the purebloods. At first, we found no such ruins or signs of the purebloods. The crown turned desperate for answers, ready to pull the plug on the project. Then we struck gold. Miles beneath the earth, we found the chamber of a Vestige.

"This proved very noteworthy to Northstrand. To them, it could prove a necessary deterrent for any who would oppose the crown. The only problem was that only purebloods possess the power and knowledge of opening the door. We hoped to test what made a pureblood special, and to rebirth the race of the ancients. Luxembourg Labs dubbed it the 'Alpha Project'. We were the start of a new race. That's where you come in.

"We tested animals first. Spiders, lizards, rats—you remember the wendigos, don't you?"

I shuddered at the thought of them.

"Horrible things. They escaped before we could deal with them. This put more strain on supply routes and the increased tension on our alliance with the proud glow-gnome people. This brought in the Northstrand army and navy. The military wanted their grubby fingers on our research.

"Then the great war broke out. Our allies sought to weaponize our findings. Our serums and tests turned to soldiers and prisoners of war, thus breeding the saryx disease through myst. Myst and its power and functions became weaponized as well. We prototyped airship gliders."

I thought of the Sirius.

"Ultimately, Cerra wanted out," he continued. "I can't say I blamed her, but we were under contract. By this point, we only had one thing left to give

—our lives. Six of us laid down our humanity for our research. They gave us titles in place of names, signifying our new birth. Cerra thought it just another way for them to dehumanize us.

"The hypothesis was that we could procreate pureblood changelings through ourselves. All attempts failed. A few scientists fled.

"The war waged on worse and worse. Your mother bore the burden of its strain and underwent treatments. A changeling under the serum produced unique results. Fertility is tricky with natural-born changelings and was next to impossible in our tests. Sad to say, the only other woman left succumbed to hysteria and lunacy after treatments. Everything rested on your mother.

"She followed through with it. Of all the other scientists, she chose me as her male donor. Memory slips me of the egg donor. She delivered a litter of six children: you, Jasper, Edith, Clement, Russell, and Desmodius."

"Des is my brother?" I said in surprise.

"So you've met him, then?"

I recalled our dance at the Canary Cage tavern. I found myself ashamed and disgusted for having feelings for the big cat.

The High Wolf took a deep breath and resumed his long-winded speech. *He reminds me so much of Minnie.*

"Your mother fussed over you," he said. "She loved you dearly. It pained her that the government only saw you, saw all of us, as the property of the project. They abducted Clement and Russell as leverage to keep the project movement going. Your mother then betrayed us all. I'm unsure how she did it, but she smuggled you and Jasper out through the channel.

"Once the war was over, our contract expired, as did our funding. We were about to lose everything unless we produced a key to the Vestige. They put your mother through hysteria treatments to avoid the death penalty for treason. I begged her to do it.

"When she finished, she escaped. Without her, there could be no new litters, nor leadership. Division rose, and many succumbed to madness. The saryx disease broke loose through the caves, victimizing innocents and making even more monsters.

"Worst of all, I never got to see my children again. Only Edith, the runt of the litter, and Desmodius stayed under my supervision. But it pains me to say I'm too sick to visit them, lest they catch my disease. Edith has been in intensive care since birth, and Desmodius has proved himself nothing but a failure. But you—you, Sinopa, could be the one we've been waiting for."

"What?"

"You can help us," the wolf said.

"No."

"We found the pureblood's Vestige: the 'War Pig,' Machina of the ancients. It can be our deterrent. They can't treat us like cattle anymore. We can stand up to the navy. We can build a nation, a changeling state—Northstrand, Aerogapolis, the islands, none will—"

"I'm not helping you start a war," I stated flatly.

. The wolf growled, "I was hoping you would see it my way. Surely, after how these men have treated you, you wouldn't defend them?"

I shook my head. My hand never left the grip of my sword. "I'm defending no one. I'm here to save my friends, which, by the way, you kidnapped."

The wolf raised an eyebrow. "Best check your accusations, young lady, before you say something you'll regret."

"You don't scare me."

"I do not wish to. Your friends are in Fenrir's care, but you're still my daughter. I'm not playing that card. You will open the door."

I approached him with my sword extended.

"I don't take kindly to threats, 'Dad.'"

The wolf stumbled back. His swivel chair crashed to the floor.

"Sinopa, my child, you wouldn't kill your own father, would you?"

I smiled. "'I do not wish to,'" I echoed. "Let them go. Unlike you, I'm not afraid to play my hand. Now you listen here, and you listen good: I'm *not* your daughter. You hear me? You are *not* my father."

Something pricked my neck. Suddenly, a figure roared and wrestled me to the ground. On my back, my saber clashed with a pair of daggers. A growling Des stood over me. My muscles tensed and froze.

He rolled me over. Des looked proud as he clamped manacles onto my wrists. The High Wolf crawled over to me in shock.

"What's a matter with you?" he asked Des. "You don't tackle your sister. Fix her now. Boy, you can't do anything right, I swear."

Des stared at him, confused. He turned to me and back to his father.

"That's right. I gave you one job, one task to prove you're capable of the birthright you so desire. Yet your bounty has come on her own accord. Fix her."

His eyes narrowed on me. Des sat me in a chair. The High Wolf continued to scolded him.

Des sheathed his daggers back to his waist. He removed a pink dart from my throat. It was labeled "weevil spit." He turned to leave.

"And where do you think you're going?" said the High Wolf. "Uncuff her. Use some common sense."

"But she tried to—"

"Think! We're all family here. I didn't search all these years to see her chained on a leash. I want to see her—even if she wants me dead."

A vein in Des's neck bulged. He stomped toward my chair and broke the manacles with a roar. The door slammed behind him as he stormed off.

"Less attitude would be appreciated next time," the wolf muttered. "I swear, he's worthless."

The High Wolf hunched over and gave my saber to me with both paws. I rubbed my neck. My legs were still numb from the dart.

"As I said, I know it must be hard to take in," he said. "We may have gotten off on the wrong foot. But I want you to trust me."

"Trust you?" I echoed incredulously.

"Yes. My life is yours, should you wish to take it."

I took the blade in my hands. He dropped to his knees and raised his neck.

My 'father' blinked, waiting. "Go ahead. I'm not going to stop you."

The mangy-hided mutt shook on his knees. His bony arms sagged to his side. He was defenseless.

I struggled to my feet, my blade extended before me. His almond eyes stared up from waist-level.

"Just know that you are my daughter, Sinopa. Nothing you can do will change that. And I'll still love you either way."

I raised the blade over his head. The High Wolf closed his eyes.

Why am I shaking? He deserves this. He hurt me. He hurt my friends. Didn't he?

I lowered my blade slowly and shook my head. The High Wolf looked up at me.

"I thought you weren't afraid?" he said.

"I'm not a monster like you. You're just lucky you still know where my friends are."

The High Wolf hugged my legs, tearing up. I swayed unsteadily, still weak from the weevil serum.

"Cerra wouldn't have hesitated. You are my daughter."

I pried him off. "The jury's still out on that." My stomach growled.

"Look at me, going on. You must be famished. Come, Sinopa; let us eat. Bring in that handsome hound of yours."

I stopped in my tracks. *How much had he seen between Max and me?* "Well, we're not dating or anything," I tried to explain.

"I didn't ask if you were. So you're married, then?"

My cheeks reddened. "What? No, no."

"Any nobleman willing to treat you half as well has my blessing."

The old man was getting more infuriating. "How many times do I have to tell you we are not a thing?"

The old changeling chuckled. "Spoken so much like your mother. Bring him in; let me see him with my own eyes."

CHAPTER TWENTY-SEVEN

The High Wolf buzzed the guards outside, and the sizzling of steam burst through pipes. The screeching grind of metal reverberated through the hall, and the door slid open. Footsteps raced forward. I shook my head in annoyance as the needy thorn in my side called for me. At least that's how I felt at the time. My migraines returned and sweat settled on my brow. I was almost feverish and I felt sick. But from what exactly remained to be seen.

The door of the library pushed open. Food was being prepared in the kitchen. Jackals led him under armed guard to the library.

Max proved weapons-grade stupid. He exploded through the door of the inner sanctum. The guards wrestled him to the ground, shouting that no one was permitted to see the High Wolf.

The High Wolf cleared his throat, and Max brushed himself off.

He looked up and saw the old creature leaning on a cane, extending his hand.

"Son, my name is Belphegor Loki, the High Wolf of this colony. You can call me Luck for short. I understand you have feelings for my daughter."

I facepalmed.

Max looked up and gulped dubiously. He squeezed Luck's hand with both of his and shook it. "Yes, sir, she's a very fine lady," Max replied.

"Is that so? Sinopa, would you mind stepping in the kitchen for a moment?"

"Uh, yes," I said, uninterested in leaving.

The old creature shrugged. "Fair enough. Young man, what are your intentions toward my daughter?"

Max looked dumbfounded.

The half-buck-half-wolf's cheeks unfurled in a sinister grin. My face turned pink. I had known him for thirty minutes and he'd already embarrassed me. A bit of drool trickled in Max's stupor.

"Best be treating her right," said the wolf.

"Yes, sir. Very much, sir," Max said.

"I have eyes everywhere. I see everything. Should you want her, you must prove yourself. Nothing escapes my sight. Should she stub her toe or shed a tear, I'm holding you accountable."

Max's sad dog eyes turned to me. I shook my head. *Don't encourage him.* Max charged and hoisted me off my feet and slung me over his shoulder, determined not to let me stub my toe.

Luck laughed as I beat Max's back on our way to the dining room.

Max set me down steaming mad. He pushed my chair in and babied me.

Luck was having a ball with it. His smile missed several teeth. He took more medication before we ate.

I sat beside my "father," which I refused to call him, while Max made goo-goo-eyes at me across the table. I kicked him each time I caught him staring. This was an all-out assault to "win me back" and prove himself to Luck.

They had trained servants to set the meals on a cart and leave. No one saw the High Wolf and lived. Why anyone would want to see a decrepit creature like him is beyond me. Then again, maybe that was the point.

Luck enjoyed teasing Max in his newfound company.

"Sinopa, you have great taste in your company. Your lady friend is truly something as well," remarked Luck.

"Sonia?" I cried and shot to my feet. "What have done with her, you—"

"Now, darling, settle down," he said. "I told you before—they're safe. They'll be joining us shortly. Any harm that Fenrir has afflicted on them I'll meet tenfold." Luck pulled at his collar. "Sadly, we have little time together. Arrangements are being made. We must be quick to make our move. There are two tasks I ask—no I beg, you to perform. One, I have seen your outbursts. Your temper is out of control. The saryx virus has overtaken you. We must begin treatments immediately to stop its growth."

"That red vision," I said, "and the—"

"The very same. All of the project founders contracted it. At the high presence of myst, it mutates your thyroid's systems and hormones. Given my little girl is becoming a lady . . ."

Max smirked. My heel stomped on his foot.

"Two," the wolf continued, "you must fulfill your birthright, but your life is more important at the moment. Your body is going through many changes. It pains me to see you have inherited your mother's curse as well."

"Curse?"

"The arcane arts. Your mother was a prodigy in many more ways than one. The saryx virus has remained untested in combination with sorcery, but if my observations are correct, it has made you stronger."

"She's already strong," said Max proudly.

I kicked his leg to shut him up. Water welled in his eyes as he bit his tongue.

"That she is," Luck said and nodded. He patted my arm before I could pull it away.

Luck got up and shuffled to fetch another drink from the cart. While he turned his back, I motioned Max to zip his lips, or I'd cut his throat. I shivered, crossing my arms. *Why do I feel so cold?*

"So, how do we begin treatments?" I asked.

Luck rubbed his chin, leaning on his cane, then held his head in pain.

A voice flooded my mind. "Kill, kill, eat, win!"

Luck collapsed to the floor.

"Mr. Loki!" Max shouted.

We helped him to his seat.

"Are you all right?" I asked.

Luck slowly shook his head. "Yes, thank you. My strength is failing me as of late. As long as my daughter is by my side, I shall be fine."

189

I remained unphased by his words. "You sure?"

"Positive. I just need a bit more medicine to keep my spirits up. Your treatments start immediately. Eat. Get some rest. Things will work better. We could go all night, but it wouldn't be very effective. Son, would you escort Sinopa to her room? When you are finished eating, of course. Protect my angel. Let not my princess's feet even touch the ground."

I rolled my eyes.

"Yes, sir," Max said and nodded like an obedient dog. "Did you hear that, Kiera? He called me his—*oof!*"

I thrust my foot between his legs. Max winced and squeaked like a field mouse.

"I say, boy, are you all right?" Luck asked.

Max's lips protruded in a pout, but he nodded. I instantly regretted my decision. *What's wrong with me? I like him.* I wiped the sweat from my brow. *Why am I sweating so much? Maybe I am sick.*

"Bathroom's down the hall should you need to use it. I shall turn in for the night. It was nice meeting both of you. I'm glad my empire is in safe hands. We'll begin treatments in the morning."

"Why should I trust you?" I spat.

Luck's lip puckered. "Come now, dearie, that hurts. It really does."

"Where are the sorcerers?" I demanded.

"What are you talking about?"

"Don't play dumb, old man."

"Maybe he doesn't know," Max said.

"I need to sleep," the High Wolf waved it off. "It's the best way to keep both our saryx in check. Goodnight, my daughter."

"Yeah, whatever," I muttered back.

Luck sighed. The old man hung his head low and shuffled his feet away.

"Don't you think that was a little harsh?" Max asked as he studied me. "He wants to bond with you. He's your father."

I glared.

Max cupped his crotch in self-defense. "The man has yet to prove it to me," I said grumpily.

"I thought you said you didn't know your parents."

"I don't, but this definitely isn't one of them."

Before us on the dining table was a soggy mush of roots and wheat. "I can't eat any of this slop. Can you?" I asked.

Max licked his lips with the meal all over his face. "I'm sorry, what?"

"You disgust me, Max."

He continued eating. My stomach roared as I stared down at my plate, unable to lift my spoon to it.

"I'm not hungry," I sighed.

"You haven't eaten anything in days," argued Max.

"I'd rather starve than be poisoned."

Max leaned over and sniffed my plate.

"It's clean," he said confidently.

"Huh? What makes you so sure?"

"It doesn't smell like the food at the banquet. Poison smells sweet and syrupy. I know my food." Max paused and turned toward me. "Why would your father want to poison you?"

I didn't answer him, but I jammed my spoon into the lumpy mass. It tasted bland and had the texture of runny mashed potatoes.

Max eyed me, drooling, from the other side of the table. "Are you going to finish that?"

"I'm done."

He grabbed my plate and readied himself to shovel it down but stopped short. He put the plate down, got up, and came around the table.

"What are—hey! Put me down!" I squealed.

Max giggled, carrying me down the hall.

"This is not funny. Put me down! You know I don't like being picked up."

"Your father said to take you to your room after you finished dinner."

I beat my fists and cracked my tail like a whip into his back.

Pink paint covered the walls of "my room." Luck must have thought I was four. The furniture was plain. A double bed stood in the center beside a small nightstand.

Max plopped me down onto the mattress with a bounce.

"That was not funny," I sneered at him. I sat sulking on the bed.

"Oh, come on, it was *kind* of funny," he replied.

I turned my head and crossed my arms.

"Kiera? What did I do wrong this time?"

It figures the idiot wouldn't be able to figure it out. "Please talk to me again. I can't bear it when you won't talk to me," he whined.

I sighed.

"You still mad?" he prodded.

"A little," I answered.

"Come on, smile. We made it. We're safe. Show me some teeth. *Cheese.*"

"I'm fine. Leave me alone."

"No, you're not, and I can sense it."

The bed creaked as he crept closer. He grabbed me and wrestled me to the floor, tickling me in the ribs.

"Stop. Hey stop!" I squealed.

I smacked his fingers, trying to remain bitter.

He licked my face and aggressively tickled me. I resisted laughing.

"Forgive me," he teased, in a villainous façade, tumbling with me onto the floor. "Submit."

"Fine, I surrender," I relented.

"What?" He dove for another attack.

I crossed my legs to ensure I wouldn't pee with laughter. He shot around them. My eyes watered. "Stop, please!"

"I wanna hear it," he insisted.

I doubled over. "Stop and I will," I shrieked.

He counted to three and pulled his hands away.

I breathed heavily and crawled away, laying my head against the box spring. I smirked and half trusted him not to tickle me again.

Max waited expectantly, "Well?"

"I forgive you," I said and chuckled.

He licked my cheek, sat beside me, and squeezed my hand.

"I guess we don't have much of a choice but to go through with this, then," I said.

His head turned.

"The treatments, I mean," I explained.

Max rested his head on my shoulder. "Ah, well, they may help you. 'Cause if you're sick, that means you can get better," he reasoned. "I'd rather not see you turn into the . . . well. . . you know."

"What if this a trap?"

He shook his head with a yawn. "From your own father? He seems to love you, as any good father would."

"That's the thing—I have had dreams and visions where he . . ."

"They could just be dreams," he suggested.

"Maybe," I agreed doubtfully.

"Get some sleep. You need it. I'll take the floor."

Lucks' voice whispered in my head, "There are two beds. One's down the hall."

Max curled up at the foot of the bed.

"What are you doing?" I shouted.

"I just thought it was the right thing to—"

"Not you," I snarled at Max.

His ears buckled.

To Luck I said, "Get out of my head."

"Thought you didn't like him," the voice teased.

"You pervert!" I yelled.

Max tucked his ears back.

"Not you, Max. You've been watching us the whole time?"

"Kiera, are you okay?" Max asked. "You're talking to voices again."

I rubbed my temples and sighed. "No."

I sighed.

"Max, would you be a dear and fetch my supper? I've changed my mind."

He wagged his tail. "You had me at fetch," he grinned.

I sat on the bed, hoping my headache would subside and, wondering how all this was possible.

"Powerful magic, my dear. Those searching and longing," it answered.

What does he know about the sorcerers? How well can he read my thoughts? Is it even safe to sleep?

The voice chuckled. "My dear, you are a frightened little kitten. You are safe here. Your secrets are safe with me. I wish you wouldn't think so harshly toward me and hold yourself in better esteem. I mean, young lady . . . we are definitely going to have a talk about this Max fellow."

You're not my father, and I can do or see whomever I want.

"Your mind is disgusting. I forbid these thoughts, young lady. At least Max acts like a gentleman."

Stay out of my head, then.

"Treatment starts from the inside out, and since there are no Coatls, like in my day, I must observe and correct you myself. Luckily, we are of the same lineage, and are close by."

Max returned with my plate.

My brain hatched an idea.

"You're smiling? I see you smiling," Luck said in my head. "What are you—don't you dare. Sinopa, I—"

I began integrating the demon in my head.

Where are the sorcerers?

"Max, would you be a dear and sit down beside me—*on the bed*?"

Max raised an eyebrow, confused.

"Young lady, I forbid this!" Luck reproached me.

Tell me where the sorcerers are.

"I'm unaware what you're talking about. All magic's out of my jurisdiction. What do you mean, that's not good enough? Young lady!"

I pecked Max on the cheek. He gulped, twiddling his thumbs.

"Fenrir lined the cave with moonstone. Not even my eyes can see everything," Luck whined.

Still not good enough. "Max, I feel it's a bit drafty. You care to share the bed?" I asked sweetly.

Max stumbled over his words and scratched the back of his head. "I . . . don't know. I'd feel much more comfortable if you had the bed," he replied.

"You're bluffing," said Luck. "I can read you; you're bluffing. You'll never force him. Even you doubt yourself."

"I'd feel safer with you close by," I said, stroking Max's arm.

"I'll only be at the foot of the bed," he gestured. He stood up.

"Max, stay," I commanded.

His ears shot back.

"I don't know any more than I told you. I beg of you!" cried Luck.

You better not be lying.

"I don't want you to sleep on the floor," I said to Max.

Max's eyes darted to the exit.

"No funny business?" he whispered.

I drew an 'x' over my heart. "Promise."

He sat down beside me while I slept. When I rolled over, I caught him sneaking to the floor, and I let him have it. He'd earned it.

For the first time since this journey began, I didn't have any nightmares. However, my slumber was still not the restful nothingness I had longed for.

CHAPTER TWENTY-EIGHT

L uck called me in the stillness of the night.
What is it now? I groaned.

"We must begin treatments immediately, my daughter."

Can't it wait until morning?

"Saryx never sleeps. Neither will you. It makes you vulnerable to it when you do."

I thought you said sleep was good.

No response.

In my sleep, the form of a man stood before me. He was lanky and human. Thick-rimmed glasses sat on his face. I recognized him as the figure who had helped me in the library.

He said, "I shall aid you in your battle, my daughter. But it is your choice to fight."

Why would I not want to fight?

"It knows you. The disease feeds on your sensations, your fears, your pleasures, your passions, even your most basic instincts, and perverts them into twisted delights. Not all at once, but slowly you give into these new curiosities, naughty secrets, and sinister vices. You gradually allow the beast control, and you become animalistic—depraved. Saryx deprives you of both love and conscience."

What makes you so sure it will happen to me? I'm a good person. I have plenty of self-control.

Luck didn't speak. His form faded, and I recalled the red tunnel vision. Max had been beneath me, pleading for me to stop. Sonia had barely brought me back in the tunnel.

That's enough. What do I have to do?

"Allow me to get to know you. Your fears. Your pursuits and desires."

You're still not my father.

"Oh, sweet pea, I know I haven't been the best."

You haven't been there at all. I want a blood test.

"That can be done. Anything, if it means I can hold my baby girl. I need you to trust me. Let me in. I can only see what you allow me to see. I'm not that strong, and I will not drug you, either. Keep in mind, your condition will only get worse the more you fight me."

Again, what do I have to do?

"Take my hand."

The form of the human man appeared again. We shared the same color hair.

I took his hand and felt myself sinking.

"Relax. Let yourself go."

I took a deep breath. My body plummeted. My dress flapped and the wind grazed my cheeks until a slimy black web caught me mid-air.

"Tell me, my daughter, what do you fear? We must drive out your demons before you."

It was hard to silence my thoughts, especially in my sleep. Water rose beneath the web. Wendigos screeched in the distance. Sonia drowned beneath me and I was helpless to save her.

"Come, my dear, you are thinking too physically. Speak your fear. Name your demon."

Big Papa unfolded the ends of the web like a blanket and made me squirm over the edge of the water like a spider dangling over a flame. I shook my head with tears in my eyes.

"How do you feel? Terrified? Confused?"

The giant Pater spider spat a bucket of water in my face. I wouldn't give up. I fought harder. Bubbles rose where Sonia had been.

Tears streamed down my face.

Weakness. Helplessness.

The strands of silk tore. Big Papa's face faded. The water receded with no sign of Sonia.

I fell onto a grassy meadow and rolling hills, the same one I'd dreamed of visiting beyond the window of my locked room at the village bildungsroman.

Luck's voice turned gravelly. "What are your dreams, my puppet? Tell me your heart's desire."

I lay on the grass and caught my breath.

I know I can't fight it, but do I really want him to know my fears, my heart?

As I stood up, blades of grass stroked and consoled me. Above me, an endless azure canopy spanned.

I didn't know what to say. I had always wanted to know where I came from. The city of Aerogapolis stood in the distance. I had always wanted to fit in. The docks rose from the sea of green. I walked toward them, but they were only a mirage. I could never reach them, no matter how long I walked. Now, alone in this maze of madness, I wanted a friend. I dreamed of a shelter.

A log cabin sprouted from my childhood farm. A place I could call home. I could bake plum tarts. Max called from inside. Two, maybe three, children played around the hearth, and for once when I lay down to sleep at night, I'd feel safe. I could be happy. I could find comfort in knowing that, when I woke up, they'd still be there beside me.

I dreamed of love. That was my peace.

The logs took themselves apart piece by piece and disappeared into the sky. The field of dreams wilted. The stalks crumbled into sand. It thrust me past the docks to the coastline.

I called for Luck. The moon rose above the sea, as lonely as ever. The sea breathed in and out. Romero stood beside me.

"Name your iniquities," his voice slurred. It was the High Wolf of before, but then returned gentle and plain. "Toss aside your guilt. Lest it tether you down and consume you."

I wasn't sure whether or not to continue. I didn't want that evil side of him knowing my darkest secrets.

A pail of blue spheres like pebbles lay beside me on the edge of the water. I struggled here the longest. I dipped my toes in the sea foam. It rinsed the salt and blood from my body. I waded, but I moved as if held back. The spheres dragged me back to shore if I strayed too far from the bank.

I picked up a sphere. The pebbles were forget-me-knots. *Go figure.* I wanted to go home. I wished I could forget how I had left Angela to work the bar alone.

Her face appeared in the crystal blue. To be honest, it startled me, and I tossed it into the water. The image of Angela rippled in the basin in front of me. I carried the pail of pebbles to the dock and began emptying myself.

I wished I could forget Jasper's death and his thousand-yard stare at my hand. I wished I could have been stronger. I wished I could have prevented what they did to me at the goblin village. Tears fell as I dropped the sphere in the water.

I heard Max speak over me, "It's okay. I got you. I'm right here."

I looked around and saw him looking back at me from the rippling water.

"Max. I hurt you most of all."

"You can't blame yourself, you know."

"How can you say that? This is all my fault."

His arms draped around me from beyond the veil. His velvety paws rubbed my scar tissue. My underbelly.

"No, no, it's not," I cried.

It was strange; it was as if he were two different people. He was the one holding me. And the one looking back at me from the water.

"But I've hurt so many people. Even you. Especially you."

"Let it go."

"Easy for you to say. You really are stupid, you know that."

His ears tucked back. His reflection turned and walked away.

"Wait, no, come back."

His arms squeezed tighter the more I called his name. The waves crashed against the beach. The gulls cackled through Pater's voice, "Worthless, stupid, unlovable."

Max's voice whispered in my ear, "It's okay. I'm here. I got you. I forgive you, Kiera."

The final sphere sank in my hands. It felt like a leaden weight. My arms strained under my burden. I held it out over the water. I peeked at it through one eye. My fingers let go one by one. The weight dropped with a satisfying plop.

The waves crashed, and the moon appeared whole. Then the defeated moon rested from its suicide and shriveled like a deflated balloon.

"Good. Good." Luck spoke in his normal voice. "I'm very proud of you, my daughter. The first step to recovery is acknowledging your problem. One more, then you can get some rest."

What happened? Your voice changed. Your personality, too.

"Just as you are most vulnerable while you sleep, as am I."

You're sleeping?

"Of course. How else would I scry? Now tell me, my daughter; you are afraid of being weak. You dream of love and a family—admirable. You are fettered by the grip of your abuse and your victims. Correct? I don't wish to put words in your mouth."

In a way. I don't know about calling them victims; it feels strange admitting it out loud.

"Tell me."

Chains lashed and snatched each of my limbs. They pulled me in all directions until I was suspended in the air.

"Where do you find your strength?"

My fears manifested around me. The safe, happy cottage I had pictured burned in the meadow, out of reach. My abuser spat in my face and called me weak. I tensed my muscles and strained for a hint of myst.

"Ah, bup-bup! Your thoughts are too physical. Your powers are weak against this disease within you. Something outside yourself."

I breathed. My wrist glowed. I pushed Pater back. He rose to twice his size with a whip.

I'm strong; I can fight it.

Luck's voice changed. It turned gruff and familiar. "Submit, vessel."

With each crack, flashes of red clouded my mind.

"I can give you love."

Thwip-CRACK.

"I can make you strong."

Thwip-CRACK.

"You will be in control."

Pater's face flashed into that of the dark wolf. Crimson saliva trickled from its mouth. My eyes watered with each lash to the face. My cheeks flushed hot. Every sentence was punctuated with more lashes.

"That's it. Let yourself go. Feels good? Don't it? Just one bite. Only a nibble."

My chains sagged. My muscles bulged. The High Wolf howled in victory.

"Kneel, my bride. Together we shall rule."

Luck called faintly, "Your strength, Sinopa. Where's your strength?"

The saryx shouted. "I'll keep you fed, if just for a little while. A quick fling means no attachment. No responsibility. Less pain, right? No one's perfect. No one has to know. You wanted your innocence, right?"

A voice called over me, "Kiera."

My legs shook. The bristled hide squeezed my shoulders.

The demon continued, "Look how strong my little girl is. Daddy's proud of his little monster."

"Kiera. Kiera, wake up," Max called.

Darkness clouded my vision. Its cold skull rested on my shoulder. "Feed . . . must feed . . ." The head slithered away.

I screamed out as its fangs burrowed into my back.

My body shook.

"Kiera, wake up!"

The head tore again, peeling at my skin like a greasy plantain.

The beast spewed chunks down my front as it spoke.

"It makes no difference. Whether you sleep or wake, I am there." It swallowed the skin in its mouth, slurping up the end.

"You are powerless against me. Whether or not you fight me, I feed. I grow stronger. I am the stillness of the night. The creature within you. I know your every waking thought and your darkest desires. I am the beast. I *am* you. We are one. Let us consummate our marriage."

Two black wings rose from my back.

"A gift from your first love. Fancy thinking the beast was something you could fight and kill. Kill, my bride. Eat. Come to me. Feed on your enemies. And when it's over . . ."

The beast cackled. My vison tunneled in the dark.

No, no, no, I cried.

Its face appeared from the shadows, its mouth agape as my own. It's jaw unhinged in fours.

It spoke in my voice.

"Win."

It lunged. I screamed.

A canine face lay in front of me. His eyes mismatched, soft and concerned.

I was awake. I buried my face into his shoulder and wept. Max held me close. He wiped the tears and sweat from my face. Blood and ichor had poured from my nose and cheeks. As Max patted my back, I cried out in pain. He flicked on the light. Blood seeped through the back of my dress like two ink-colored wings.

It was more than a dream. The disease was taking over. Max promised to protect me. How could he save me from myself?

CHAPTER TWENTY-NINE

M ax held me close and never left my side. Every time I attempted to tell him my dreams, he hushed me and squeezed me tighter. Apparently, he'd been trying to wake me for an hour. The dreamscape had held me tight. I now realized that it was his whispers from beyond the veil.

I struggled to keep my eyes open. My head never left his shoulder. His heartbeat thumped in my ear. So gentle. So calm. I counted them in his tender grip. As I started, my eyes closed, wrapped in my furry blanket.

I woke up alone to a knock on the door.

It was Luck. Desmodius stood behind him at sulking attention.

"Change of plans," Luck said. "My health is sinking faster than expected. We must begin your treatments immediately if there is to be any hope of saving you."

"Where's Max?" I asked, searching the room.

"He's volunteered to help as a catalyst for your treatments. Spare blood samples and what-have-you's. I approached him about it while you slept. It was his decision, not mine. Desmodius will oversee both of us to prevent any future flares or injury they might cause to you or me. He's the only one I trust with this."

Des huffed, shaking his head.

"Are you ready?" Luck asked me.

"Is Max safe?" I asked.

Des nodded.

"Then that's all that matters." I couldn't bear to hurt him again. I'd rather die.

Des led us along a corridor lit with blinking red lanterns. Metal grates spread across the lab floor. Myst rose beneath us. Large green tubes stood upright, some with figures in them. Bubbles rose within the tinted glass. Masks and tubes ran from their face and stomachs. Each changeling's skin appeared shriveled and mutated—humans crossed with mice, horses, and bats.

"This is where those who have failed lie in sleep for a cure," said Luck. "The other four rest here. Let us pray you are not one of them."

We reached an empty chamber.

"Prepare the volunteer just in case she goes under."

Des left us, and went further into the shadows, obscured from view.

Luck began going over several types of triggers like heightened emotions, tiredness, loneliness, and yearning that could cause saryx tremors in my system.

"There's one natural way to yield relief," he began, rolling up his sleeves. The horned wolf stuck a needle into his forearm, extracting a black ichor from his veins.

"Here's your blood test," he said and chuckled. "It's the same color as mine. You can remove the poison manually. It's only a quick fix. I have a spare needle."

He showed me which vein to pump and hugged me, holding my first vial of saryx fluid. "I'm proud of you, my Sinopa."

It felt good. Maybe he was who he said he was . . . maybe.

He lay me down in the pod. Restraints strapped me inside so I couldn't break free during my rage. Needles stuck at my ankles, wrists, and neck.

"All right, my dear. Whatever happens, always remember I love you."

That's reassuring.

The glass door to the pod shut. I lay inside it and it reminded me of a see-through casket. The bed tilted upright while the restraints held me to the wall.

Luck pressed a button, and a mist sprinkled against my face. Needles sunk in and prickled my ankles. I could feel my energy at once restored. The mist clouded the glass. The world muffled outside, save for Luck, calming me on the loudspeaker. "You're doing well. Relax. It should be over soo—"

I saw Luck grab his head. I called to him feebly from behind the glass. He fell out of his chair. His body wriggled on the ground.

His mass grew. His back straightened. Luck's coat lay tattered on the floor. All my cries were muffled behind the glass. A second horn grew and curled like a ram's where it had been broken. Luck's muzzle widened. His eyes narrowed. His chest grew. A single batwing ripped from his back in a scream of agony. I felt everything he felt. It was as if I were watching myself.

The grizzled voice guffawed into the loudspeaker. "You thought you could escape me, Cerra," it roared. "I have you now. You will love me. You will be made new."

The second set of needles sucked the blood from my wrists. The High Wolf's face pressed on the glass, smiling like Jasper. His needle-like claws tapped on the glass like I was a fish.

The two needles, full of dark fluid, edged closer, ready to inject my throat.

"Foolish brat. You connected to him, and I spread. You just gave me the upper hand over my slave. Any last words?"

I begged Luck to stop.

Both needles pierced my neck like a vampire, breathing venom into my bloodstream. I lost my vision for a moment. Everything turned to black, then a still red. Images formed. My heart rate climbed. The straps broke. I broke the glass. Ichor covered my body and I was reborn as a swamp creature.

"Rise, my spawn. Kill. Eat."

Max raced into the room, followed by Des.

Like a moist butterfly, my damp new wings furrowed in wet sludge, one bat-like, the other feathered. My face had lengthened into a canine snout, with fangs exposed over my lips. Webs stretched between my fingers. Bratwurst links had replaced my slim lady fingers. Devil's needles shot from my once-little kitty claws.

I wanted food. I wanted pleasure. I was ready—no, born to kill.

"Kiera, what happened?" Max cried, looking on at the scene.

I licked my lips at the fresh meat.

Des drew his dinky little daggers from his side.

Child's play. I lunged.

Max turned and ran. Des's body flung like a rag doll into a green tube. *Always one for the chase, I suppose.*

"Kiera, this isn't you!" Max yelled.

My talons plowed through the floor. I galloped after him.

Max weaved through machinery and tubes. I smashed through the glass. Nothing could stop my kill.

I growled in my bestial body, "The chase only makes me want you more." Glass dug into my hide, trapped in fur, skin, and scale. I leaped and my wings glided me over rubble with a roar.

"Kiera, stop, please!" Max pleaded.

My voice spoke in doubles, "Fool. I am not Kiera. I never was."

My vision and thoughts narrowed. Everything within me turned primal. *Must kill. Must eat. Must win. Much win. Very much win.*

Max's back pressed against the barrel of a tube. My tongue shot out like a chameleon and licked his face. He slid limply to the floor. I juggled the bean bag of fur, salivating at the mouth.

"Please, Kiera. I beg of you."

I slammed him into the tube with both hands. The glass cracked and green liquid trickled down the side.

My voice snarled in my new feral language.

"Idiot! You don't get it, do you? I don't love you. I never will. You're stupid, weak, and a coward. *That* is why you must die."

My claws peeled his breastplate like a cheap plastic wrapper. They clicked and pricked his skin, giving them a ruby gloss. My tongue sucked like a weevil into his wound. He grabbed it, and I pulled him in. His fist sank to the back of my throat, gagging me. His other fist punched me in the nose like a shark.

With each blow, the smell of blood turned from peach to iron. Color returned to my vision. My beloved lay limp before me.

A prick hit the back of my neck. Desmodius stood behind me, panting with an empty syringe in his hand. He dragged the limp body of the High Wolf. My world shattered. The black wolf, Fenrir, who had attacked Romero and Sonia before, approached us.

He patted Des on the shoulder, "Well done, little cub. The key is ours. The crown will fall to us."

CHAPTER THIRTY

S hackles held me to the wall with my arms above my head. My night vision was *slow* to kick in.

Three two-foot-tall vials of saryx juice stood in front of me. My form had returned to normal, give or take some stretch marks. Two gimp wings rubbed the wall behind me. My jaw ached as if it had been stretched open in a vise.

A metal gate rolled open in the dark. Footsteps approached.

Fenrir approached carrying a torch, with Desmodius in tow. "Rise and shine, sunshine," the wolf laughed, tossing a bucket of water in my face. "You've been out three days. Blood loss will do that to ya. What's the matter?" Fenrir elbowed Des in the ribs. "Cat got your tongue? I'll send him away if you'll play nice."

"What do you want?" I choked.

Fenrir grinned. "What do I want? You've already given it to me."

His eyes darted to a tank full of saryx fluid and blood, then back to me. His mouth salivated.

"Look at you! You've recovered without a scratch. Hardly any stretching of muscle or extreme aging. All except those wings, of course, but they build character. Easy on the eyes. It's like some treatment finally worked to preserve your form. Are you taking any medicine?"

I shook my head and thought. The only medicine I'd taken was . . . Minnie's brew. Of course. They kept her looking young.

"Well, maybe," he tapped on the canisters, "you've just got good blood. You've given us enough pureblood to open the door. We can finally take back the earth from these humes. You're our heroine in this fallen earth. I should ask you, my dear, how can I help you?"

"Let me out of here," I suggested feebly.

Fenrir snapped his fingers, and Des unlocked my chains.

"You're free to go, princess, wherever you choose. Just stay out of trouble."

"Where's Max?"

Fenrir snickered "Where do you think?"

"If you've hurt him, I swear . . ."

"Sucker's crossing the rainbow bridge," Fenrir retorted coolly.

My heart sank. "What?" Fenrir grinned. "You heard me."

I shook my head in disbelief. *I couldn't have killed him. He promised I couldn't. Max is . . . dead?*

"Come on, Prince, let's go," Fenrir said, motioning to Des. "You have a coronation to attend."

Tears streamed down my face. Des lingered in the doorway.

"Cutswell, do you hear me?"

Des sighed and glanced at me over his shoulder before leaving.

I'd killed Max. I couldn't believe it. They were right. I truly was a monster. This was the final transformation. The beast had won.

When the tears refused to come any longer, I stared at the dried blood on my hands.

It took me a while to compose myself. I scraped myself off the floor and wandered the halls. They held many prisoners here. Moonstone lined the walls in shimmering white. Sorcerers lay either dead or dying in most cells. I'd given up on trying to find Cheryl.

I walked past the cells into a camp. There was no way I could save them now. I was a murderer.

Music blared in celebration. Fires crackled. Tents sprouted up everywhere in joyful exuberance. A torch illuminated a myst-powered lift similar to the one from behind Temple 42. I walked past the camp and toward it.

A voice called out to me from the revelry. A stinging sensation pricked my shoulder, and a pebble clattered to the ground. Sonia appeared behind me and flung her arms around me.

"You look terrible," she began, pulling away.

"Sure feel like it," I said.

"Thank goodness you're here. I figured out how to save the sorcerers. Jasper's men are going down. You see, they're planning an ambush for the army, and—"

"Don't care," I cut her off.

"Beg your pardon?"

"I don't care," I said. "It's not our problem."

"Sinopa, people will die. What happened to justice?"

"I wouldn't be much help, anyway. Scrape up Romero and let's go."

"He's locked up at the moment. What happened to you?"

I couldn't look her in the eye. "The same thing that always happens. I get attached, and no matter what I do, they slip away."

I walked straight ahead to the lift. Sonia trailed after me. "So that's it? You give up?"

"Yep. Seems about as good a time as any."

I started the lift, leaving her on the bottom. The dust cleared, and my head with it. Giving up seemed, at the time, to be the first reasonable thing I'd done. I was no soldier.

The lift brought me to the camp of the Ammonites. Most of the camp lay empty. They'd all rallied with the army to storm the quarry in the morning through the channel.

I remembered what Lot had said. The Ammonites were traitors, too. I hadn't understood what he meant at the time, but it felt true—I was just like them. Although, I hadn't sold the secrets to ancient Machina and broken sacred traditions. But I did abandon my family. I'd betrayed Max and hurt those I loved.

A light shone through the large war tent.

I pulled back the curtain, and the magistrate sat inside sipping a cup of tea. The tent appeared to be an elaborate house of luxury. *No roughing it here.* A single-sized bunk sat in the corner next to a small woodstove, and an armchair. Several trunks surrounded one wall, and a chest of drawers piled high with junk took over the other. Only the best for the magistrate, I assumed.

He sat in the armchair. He wore a jacket similar to Romero's. "Care for some tea?" he asked casually.

I nodded.

"Ah, so the conquering heroine awakens," Beauregard said. "I was wondering when I'd finally get to see the princess herself."

I remained silent. I didn't even care to check the cup for poison. In my mind, I was ready to die, anyway.

"Come, now, dearest. Where's the fun in winning if you are just going to suck the life out of it? Didn't my pupil teach you even the tiniest bit of sportsmanship?"

Winning. The beast really had, hadn't it? "Excuse me. Monologue away," I said "That's what you're supposed to do, right? And I'm supposed to deny it—like in an opera? And I pick myself up and you get away."

"What's on your mind?" he asked.

"What do you care?"

Beauregard walked over to me and dusted off a box. "Do you like chess? Leopold fancied it, but," he paused. "To be honest, he was never very good. The trick is to guess your opponent's moves and plan accordingly. I have nothing to gain or to lose, no matter what you say. I'll win either way."

"How do I go on—knowing I've killed someone I've cared about?"

"That's it? First off, you didn't kill him. He's fighting. He's in the medical tent should you wish to visit him. Had you though, you should have patted yourself on the back. You would have done what your teacher never could."

I took in his words, but they only half registered. This had to be a trick. I quickly changed the subject. "So what's Romero's deal with you?"

"I suppose I could tell you, but wouldn't you rather see it for yourself?"

He pulled from the jacket a blue forget-me-knot and tossed it my way. The sphere slipped from my fingers into the air before I caught it again.

I attached the knot to my neck. Romero's memories flooded into mine. I experienced everything he'd experienced.

My feet raced. Coal stank in the air. Wind beat in my face as I rode the Sirius over water. I raced to an island. Steps ran down deep into a mine. A young blonde lady struggled, tied to a support beam in the center of the quarry. Her stomach was round and swollen, and red sticks surrounded her. Beauregard stood on the catwalk above. A rope snapped. A blood-curdling scream burst forth.

I couldn't look where the girl had stood. Then flashes and crashes of metal. My sword clashed against Beauregard's. Only his was faster, and so were his legs. No matter how hard I tried, he got away. My memories then became doused in alcohol. Mutterings of changelings and revenge. A journal opened with the image of the door. Between hangovers, I searched for the pureblood and I searched for Beauregard.

I yanked the tick from my neck.

"He was using me," I whined.

Beauregard nodded.

"The woman's death wasn't part of my plan, but he wouldn't listen. Sometimes you must let them believe what they want and adjust accordingly. But yes, he was using you. He was trying to use you as bait for me, as I did her for him."

"So, the extra ring Romero wore?"

"It was hers." Beauergard paced the floor like a professor. I could see the similarities to Romero all ready. "Eleanor Addison Pratchett, she descended from the noble house of Northstrand. Leopold had confided in me how they had been lovers for years. Sweethearts since the academy. She named that ramshackle bird you flew here. It was her 'wishing star' or some mushy crap. Here's another sphere you might find interesting."

I barely caught it. I was hesitant to attach it.

"Go on," he urged.

I inspected the inside and saw a goblinoid figure. Intrigued, I attached the sphere.

It placed me in the shoes of a tall man. In his company were three soldiers. They walked through a cavern, reaching a goblin village. The village extended into the tree line and small huts dotted the forest floor beside an open meadow. A goblin man named Pater greeted and took them to an "inn."

Uh-oh, I know where this is going.

Beauregard found me and gave the orders to raid the village. The meadow and huts burned to the ground, and Pop-pop with it. They brought me to Nantucket to escape Luck's search and prevent the Vestiges from being found . . . until now.

I handed back the sphere.

"Scary, isn't it?" he smirked.

"You're insane," I murmured.

"Am I? I have many more of Leopold's memories if you are interested."

"You destroyed my family. My home. You killed Havish."

"Me? No. The army, yes. I have much more important things to handle. If it makes you feel any better . . ."

He placed Romero's flintlock in my lap.

"He won't be needing it anymore. Whichever side you choose, I hope it brings you good luck."

I pointed at him and fired. Click.

Beauregard just laughed.

"Good luck finding bullets." He gathered up his tea things. "Bobby pins are in the top drawer should you decide he's worth saving. I won't stop you; I fancy a challenge. It's much more satisfying knowing the thing I gave my flintlock to all those years ago survived. But just remember, he used you. Don't put it past him to do it again."

Beauregard exited the tent.

I pulled open the drawer and snatched all the bobby pins. I wasn't letting Romero loose, but they could come in handy.

Sonia was right. They still needed to go down. After what he did to Havish, Beauregard was on my list, too. What could I do with just Sonia and me? We needed more people. Without allies, we didn't stand a chance. I needed answers. I wandered around and searched the camp, hoping to find Lot.

Instead, I found a medical tent. I took a deep breath, stepping inside. A million conflicting feelings washed over me as I surveyed the scene, yet I was dead inside. I found myself shocked, unable utter a word. Inside the tent, a brown canine changeling lay motionless on his back. White bandages mummified his chest. His crooked ear flicked away a fly. This was Max—my Max, and I had hurt him. I turned and exited, unable to look. *I'd done this. I'd almost killed him. Maybe I really am a monster.*

"Kiera?"

I took another deep breath and reentered the tent.

More bandages wrapped the back of his head where I had slammed him into the glass. I stood beside him and squeezed his paw. His mismatched eyes stared up at me. He smiled weakly.

"How do you feel?" I asked.

His tail wagged. He groaned, reaching across his chest, and squeezed my hand with both of his.

"Much better now," he said.

I faintly smiled. It was hard to survey the damage I had caused.

"Don't blame yourself. It was not your fault," he told me.

It was as if he could read my thoughts. I ignored him. "Can you walk?"

He shook his head. "Don't know, haven't tried." I patted his shoulder. "Rest up, buddy. I'm going to find us a way out of here."

"Wait, Kiera."

I turned around.

"Stay with me. Please."

I pulled up a chair and sat beside him. I couldn't muster up words so I just held his hand and hummed a tune, stroking back his ears. Luckily, he didn't want to talk. He just wanted company. I kissed his hand and held it close to my heart. Max beamed from the hospital bed, staring, and giving me that irresistible smirk. His chest rose and fell in long pauses. No doubt, I had overwritten his scars.

Max chuckled out of thought. "Such a pineapple, twice as sweet," he said, gesturing to me. He followed my eyes to his bandages. "You know I got lucky."

I nodded, pretending to understand. Max's ears tucked as if waiting for a response.

He cleared his throat. "Aren't you gonna ask how?"

I raised an eyebrow. "How so?"

"Because an angel like you hasn't left me yet."

I blushed and kissed his forehead. He really did deserve better than me.

Eventually, his eyelids grew heavy and whisked him off to dreamland. I walked across the camp. A faint light came through the opening in the canyon wall above, and a silhouette stood in the moonlight. I readied my saber and made my approach. Lot, battle-scarred and weary, looked over the chasm.

"Evening," he called when he heard my footsteps.

"You're not heading to the chasm?" I asked.

"No, I can see through the ruse, unlike the others. What about you, Miss Detective? Did you save those you set out to rescue?"

My feet dangled over the edge as I sat. "I couldn't even save myself. I'm such a monster."

"No. A monster wouldn't have come down here," he reasoned.

"They created me to destroy everything in my path: humans, animals . . . even those I love aren't safe."

Lot raised an eyebrow. "Says who?"

"Says my father and the rest of the changelings. The humes see me as a beast, too."

"Yes, but why should their opinions matter?"

I didn't understand. I considered sliding off the edge of the cliff and just letting anything happen.

"Should I build a tower out of bricks, whose tower is it?" he asked me.

I exhaled. "The person who built it, I suppose."

"And I would get to define its purpose, would I not?"

I brushed back my bangs, impatient with the riddle. "Get on with it." "My people believe in a creator beyond parenthood. This is the reason we've been hiding underground all these years. I believe He made you for so much more."

I rolled my eyes. "Yeah, right. I'm worthless and stupid. I nearly killed my friend, and I murdered my brother." "Ah, but who would define your worth?"

I was ready to punch him.

"I'm not trying to force this upon you," Lot said. "Just think about it. You have help should you ask for it."

I sat alone on the cliffside for an hour. I was never the religious type—mostly because my demonic appearance kept me out of places like that.

What is my real purpose other than destruction? I didn't want to become a weapon. I didn't want to hurt anyone again. Things had been so much simpler before the city.

I found Lot and he helped me pray. We prayed that I might be a vessel of good, that he would help us escape this place, and that I might find my true purpose.

I considered it strange—something as repulsive as me speaking to something considered holy. I can't say I entirely understood it, but my spirits were lifted.

Lot talked with me until I found my strength again. I had made a promise to Cheryl. Those sorcerers needed saving, and Cobarde's "missing" changelings did too, while we were at it. This consul that Beauregard had duped didn't know what he was up against. If Fenrir got his paws on the Vestige, they'd be massacred. Fenrir, Beauregard, and Cobarde—they were all going down.

And Luck… if they hurt him, they would be sorry. I just hoped he was alive. Fenrir would have him under lock and key.

Whatever the saryx did it wasn't pretty. Luckily for me, my symptoms mitigated—for now. If he even lived, the disease warped him unrecognizable. This new Luck couldn't be stopped alone.

If we were going to leave here, it would be with guns a-blazing. Also, I'd feel better if someone would put me down should my condition flair up again. We had best get some more firepower, and I knew just the guy. It was time to visit an old friend.

Watch out, Leopold. It's showtime.

CHAPTER THIRTY-ONE

I felt terrible waking Max. Sneaking through the tent flap, I gathered my strength and placed my glove on his chest. My fingers pulsed and evened out his skin.

Max whimpered awake.

I shushed him and continued mending his wounds. My migraine kicked in again, but I would fix him if it killed me.

I welcomed death just so long as I wasn't a monster. They needed to live. My friends deserved to live. And if my life meant they were safe, then so be it.

Max wouldn't let me leave so I helped him to his feet; he was coming with me. Lot offered his help, and we brought Max down the lift. The quarry lift was structurally sound enough that we could all ride.

Together we devised a plan. Lot set out to fetch Sonia and gather any enslaved gnomes for a militia. Meanwhile, Max and I were to free Romero and the unguarded prisoners in the cellblock.

Footsteps echoed in these halls. Step one: keys. If there were any. The cellblock, like I said before, remained relatively unguarded. I'd seen maybe three guards total. Max was heavy on my shoulder. He could walk, but I felt better helping him along.

The elevator gate opened, and we broke on three. Max and I made for the prison. I still refused to believe he wasn't upset with me. There wasn't enough reprimand. I should feel more guilty. My mind turned over and over, asking what was wrong with me.

Max fixed his eyes on the trail ahead the entire time. His tail buffeted slowly. His body remained frail, but his tail wagged. He seemed happy to be on the mission.

One guard approached. Judging by the jingling of metal, this may be our ticket. We ducked into an open cell and hugged the wall. Torchlight approached, and on the guard's waist was a ring of keys.

"How do we get the keys?" whispered Max.

"We? No, I got this. Just stay here, okay?"

His ears tucked as if hurt. He nodded.

"Not a peep," I reminded him.

He bared his teeth and waved me on. I knew he wouldn't like it, but it was the only feasible nonviolent method I could think of.

I did my best Sonia impression. "Yoo-hoo. Mr. Watchman?"

The guard turned to me. His face was that of a cougar.

"What are you doing here? This place is restricted."

"Yes, I'm sorry," I said, approaching him. "You see, I've lost my way, and I was wondering if you could help me find it." I let one bra strap slide off my shoulder.

Max growled in the cell. "What was that?" asked the guard.

I grabbed his forearms. "What was what, puddin'?"

"I thought I heard something."

"All I heard was the sound of your heartbeat. I got locked out of my room, and if you'd be so kind as to hand me the keys, I could try them and be on my merry way."

"I could help you," he offered.

"You'd do that for me?" I pulled him close and kissed his face.

Max snarled and barked. The guard tried to pull away. I yanked him closer, more aggressively. Time to change tactics. I fished out his dagger and sliced his throat.

The guard gargled to the floor, pouring out a red mist. *So much for nonviolent.* I shot Max a stern look as he approached. His snout drooped.

"You're disgusting," he whined.

"Shut up and help me drag the body, Mr. Loose Lips."

I struggled to keep it together that I had killed someone. Was death really unavoidable?

Max muttered how *I* really had loose lips and yadda, yadda, yadda.

I gave Max the guard's weapon, and he still went on and on about how I'd kissed him.

"Relax. Our kisses are real," I said, patting him on the back.

"I'm not sure what to believe anymore. You said your name's not Kiera?"

I shook my head.

"What's your real name, then?"

"Why does it matter? You can call me Kiera if you like. I don't like it, but—"

"Kiera," he grabbed my shoulders and turned me to face him. "I want to know you, the real you. Warts, scales, horns and all."

My eyes went to the floor. Sinopa."

"Kinopa? One more time?"

"*Sss* like a snake. Sinopa."

"That's kind of pretty," he decided.

I smiled. "Keep practicing your *s* sound."

"Now do me," said Max.

"What?"

"Ask me anything. Showing your underbelly, remember? I did you. You do me."

I bit my cheek. "You're not mad at me for the, well . . . ?" I gestured toward his chest. "Maybe a little," he admitted. "Mostly because you called me stupid."

"You could understand me?"

He nodded.

I held two sets of keys in my hands, ready to let them all fall to the floor.

"Look, Rin—Kin—or Sin—"

"Kiera is fine."

"I'm going to master it one of these days."

"It shouldn't matter. You're my packmate. When we get out of here, we'll talk more. You still owe me that date."

He smirked.

Whether you want to call it stupidity or loyalty, his forgiveness knew no bounds.

"Here's a set of keys," I said. "Meet me by the entrance in an hour. Don't get caught."

"Got it."

I grabbed him by the shoulder before he left. "Wait. Don't go dying on me," I said, pecking him on the cheek.

Max blinked.

"Was that my kiss from before? You aren't giving it back?"

"Ha. Don't count on it."

Max smiled. "I'll be needing it back, then," he winked.

"I'll hold it close to my heart. Now get moving, hot-shot."

"Well, I was until you stopped me."

I threw a rock at him and snickered, racing the other direction down the corridor. Next stop: Romero. I remained undecided about whether to bust him out.

Lucky me—the other two sentries were in my block. I would have to pick them off one at a time. No way I could fight both of them at once.

After some ninja-like skills, if I do say so myself, and vampiric seduction, both guards lay motionless in a cell. I grabbed their sabers and donned their armor. It was sweaty, far too large, and reeked of BO, but it would have to do.

I wandered along till I found a large cell at the end of a hall. A man lay inside, beaten up. His face swelled. Chains held his arms above his head, and a long button jacket hung open with red *x*'s on his chest.

I fumbled with key after key, until I found the right one.

Unsheathing my sword, I stared down at the pathetic excuse of a man. "Beauregard told me everything," I hissed.

He remained silent and stared at the floor.

"You give me one good reason not to end you right now. You used us, and we trusted you."

Romero spoke unbearably calmly, "I couldn't go through with it. Remember the lift?"

"All this—the teachings, the deals, the charades—it was all to catch him, wasn't it?"

"That's not—"

"You couldn't care less about us."

"That's not true. Kiera, we need to go. This place will—"

"Let you out? Why should I?"

"Kiera, calm down."

"Even that name is part of your routine. Who is she? Who's the real Kiera? Riddle me that before I blot you out of existence."

"I was cocky and stupid. I told you before and hate myself for it. We continue down this road of fantasy and masquerade, and we lose ourselves." *Ouch.* Romero looked up at me. "The bottom hurts, doesn't it, kid? I can see in your eyes you've hit it, too. You're bluffing. I can tell. You're still a terrible liar."

I pulled out my flintlock with my other hand and cocked the hammer back.

"You didn't answer my question," I said.

"You need me. I need you."

I turned the gun from him to myself.

Romero sighed. "Fine, put it down," he relented.

I turned the gun back to him.

"I lost the only girl I had ever truly loved. Ellie and I had cruised the entire coast as pirates and treasure hunters, of a sort. We grew closer with each passing day. She was my sanity; I was her shield. We had gone through alias after alias and disguise after disguise with time. It's tough being popular."

Even under the barrel of a gun, he never dropped the act. "Her becoming pregnant was rather unfortunate. She wanted more than anything to keep the baby, and despite my heeding, she insisted on tagging along. Kiera was the only name we could agree on."

"What happened to her?"

Romero shook his head. I remembered how round Eleanor had been when I saw her through the forget-me-knot.

"I'm sorry," I mumbled.

"Don't be. Now you see why people like them must be stopped. Cobarde, the Order—heck, even the magistrates were made to keep countries in check.

But no one, not a soul, keeps them in check. That's our job—yours and mine. Let me out of here, kid. We have one final act."

"How can I trust you?"

"You can't," he said with a smirk.

"I really don't have a choice in this, do I?"

"You can have my sword if it makes you feel better," he offered. "I owe you that. Should you wish to strike me where I stand . . . It's been an honor having you as a pupil."

I pulled the blade back and stopped an inch from his skin.

"Consider that a warning," I said. I pulled out my keys and tried every lock, but none worked. Romero said the magistrate had the key. *I wish he said that earlier.* I started with my bobby pins at his shackles.

He rubbed his wrists. "I ask your forgiveness, Kiera."

"For using us?"

"Nope." He pecked my cheek and shackled my wrist.

"Hey!"

He hobbled as fast as he could out the door. "Stay safe. See you at the quarry."

"Hey, come back here! Romero? Romero!"

CHAPTER THIRTY-TWO

I regretted not killing the sneak. When I found him, I would wring his neck. One thing for sure: if he wasn't dead already, he would be.

I pulled a bobby pin and began picking the shackle on my wrist. The angle made me feel blindfolded. I went through two pins until it clicked.

Max had been busy. Several sorcerers and weary changeling inmates warmed the halls. I surveyed the cells, freeing many of them. No sign of Cheryl in the chaos.

In the corner of a cell, I found a man in prison rags. His frame stretched large and muscular. It was Rudolph! I frantically fidgeted with the chains of the man clinging to life. None of my keys worked. I quickly force-fed him some water and cleaned his wounds.

Max raced into the cell out of the roaring crowd. "Need help?"

I nodded, and he started going through his keys.

"How did you find me?" I asked.

"Followed my nose."

"Great. Just what every woman wants to hear."

"What? You have a distinct smell. It's unique, and while not girly, its—"

I clamped his snout. "Quit while you're ahead," I advised him.

Max unlocked the manacles. Rudolph stood up with a hobble. His eyes narrowed in the torchlight. "You," he rasped.

I nodded.

"Max, you know the way to the lift, right?" I asked him.

"Yes. Why?"

"Get these people to it. The lift should hold plenty. They'll at least be safer there, for the time being."

"How can I help?" Rudolph groaned.

"How do you feel?" I asked, helping him to stand.

"Terrible."

"Then there's no way you can fight."

"Nonsense. You really don't know what is going on down here. Do you?"

"It's an ambush, right?" I countered.

Rudolph nodded. "We must secure the Vestige. The army wants their research and mutants. Um, no offense."

"Taken," Max growled. "Right," Rudolph continued. "Well, they want their nation. Both sides have leverage. Beauregard is ready to play both sides. The army rigged the place to blow if negotiations go awry. On top of that, my country hasn't been . . . well . . . they hold your kind in the quarry."

It made sense now. The dynamite, the missing changelings and sorcerers —everything clicked. The missing changelings and the sorcerers were just their bargaining chips, and if the army couldn't have the Vestige or their research, no one could.

"So what do we do now?" I asked.

"You have a way out?" Rudolph asked.

I paused. Honestly, I hadn't thought that far ahead.

"Yes," said Max proudly. "The sewers run to the city."

Guess his nutshell of a noggin wasn't totally useless. Maybe he would recover after all.

"You're positive?" Rudolph asked.

Max nodded.

"Otherwise we're going out swinging to the docks till the roof caves in. Most of the changelings should prepare their assault on one side of the quarry. Using the lifts is asking for a target on your back."

"What about the army?" I asked.

"They're stationed in the channel with the consul, I presume. Is he all right?"

Max and I turned to each other. "He was alive last we saw him," I said.

"Good. I'm not sure what Beauregard and these beasts are planning, but I fear the consul is in danger. The last thing this place needs is a power vacuum. What are our options? Do we have any manpower? Any rebellion? Resistance?"

"We could gather the prisoners and see," suggested Max.

"Most of my soldiers died, or they remained trapped in the quarry," Rudolph said.

"Could you lead them if they're there?" I asked.

"It would be my honor. I'll meet you at the lift." He stumbled off into the crowd with one of my sabers.

"Who was he?" Max asked.

I bit my cheek, unsure of what to say. I couldn't tell him Rudolph was the other guy.

"Nobody," I mumbled.

"He seemed to be somebody."

"Just an old friend." I waved it off. "Now get moving. You did lovely. I'll free the rest. These people need you."

Max smiled. He stood in the hallway and let loose a howl, and people started funneling toward him. They swept him off into the sea of rags and fur.

I patrolled cell by cell. I couldn't bear the thought of one person left behind. The halls were now still. Whether it was a good silence, the jury was still out.

I had to work quicker. My ears caught wind of sniffling at one of the end cells. The room was dark. I couldn't see beyond five feet in my night vision. Rudolph had taken my torch.

The key to the room was rusty and more ancient than the rest. The door clanged against the bars. A little girl's voice screamed. "Stay away from me!"

"It's all right," I attempted to soothe her. "I'm here to help you."

The girl was in nicer clothes than the rest of the inmates. Her room had small drawings nailed into the wall. An IV pumped saryx fluid from her elbow.

"This is another one of their tricks, isn't it?" Her face scrunched at me—

changeling features, too hard to make out in the dark. "That big bad wolf put you up to this, didn't he?"

Big bad wolf? Fenrir or High Wolf? "No, I'm here to help you out," I assured her.

I stepped forward.

"Lies. Get back!" she cried.

I stepped closer.

Closer. Her face was white, covered in pale fur. Tufts of blonde hair ran down her head in curls, and on both sides stood two jumbo mouse ears.

"I said get back!" she shrieked.

Her hand swung out and flung me into the steel bars. The IV left her arm. Ichor dripped onto the ground and blood ran down her arm. She began crying. My world spun. I barely got my balance as I stood up.

The girl flung me without even touching me. It must be magic. I staggered over to her in the corner.

"I said get back," she sobbed.

"You're hurt; let me help you."

Blood trickled down her arm. Whatever they had stuck her with had run up her veins.

"No. Leave me alone."

I fell to her level and grabbed her arm. My hand glowed. Her eyes shut tight in fear. The wound sealed, and she opened her eyes. The girl rubbed her cut.

"Th—thank you," she stammered.

I smiled, holding my aching head. I would feel that in the morning.

"Sorry," she said.

"It's okay. What's your name?"

The girl blinked her misty blue eyes. "Edith."

"Well, Edith, let's get you out of here, okay?"

She shook her head. Her legs were small, frail, and almost shriveled. She was small. Unbelievably tiny. I picked up her fragile body and carried her out of the cell. Edith wept as we left, but soon she cried herself out and was asleep over my shoulder.

Little did I know how pivotal she would become in my life. I'd gathered three allies. It was time for us to bring the fight to them.

CHAPTER THIRTY-THREE

M ax got all the unable-bodied sorcerers and inmates up the lift. The few remaining were changelings who'd crossed the High Wolf or Fenrir for disobeying the teachings by showing compassion or insubordination. They were ready for payback.

We armed them with shovels, and what few tools we had. Lot took several to run a guerilla operation. With the sorcerers free, the changelings were next. They were our reinforcements. Rudolph was to prepare the frontal assault with his unit.

Max and I had two goals: find Sonia and stop the new High Wolf. If we could get through to him, we could prevent the ambush and call off Fenrir's men. They must have taken Sonia with them while clearing the camp, kicking and screaming, no doubt. There was no chaining that bird down.

The only problem remaining was what to do with Edith. Despite everyone's objections, I carried her with me and joined Max in the last working lift. She was coming with me and that was final. But even Max growled at the idea.

I couldn't trust her to be left alone in her condition. If she really had the saryx disease, she could wipe out the remaining survivors without a second thought. No one else needed to die. Not on my watch.

If Cheryl was alive, she'd be there. I had made a promise to her son, Simon; one I intended to keep.

Max glared at me as we rode down the shaft to the quarry.

Beneath us was a wide, funnel-shaped pit with a clearing at the bottom. Rings of pueblos and tin roof huts surrounded the center. The back wall comprised endless rows of cells carved into the stone and earth.

It was then that we realized how risky our plan was. Crossbow arrows shot at the bottom of the car. Shouts rose. Soldiers rushed toward the lift. *So much for stealth.*

They'd reach the bottom before we did.

I squeezed Edith tight and looked to Max.

"Any ideas?" he asked.

"Just one," I said.

"Let's hear it."

"Jump."

Max whimpered unsure of himself.

The lift inched closer to the roof's edge. I grabbed Max by the arm and pulled him near, readying us for the jump. The ground seemed miles away. We neared the edge of the roof.

"Now!" I screamed. I leaped and skidded on the metal roof sideways. My arms braced Edith for the impact.

Max hit the roof with a hard thud. His nails made a screeching sound as they scraped down the side. Max whined, gaining no ground. I set Edith down and dove over to the other side of the roof. My hands snatched his paws.

"Gotcha."

Max's legs flailed and kicked. I summoned all my strength to pull him over the edge.

They raised more alarms. The camp lit up. I hoped we hadn't made things even harder on Lot. We scrambled to our feet. Edith began to stir. My best guess was the Order had been drugging her. I tried to calm her as we ran to the unguarded tunnels.

As we entered, the Order of the Archaeopteryx met us with praise. The camp was dark. I lit a torch. A circle of heads stared at us, chuckling. We were surrounded.

"What are you doing? Put that light out!" Fenrir stalked closer. His eyes glowed white. Max stepped in front of me and growled a warning.

"Loyalty. How cute. Such weakness is unfit for true soldiers," Fenrir said.

"True wolves protect the pack above all else," Max replied.

"Where's Luck?" I asked.

"Ah, and who could forget the chosen of her people? It would seem she's been snooping around, much like her father."

"Where is he?" I demanded.

Edith quivered at the sight of Fenrir.

"And how is my little pet?" he spat, eyeing her.

Edith squirmed, flailed, and did everything she could to escape my clasp.

I pulled her close as she burrowed her head into my chest.

"Where's the High Wolf?" I asked for the third time. "We wish to speak with him. It's important."

"The High Wolf is undergoing treatments. He won't be seeing visitors," answered Fenrir.

"Then who's in charge?"

The coal-colored wolf's pink jowls curled in a devilish grin. "Speaking," he said.

"Don't you know you are walking into a trap?" I asked.

Murmurs rose amongst the order.

"Nonsense," argued Fenrir. "We have the home turf. If they want their disgusting humes back, they must leave the cavern. Besides, what are they to us, anyway? My pupil Jasper's plan was excellent, yes, but no longer needed. Why have only a slice if we can have the whole cake? The wreckage is a pea shooter compared to the entire Vestige."

"And I'm telling you, the army doesn't care about the sorcerers. They're just as heartless as you."

Fenrir stood to his full height and approached me. Max stood between us, but Fenrir stood a foot or two taller.

"Out of my way," Fenrir sneered at Max.

Max barked, baring his teeth.

"So be it," said Fenrir, reaching for his weapon.

"Enough!" Two voices spoke in a chorus.

A hulking figure shook the ground as it approached. Those closest to it bowed one by one.

"You are not to harm her," the voices spoke.

The monstrous form of the High Wolf stamped toward us.

Fenrir turned and stood dead in his tracks.

Luck's monstrous voice cracked in a chorus. "Let me make one thing clear: you will never be the High Wolf. My throne falls to her. And with it my crown, and her husband."

Fenrir stammered in his defense. "But I—"

The High Wolf roared with a rush of wind, spit, and rancid breath in his face. "Your lust for power ends now. If you value your life you will kneel."

"As for you," he said, turning to me. "Your coronation begins now. You will open the door. We will overthrow this city, and the Age of Man will end."

Suddenly, a purple dart sank into the High Wolf's throat.

Fenrir grinned.

"No!" I cried.

The beast's eyes blinked in a poisoned stupor. His lumbering body swayed, and Max barely dodged him as he fell.

Cutswell emerged from the shadows with a blowgun.

"Well done, prince. You may be of use yet," smiled Fenrir. The dark wolf scanned the crowd. No doubt they'd heard Luck. Fenrir seemed to be silently questioning where the changelings' loyalties stood. "The High Wolf has spoken. We begin the ritual at once. You will have a new Belphegor to lead us in his daughter. This should prove her blood. Otherwise, the title shall fall to me, the last survivor of the six thrones. I shall be High Mammon and establish a new lasting throne. Let the record show this as his final order, for now, he rests, and so do we. He will lead us into battle but no further."

Desmodius roared in protest. "This is my birthright! My throne!"

"Then you should've shot earlier, shouldn't you?" Fenrir replied. "Bring them to the chamber. At least you will keep your life under my rule, unlike him. Celebrate that."

"We're not going anywhere," I said.

Crossbows cocked.

"I beg to differ. No one defies the High Wolf," said Fenrir. "You'll prove your birthright, and Luck will have his blood bath. Take him to his tent. We meet the humes at dawn as planned, Belphegor in front."

The crossbows prodded our backs as guards led us in darkness. The further we marched, the more the air turned sour and sulfuric. The walls of the tunnel turned black and volcanic.

"What do you think the birthright is?" Max whispered to me.

"Don't know, but it can't be good."

"The door," said a small voice on my shoulder.

I turned to Edith in surprise. "You've seen it, too?"

"Yes, once. Des tried once," she said.

"And?"

She shook her head.

Cutswell led the way. He was strong and combat trained. What hope did we have of defeating him?

The road narrowed. My feet ached from miles of travel over the past week. The ground turned from brimstone to paved in ancient tar and granite.

The guards stopped at the head of the column.

"She continues alone from here," Fenrir declared. "You can follow if you wish, but she is to complete the task without assistance."

I handed Edith to Max. He shook his head and followed me. He wasn't leaving my side. *Good. I'm not losing him again.*

The road appeared familiar as torches let the way. It was just like my dream. The room descended. A chamber with six stone faces narrowed on a gleaming steel door. The pathway divided two troughs of cave water beneath them. Moisture and ichor dripped from the chins of their closed mouths. The carved faces and the stalactites were the only natural stone in the room.

Behind us, a changeling of the Order pumped a canister of tar-like saryx fluid and blood into a rotating, steaming vat. Tubes emerged from beneath the cave water.

Reinforced steel and iron coated the wall with runes, preventing anyone from digging around. Exposed mechanical cogs collected rust from the lime-stone stalactites drippings. Empty hydraulic presses secured the door on both sides, powered by blood. The rotating vat syphoned the fluids down the tubes into the entire apparatus. Only a pureblood, thicker than water, could open the door.

Des stood in the mouth of the cave with his arms folded, glaring at me. "You know what to do," he mumbled. "Get it over with."

I took a deep breath, turning back to my friends one last time. It was time to face my fears. I stepped forward into the center of the chamber.

The guards looked at me. Their heads drooped as they threw a lever. A deep mechanical humming rose in the chamber.

"Yes, open the door," hissed the High Wolf's dark voice.

"Take heart, my daughter. I'm here."

Luck?

"Yes. What's left of me. We share so much, you and I. I feel I know you so well, but I have seen you so little."

What do I do? I could never open the door. What if I die? What if it takes control and . . . ?

I thought of Max, Edith, and Sonia.

"Sinopa, I'm here. I will guide you and never leave you. Quickly, now, where do you find your strength?"

I'm strong.

The stone faces sang in a chorus, releasing springs of water.

"Not good enough," whispered Luck. "How do you fight? What do you stand for?"

I stand for what is right.

The voices rose in harmony, one after the other, at my approach; some were celestial and others sang in deep, throaty drums. Water pooled at my ankles.

"Move faster, my child. You're doing well, my little one."

I calmed myself and breathed deeply. My wrist glowed. The heads gargled and choked. Black sludge poured from their mouths. The water surrounded my waist with clotted crimson ink.

My head floated light. My migraine flared, and my vision tinted red.

"Not good enough. Try harder. Where do you find your strength? Don't let it take control over you."

I'm trying. I'm strong.

The sludge crept closer toward my neck as I approached the door. My wrist glowed.

"I know you are. But not enough for this. Trust me. Outside of yourself, where do you find your strength?"

Magic. Sabers. Muskets. Flintlocks.

The light from my fingertips snuffed beneath me. I raised my chin toward the surface of the pool as it splashed at my face. The door stood three feet away. It remained locked tight.

"What else?" urged Luck. "You're smart. I've seen you. You've been through so much. What helped you bear it all? What power outside of yourself?"

The tips of my horns were the last bit above the sludge and waves.

My friends. My friends are my strength.

I shut my eyes in my final moments, accepting my fate, thinking of them. There was Romero, who nurtured me and yet was utterly full of himself; I was sure that deep down he really cared.

I thought of Sonia, my new sister—of the bruises she gave me on the shoulder and her willingness to listen and care despite her gruff attitude. Last, I thought of Max. Ah, Max, my loyal guard dog. Words failed me as my feelings for him overwhelmed me. He never quit on me. He never left me.

I'm sorry, Max. I love you.

"Do it. Do it for them, Sinopa," Luck urged.

I opened my eyes, and my vision turned from red to black. I had lost my rage. My gloves glowed like white coals. I thought of my friends and protecting them. A white shield pushed the waters away toward the door. The rest parted in a dome around me. My fist cracked an aurora of light. I looked up, and the door was only cracked—less than an inch gap stood between the metal door and its frame. Still shut.

I failed, Luck.

"No. No, you haven't. You have made me very proud. While the door remains closed, you made great strides in defense against your saryx nature. You've found your shield where I could not. I'm proud of you, my Sinopa." His voice waned. "You're worthless, stupid, and unlovable," the gruff voice snarled.

Luck? Don't leave me. I don't know what to do.

"This sin will be with you all your life. It will be your burden to carry, and I'm sorry. But take heart. I'll be with you, just as *it* will always be with you."

The waters receded. The stone faces dulled. Mouths shut. My dome dropped, and I collapsed to the floor.

Desmodius stood over me. He shook his head and walked away without helping me up.

Max placed a hand on my shoulder. "Kiera. We need to go."

I nodded. I stood to my feet.

I turned and gave one last glance to the door of my dreams. I could make out faint carvings of weevils and coatls in the stonework. The tarnished steel seemed less bright than I remembered. The faces roused calmer. I had faced my fears.

Thanks . . . Dad.

CHAPTER THIRTY-FOUR

Max and I rushed back the way we came, carrying Edith with us. Des's men didn't care about us anymore. They were too busy trying to open the door. Honestly, I didn't care to look at it anymore. I'd failed, but the weapon remained safe, for now.

We couldn't lose a single second. We had to save the hostages, find Sonia, and take down the new High Wolf, Fenrir. The last one may prove the most difficult. Come dawn, the caves would probably collapse. We had to stop the Order. I couldn't bear more blood on my hands.

The serpentine tunnels created a nearly impossible trek. Despite Max's "bloodhound nose," I was sure we were lost. Worse, Edith was terrified of the dark. So there I was, running circles in the dark and carrying a screaming child with a man who barely remembered his own name. *Ain't life a bowl of fruit?*

Up ahead, Max shushed Edith and me.

"Do you hear that?" he asked.

"Hear what?" I whispered.

Edith whimpered, about to cry again.

"Stop it, Max. You're scaring her."

"It's singing. A lady . . . not too far . . . and water."

I listened closer but caught only silence. "I don't hear anything, babe."

Edith squeezed me tighter. "Maybe it's the bad wolf after us like he got me," she said shakily.

I rubbed a small circle over her back. "There, there. Fenrir won't hurt you anymore," I assured her. "I'll make sure of it. But you gotta be a big girl now, okay?"

She nodded and buried her head in my shoulder. Her eyes squeezed shut.

I wished I had a torch to give her.

Max stepped ahead with a paw cupped to his ear. "I know I'm not crazy," he said as he listened.

"I beg to differ," I replied, "but it's our only chance of getting out of here. Maybe it's Sonia."

Max nodded and led the way toward the sound.

Loose rocks bashed the soles of our feet from the unused tunnels. The path inclined. I finally heard the running water. A faint song resonated off the walls:

"Gather wearied souls and rest. Flock, dear angels, above the ground. Come and shelter in our nest. Coatls bless you with our sound."

Max sniffled. "So beautiful. Can you hear it?"

I nodded.

"Are you crying?" I asked in surprise.

"No. Just dirt in my eye, that's all. Let's go." Max swayed forward with his hands folded.

"Are you all right? We can rest if you need."

No response. He strolled on, humming to himself.

The sound of water grew louder, and a light shone from one of the tunnels like bright daylight. Max raced toward it. "An exit! We're saved!"

"Max, wait up," I called after him.

Max was gone. I stood at the entrance of the tunnel to see luscious vines draping the arch. Steam and myst billowed out of the ground like a sauna. The song pulsed inside.

"Hear the voices that we sing. Drink our water; taste its bliss. Bind our covenant with no ring. Soon we marilith will you kiss."

"Max, come back here!" I shouted.

Edith stirred. "Is it safe to open my eyes?"

"No, keep them shut—no matter what you hear. Understand? Max is walking into a trap."

She nodded.

I adjusted Edith under my arms; she grew heavy as I wearied of carrying her. Stealth was key. Should Edith react, our cover was blown.

I pushed back the ivy curtains and entered the grotto. Bright heat lamps hung everywhere, powered by myst. Ferns and grass brushed against my legs. Water rushed in the distance. Myst billowed from the ground, obscuring my sight.

I had to move fast. It would see us before we saw it; and worse, I could have a reaction again. This was no time to turn. We were too close.

The song grew louder. The air smelled sweet, like persimmons. Moisture and humidity stuck to my face, making it difficult to breathe.

"Max, where are you?"

The song stopped. I only heard my breathing and running water.

My head started turning over everything I knew about mariliths.

What did Minnie say? Mariliths were giant serpents with tendrils instead *of wings. What else? I'm missing something. They were crafty, used myst, and seduced a horde of followers.* **Avoid the eyes.** *That's it.*

"Kiera?" Max whined.

I scanned the rainforest for him.

"Max?" I said uncertainly.

"Kiera, where are you?"

I listened for the direction of his voice. "I'm over here. Stay put. I'll find you."

"We gotta get out of here." Max rasped. "I feel funny."

A lady's voice giggled off the walls.

"Leaving so soon, our furry friend? *Sssss.*"

The water only amplified the sound. There was no way to tell which direction it came from. I moved faster. Twigs snapped. Branches stung and smacked me in the face. Burning heat formed on my cheeks. Blood trickled from my face. I didn't care. Max was more important.

He was on his knees in a clearing of fig trees. A waterfall gushed in the distance, and steam ran thick. Myst enveloped him.

The grass rustled.

"Oh, Poochie? You must be thirsty after your long journey. We have an endless supply. Boiling hot springs will soothe your feet, and cool falls will quench your tongue. We long for tall drinks of water, too. Tee-hee. *Sssss.*"

"Psssst! Max, over here," I hissed to him.

"Kiera? I can't move."

"What do you mean? I'm not carrying both of you. Get up and walk."

A twig snapped. It moved closer.

I set Edith down.

"Where are you going?" she asked.

"Stay here, okay?"

A giant figure emerged. Her scales glistened a decadent teal and sapphire. A long spine ran from her neck to her tail. The tail lashed back and forth with a long stinger at its tip.

From her back, two long tendrils lashed like whips with bud-like sprouts at the ends, covered in thorns. Her underbelly curved white. Catfish whiskers flicked from her face to her breast. I shut my eyes so I wouldn't see her face.

"There you are," she giggled at Max. "We don't like playing hide and seek, you naughty pup. It's not nice to keep us waiting."

"Max don't look into her eyes," I warned him.

The marilith hissed in my direction.

"My, that scent! So sweet. Minerva, perhaps? Those scales? Not Cerra. Definitely not. Who are you, little friend?"

Its whiskers kissed the cuts on my cheeks.

Max growled. "You mustn't hurt her."

THE BEAST SNAPPED back at him, and he quickly shut his eyes. Her tail coiled around him.

"Tell us, fluffy one, what brings you to our garden?" she asked him. "Did you fall smitten over us?"

I shook my head. "He wouldn't have if you weren't manipulating him."

"We sense jealousy."

"Hardly," I shot back.

Her body tightened around Max. I heard his joints crack. "Is that so?" she asked.

"Don't you dare hurt him," I challenged.

The marilith giggled.

"Cute. Step forward and we won't."

I stood up and trudged through the brush. I stared at my feet, unwilling to look at her.

Her shadow circled me, carrying Max in her tail.

"Well, if it isn't our little spy from the library. Here to finish us off, are you?"

"No."

"Tell us, daughter of Luck."

"How do you know who I am?" I asked.

She lunged at me, wide-eyed, and I turned my head away.

She sighed.

"Your stance, your smell—it's all him. Tell us, is he well?"

"Actually, no. He's not."

The marilith chuckled. "Good."

"That's why we need to leave," I said.

"No, I've been watching you. You are lost, yes?"

"What of it?"

Two split tongues flicked my eyelids.

"Leave her alone," Max cried.

The beast turned and hissed in his face.

"Yes, yes. That's it," she cooed.

I opened my eyes and Max's irises had turned black. Both pods of her tendrils released a gas around him.

"Do you like our perfume, poochie?"

I choked on the gas cloud. It smelled of lavender and vinegar.

"What did you do to him?" I demanded.

"Nothing. You can open your eyes, foolish girl. Our powers only bear over the feeble man. We owe the fallen princess a favor, do we not?"

I saw her face. Two round pearls stood for her eyes. Her mouth split and four pincers forked around the two halves.

"You have hunted me through the sewers and library. Now you want to help me?"

The creature smiled, bubbling with excitement. "Now that you failed, what's the point in killing you? You finally proved that traitorous Luck wrong."

"Traitorous? Wait, you were his coatl, weren't you?"

The snake's pincers pursed. Max drooled on the floor, staring over her "Yes, before he dumped me for that disgusting changeling!"

Her mouth shot a blast of water that cut through tree limbs. "He loved her, and he loves you, but us? No. We were merely his pawn. When we failed to help him open the door, like you, he tossed us aside. Now his world has come crashing down, and the caverns and sewers are ours to rule, not his. We thank you."

"He mentioned you once," I said.

She stopped in her circle around me.

"Good or bad?" she asked cautiously.

"Good," I replied.

She shook her head. "Lies. Just like he lied about flirting with that librarian. We could read his thoughts."

"Librarian? Minnie was part of the Order?"

"She's been hiding from me ever since. She didn't tell you?"

I shook my head.

The snake laughed. "Best not to ruin the surprise, then. Tell us, spawn of that accursed Cerra, do you like bets? Cerra was a betting girl."

"Not really."

The six-tendrilled snake groaned. "Pity. We'll make you a bargain, then: our people shall help your people, our harem can be your aid, and our sewers will be your escape. You've already met my Cobarde."

I had, and I knew I couldn't trust him; especially considering his distaste of changelings.

"What's the catch?" I asked.

"Smart girl. You, hmm, you're interesting. Perhaps Cerra's spawn, perhaps not. Keep us guessing. You must do us one favor: slay Luck the High Wolf."

"Never."

"Luck betrayed you as he did us. There is no more Luck. Cerra's serum killed him long ago. That is why he must die."

"I can't kill him. I refuse."

The serpent hushed her voice to a seductive whisper in my ear. "If you can't end him, he'll end you. Because of your failure, you're no longer his daughter. Our offer is more than gracious."

The brush rustled. Edith emerged and cowered at the giant serpent.

"Aw, now who do we have here? Come to Aunties." She caught the tiny mouse before it could flee. Edith shriveled into a ball while the giant wyrm squeezed her baby cheeks with its catfish whiskers.

I looked at the drooling hound, Max. His eyes dilated like a cockeyed fish. There was no one to lean on. *Could I really kill Luck? This was the perfect way to save the sorcerers. Justice would be served but is it worth it? I just found my family. Could I really give all that up? Lives are on the line, Sinopa. Focus. What's more important?*

The marilith scooped up Edith and returned to me. "Do we have a bargain? We can sweeten the deal."

"You fix Max and help us save the hostages, and we have a deal," I said.

"You must promise us the sewers are ours to keep," she hissed.

"I have no authority over the Order."

She pushed closer in my face. "True. But you do have the strength to put down that wolf mutt once and for all."

"Do I really have to kill him?" I whined.

"It's that or no deal. You can scrape up your fleabag with you. We'll even show you two the way to the surface. Do we have a deal?"

Her tendrils extended for me to shake on it.

This is for the greater good, Sinopa.

I closed my eyes and shook. I'll try my best," I found myself saying.

Her tendril pricked my veins. My head flashed with a schematic of the sewers and tunnels for miles. She did the same for Max, and with a kiss of the pods on his snout, his eyes narrowed. She was lucky I needed help. The marilith smirked at my jealousy.

The giant wyrm bid us on our way and turned to scry on her messengers.

I scraped up the still-drooling Max, and we left. I questioned whether I had just made the right decision.

Does this make me a monster if I kill Luck? Can I go through with it? Do I really have a choice?

Max leaned on my shoulder with lustful eyes, and my fears melted. I almost wished the pheromones would last. My friends were my shield. In them, I had strength. I hoped it would be enough.

CHAPTER THIRTY-FIVE

Max and I raced back through the brimstone of the depths toward camp. A clamor rose from the brigs of a cell block.

"Why did you stop?" I asked Max. "The quarry's that way."

"What about Sonia?" he asked.

Abruptly, a man sailed through the air between us. He begged and clung to my feet.

"Keep her away! Keep her away!" he whimpered.

Sonia stood in the doorway with her sledgehammer.

"I think she'll be fine," I said.

A gun blast echoed down the halls. Romero raced toward us, and stillness set in the brig. He smiled. "It's g-good to see you."

I decked him on the shoulder.

"Ouch."

"That's for leaving me," I said.

He smirked. "See you finally learned how to throw a punch."

"She's been practicing," Sonia laughed.

"You deserve a lot more," I pointed out.

"So, what's the plan?" he asked.

"We need a way into the quarry."

Romero scratched his head. "Are you thinking of a distraction?"

"You're the smart guy. Think of something," I retorted.

Romero turned to Sonia. "I may need some help on this one."

"Ha, I thought we were dead weight," she said sarcastically.

He whispered into her ear. Her cheeks rose in a devilish grin. She whispered back into his ear. They laughed like two mischievous siblings.

"That's twisted . . . I like it." Romero grinned. "All right, Kiera. You've got your distraction."

"One more thing." I handed him Beauregard's pistol. "A gift from your teacher."

"The better to kill him with. Ready to keep your end of the bargain?"

I nodded.

"Good. Be safe," he said.

Max and I trailed our wrecking crew through the hall. Corpses of at least ten men littered the floor in their wake. Rather impressive, I had to admit. Wounded rebels gathered at Romero's command, and an order of men fell in behind us. The cave exited to an upper level of the quarry. Three men with Romero pulled a giant grate away from the exit.

"It's curtain time, my friends," Romero declared. "Let's give them a showstopper."

Rudolph snuck to our left. Romero and Sonia's forces joined his.

Max, little Edith, and I rushed to the base of the quarry.

Four figures stood in the center with opposing armies on either side: the High Wolf (Luck) enlarged in monstrous glory, Fenrir in a whitewashed lab coat, Beauregard, and the high consul himself blocked the entrance.

"As I told you, consul, this is the work of your hand," Beauregard said.

"Preposterous!" cried the consul. "We would never produce an evil so foul. We're Northstrandian. Hand over our research and the Vestige, beasts. Maybe then we'll let your pets live."

"The humes must suffer," growled the High Wolf's thoughts in my head. "The humes must pay. They did this to you. It's their fault you're ugly. It's their fault she left you." *Were these Luck's thoughts?*

Fenrir spoke, "We'll never bow to a hume. Behold our true king."

The saryx-infested shell of Luck roared, shaking the rocks above. The lift gears ground as Cobarde and Heimer stepped onto the bottom floor. *Whose side were they on? Where were the wyrm's men?*

Beauregard approached them. "Now, now, children. Let us not flare our tempers. Threats against the head of the nation are not to be taken lightly."

Fenrir growled. "Whose side are you on?"

"The law's," said Beauregard. "This research and prison are in clear violation of international law. The humane treatment of all peoples was ruled by the founders themselves. Certainly even you must be aware of this."

The Consul scoffed. "These are not people, Magistrate. Take your bribe and leave. We gave you the Machina."

Beauregard chuckled. "Yes, but . . . I feel the deal's changed. Consul, I hereby place you under arrest."

The army raised their crossbows.

The consul shook his head. "Pity. Turned against your flesh and blood."

"New Archades has proved most interested in your research."

"Despicable!" The consul spat. "Fire!"

Beauregard cast a curtain of flames. All bolts were scorched. The heat radiated even from where we hid.

The magistrate raised a rifle from his back. The polished steel barrel reflected the flames. A lever action sat beneath the trigger. A blast roared, and within seconds, the consul fell dead. Both forces rushed to each other. The lever action pulled back. Gun blasts picked off the advancements with deadly precision.

I handed Edith to Max.

"Where are you going?" he asked.

"To stop Luck before he gets hurt."

He pulled my arm. "Be careful."

"I will."

"And I—I love you."

I just nodded and brushed it off. *I'm sorry, Max. What was I thinking?*

Before I had even gotten close, the beast's nose flicked, and it stood on its hind legs.

Gunshots blasted in the distance. A horn boomed up the cliff, signaling a charge. Romero's unit must have made their move.

Fenrir charged Cobarde and Heimer. Beauregard drew a massive longsword and marched behind him.

The High Wolf threw changelings aside in his strides toward me.

"Rise, my puppet. Kill."

The High Wolf pounced and tackled me to the ground. "Embrace your destiny," he snarled.

"Luck don't do this," I begged him.

"Why do you resist? Submit."

I refused to believe Luck was gone. The eyes of the beast glazed over. Drool oozed in a stream onto my face. An arrow struck him in the shoulder.

I saw Max barely juggling a crossbow and child in his arms.

"So be it," said Luck.

The High Wolf raised a howl, and several changelings turned and faced Max. He threw the weapon at them and ran.

The beast stared down at me. Its eyes blazed in an endless void. Its arms pressed my knuckles into the brick. He roared and a stream of hot myst pounded my face. It was no use. The marilith was right—the Luck I knew was gone. "Submit."

My vision tinted.

"Give in to your cravings." The dragon roared and breathed boiling myst clouds in my eyes. My throat burned, and my muscles tensed. Wings sprouted further from my back. Soon they rose and pushed me off the floor. Muscles stretched and popped. My forearms grew. Massive horns rose and locked with his. Its teeth showed.

I shook my head. I would not give in. He couldn't make me do this.

My legs threw him off me.

"I will never become like you!" I shouted. I drew my talons and charged. His fists caught mine.

"Yes, go on. Feed your anger. Fuel your hunger. Join us. You're weak. I can sense it."

He breathed hotter myst in my eyes.

My head swayed light. He let go, and I rubbed my eyes. *I must maintain control.*

His shoulder plowed me to the ground. The wind shot from my lungs. My head spun.

The High Wolf howled over me.

On the ground, my vision blurred.

The saryx called to me. "Submit. You have no power over me." *I'm not a murderer. I'm not a monster. You're wrong. I have strength. My friends are my strength.*

"Hmm, are they now?"

My vision cleared. Beyond the howling behemoth, I saw Max on his knees. A crossbow to his throat. Edith was gone.

"Choose!" the High Wolf demanded. "Them or me. I know your heart. Let go and they will live. Resist and we shall live. But even if you do futilely resist, do you really think you're human? You'd be sending the poor pooch to the slaughter, now wouldn't you? What humanity is that? Either way, you can't escape us. All humanity is sin. We are you, and you are us, and we are the beast within."

If I killed Luck, I'd prove everyone right who had put me down—Pater, Cobarde, Jasper. I'd be a monster. But if I kept fighting these urges, I'd be forced to kill Max.

The beast drooled above me. Its cavernous mouth seemed to have no end. The massive pupils blinked.

I heard Luck's voice in my head.

"You are who you choose to be."

Dad? I don't want to hurt you. I don't want to hurt anyone.

"It's okay, my child. For twenty years I've searched, and for twenty years I've suffered. My life is in your hands. End my suffering, my daughter."

No, there has to be another way. We can save you. Everything will be all right.

"My child, I love you, but you must live on. Let me save you. Beauregard will spread this disease across the globe. You must stop him. You must stop me and put me down."

I can't. I'm not strong enough.

"Not yet. You will be. Baby girl, I feel my time has come. I may not speak to you again. I want you to do one thing for me. Listen—this is important. Remember who you are. Don't let anyone tell you who you are. You're not a monster. You're Sinopa, my daughter, and I love you."

Luck don't leave me! Father? Daddy?

He was gone. Drool hit my prone body. The beast stood ready to devour me.

With tears in my eyes, I struggled to my feet. My back cracked. I turned to Max and their crossbows lowered. There was no holding back. This was for Luck.

I fanned open my wings. Anger pulsed through my veins. My knuckles cracked. My vision darkened. Everything tunneled on the High Wolf. I screamed in bestial fury.

My horns crashed into his chest like a freight train. His body flew into the sea of clashing swords. Bodies parted in the surrounding sky. My fists locked with his. His feet lost ground. The old man couldn't keep up. His eyes bulged. His head turned with more scorching myst.

Not this time. I squeezed my hands around his snout. My claws finally found meat. The acid singed my palms, and I flung him to the ground.

He lay, rattled, stunned. Now was my chance. I struck him in the gut with my knee. His head bobbed around my fists, cracking into the stone.

I pinned his arms as he tried to pin mine. My tail grew and coiled around his throat. His eyes bulged as he gagged.

My saryx shouted in my mind. "Do it. End him. Take the power and breathe in his last breath."

"Sinopa! Resist!" Max shouted. "Your strength. Remember your strength."

There was no remorse, no emotion, and no pain. The saryx had its hold on me.

A bolt crashed into my shoulder. I shrieked in pain. Cobarde shook across the way with a crossbow. Blood trickled down my chest.

My form crumbled. The High Wolf pushed off my limp body.

"Fool!" he roared at Cobarde. "How dare you interfere! You shall pay for your insolence with blood."

He charged after Cobarde in the chaos.

Luck's voice echoed in and out. "Sinopa. Hang on, my child. Hang on. Stay awake. Sinopa. Sinopa."

"Sinopa!" a female voice shouted.

An Order wolf flew, eating dirt in front of me, and a hammer clanged on the floor. Sonia stooped down beside me. She began pulling at the bolt fixed in my chest.

Bile and black fluid poured from my mouth. The puddle turned into mercury, and my horrible reflection gaped back at me. My scales stood raised on end. A devilish bat and a dove wing tucked behind me. My biceps had bulged to inhuman sacks of meaty flesh.

Something burned my cuts.

Sonia stood at my side and dressed my wound. My vision steadied, but my stomach still churned.

"Stay with me, puddin'. Max is gettin' help."

As the sludge drained from my body, my form shrank back to its normal size.

A horn sounded. Cultists stormed the quarry. The changelings fled as reinforcements stormed the ground with magic. The wyrm had held up her end of the bargain.

Sonia poured a moon juice tonic down my throat. My bleeding stopped and my stomach settled. Dynamite detonated above us. I turned to see Cobarde pulled from the end of Beauregard's sword. Heimer lay beneath him, tensing before he swung the killing blow. A dagger stuck into the wall, sending fragments of rock flying.

Beauregard turned to see Romero behind him.

"You missed," he said.

"I never miss," replied Romero.

Changelings barred their approach. Both sides made quick work of them, and their swords clashed.

The army dropped a plunger, and then another. Blasts of boulders and stalagmites rained around us. Cliffs collapsed in a landslide.

Beauregard disarmed Romero. He pulled his flintlock. Empty. Beauregard's longsword rested at his throat.

The screams of chaos drowned out every word spoken. His sword lowered and Beauregard raced toward the lift. Romero glimpsed me and sprinted my way. He stooped to my side. All three were by the lift, poised to escape—Fenrir dragged the High Wolf who was screaming after "his spawn."

Rocks fell into flocks of screaming soldiers, crushing those out in the open. Most of the army lay dead. The few remaining changelings had been abandoned by their king.

Romero glared at Beauregard, who smiled back with a wave.

"Romero, apply pressure to her wound," snapped Sonia. His fingers reached for his pistol. He shook his head, thinking better of it.

"All right, kid, let's patch you up," he said to me. "Stay with me, now, you hear?"

The world was crashing all around me in more ways than one.

Something pricked my side. My eyelids jolted open. Strength returned to my muscles. Romero removed a needle from my thigh. He slapped my cheeks.

"All better. Let's go."

CHAPTER THIRTY-SIX

The few survivors raced across the quarry toward the light at the end of the tunnel. Romero and Sonia held me on both sides. Boulders crumbled down around us. Rudolph and Lot stood by the cave, funneling in their men.

Sonia grumbled, "Where's that disgusting dog? He said he would get help."

Romero pulled my arm further over his shoulder. "Leave him. This place is coming down."

My tail dragged across the ground, my boots dug ruts across silt and sand behind us. They carried me through the falling hailstorm to the exit.

Bits of gravel struck my face. Dust and sand stung my eyes. My vision tinted. The saryx refused to surrender. Its thoughts became my own. *Why do they hold me like I'm their prisoner? Foolish humes. You know not the schemes of man. Their hatred must be avenged tenfold.*

"Romero, move faster," Sonia nagged. "I think we're losing her. She's turned from blue to white. Sinopa, stay with me, puddin'. We'll get you those plum tarts you like. That sound fun?"

Her voice broke. "Allow me to save you," she whispered. Her lips kissed my cheek. *Foolish bird. I'm beyond repair. No, we need no fix. We are natural. We are one.*

My throat glowed a dull white. *What is this? Stay back.* I coughed in the soot and dust around us. The debris felt larger.

"Romero, say something," Sonia insisted.

Romero sighed. "Kid, from the moment we met, you've been nothing but trouble." *Yes, fuel that hatred. Let us feed. Let us breed.* "I believe you chose that name—Kiera—just to spite me all the more. As if you were my blood child, you've been an absolute pain in my side, but I wouldn't have it any other way." *No. Stop. Silence, human!* "I'm proud to call you my apprentice, and the closest thing I have to a daughter. And as the curtain will certainly fall for all of us, it's been a pleasure fighting by your side."

His lips touched my other cheek. My throat burned like embers. The saryx shrieked and pleaded to stay but had no place in my heart. My friends were my shield. Through them, I clung to sanity.

The ground cracked in plates beneath us. The pebbles had turned to bits, and the bits to stones and boulders. My friends snaked and weaved me around fallen stalagmites. The hail of stone pelted our heads. Salt and silt chalked the air.

The plates sunk beneath us. Someone hoisted me over the lip. A large rock cracked Romeo in the shoulder. My lungs wheezed and coughed. Sonia spread her wings in a feeble umbrella and flapped the dust away.

CRACK. The ceiling above us split. A boulder as large as a stagecoach hurdled toward us. Sonia stood me on my feet. Romero shook his head. I braced for impact. A dark shadow cast over us. Dust continued to rain, and then nothing. The boulder had stopped. It glided aside as a green dome cast over us.

Across the way, a woman leaned one of the wyrm's men and cast a smaller umbrella over herself.

"Hurry!" Romero shouted. He grabbed my arm. Rocks pinged off the emerald canopy. Boulders split and rolled as the field warbled. None of us knew whether it would hold.

The air ran clearer under the dome. It rushed, brisk and cool. I could almost jog.

The woman met us at the entrance to the cave. Her hair stood ragged and frizzed. Above her button nose, an eye had been put out. This was Cheryl.

A blur of brown fur raced past me covered in gray soot. Max handed

Edith to Rudolph, who took her frail body with confusion. He spoke to Cheryl in guttural growls and yips, and she nodded, seeming to understand. I couldn't believe she was alive, let alone sane.

"Out of the way, mutt," snapped Sonia.

"No, wait," I mumbled. "The sorcerers."

"They're upstairs in the camps," Max explained. "They'll be trapped, but safe."

"Forget them. You're more important right now," I told him.

"I got them," Max said.

"Max, wait." I coughed. Romero and Sonia turned me around to face him.

"I have to do this," he told me. "I'll be a good boy then. The chief is counting on me."

"Max, it's suicide."

"Maybe, but—"

"Hey, lovebirds, need I remind you this place is caving in?" Sonia spoke up.

"I—I can't lose you again," I said to Max.

Max came closer. "You won't. I promise. This is the right thing to do. It's what we came here for. If it will make you happy, and if it means somebody will like me, then maybe—"

"I already do."

His arms wrapped around my neck in an awkward hug. Sonia and Romero stood by as third wheels. Sonia roared that I still didn't seem to realize the danger.

"Careful; watch the horns. They're sharp," I warned.

"You'll never be a monster to me." he said, kissing my cheek.

"You missed."

He raised his eyebrow, confused, and tried again. I pulled his snout to my lips.

My tail stiffened on end. His arms enveloped my waist. My heart leaped. For once in my life, everything felt right. I was safe. The world could cave in, and the sky could fall, and I wouldn't care. I found my one.

He pulled away. His eyes shyly darted to the floor. "Was that my kiss back?"

I playfully raised my finger to his lips. "Perhaps. You'll get the other when you get out of this, hero."

Sonia gagged.

Max smiled and backed away, not taking his eyes off me. Shale and stalagmites continued to rain in the quarry. His feet appeared to be glued to the floor. Cheryl and Lot passed him with a magical umbrella overhead.

"Get!" Sonia shouted.

Max raised a howl, and a few dazed changelings followed him in a mad dash. He stopped at the other end and blew a kiss. My tail flicked in delight. The tunnel collapsed and then nothing. Buried earth stood between us.

"You sure can pick them," remarked Sonia, guiding me to the light.

"What's that supposed to mean?"

"It means you can do better," laughed Romero.

"I think he's kind of cute," I huffed.

"If you're into rocks for brains. Is that really the best you could do?"

"If you can do better, prove it."

Sonia remained silent, and Romero grinned ear to ear.

The sun rose over the sea between the great divide. A swarm of survivors, of all sorts: race, breed, and heritage, piled on the steamboat in the harbor. Rudolph stood by the dock and approached.

"Well, look what we have here," he snickered.

As he strolled over, two streaks of purple struck both Romero and Sonia. Their knees collapsed and they took me down with them. An arrow stuck into the side of the canyon, and a hefty cord pulled at the shaft.

Desmodius ziplined between us and the ship. He unsheathed two scimitars and roared. "No! You will not escape. You took everything from me. My home. My honor. My father!" He grabbed his bloodied abdomen and wheezed. Both his blades fell in the dirt. "You'll not get away. I've searched for years. Years! Luck swore the throne to me. Now you've gone and ruined it all."

Rudolph held a dagger at his throat and turned to me. "What do you say we do with him?"

"Kill him right there," said Sonia, rubbing her temples.

Romero agreed.

I swayed, standing to my feet. "Heal him."

"What?"

"He tried to kill us!" Sonia argued.

"He's my brother, Sonia. Master Rudolph, heal him." I staggered over in front of him.

Desmodius growled in my face as Rudolph healed him from behind. His mouth shut, and he locked eyes with me.

"You're more than welcome to come with us if you like," I offered.

"Like hell he is," shot Sonia.

Des stood. He didn't reach for his swords. Overhead, a large airship the size of a fortress approached. Red trim and massive wings cast shadows over the cavern as it rose. Creaks of wood echoed off the sea, and then it drifted away from us.

His eyes turned to the ship, then back to me. He pushed past me and kept on walking.

"You're welcome," I called after him.

Des kept walking up the shore, holding his sealed abdomen. Rudolph helped me onto the deck, and two changeling rebels fetched my friends.

"What now?" I asked.

Rudolph shook his head. "Now?" he paused. "They'll have my head or my title for this. I've failed as a Master. The consul died on my watch. We can trust no one anymore. Beauregard played all sides for the empire. He's forming an army. News of the consul's death could spark war in this already fragile climate."

Romero hobbled over beside us. "I know one nation we can go to. It's safe there. We train, keep you safe, and strike when we're ready. Beau has started a war and we're going to give it to him."

"Rest sounds good right now," said Sonia, leaning on the rail beside Rudolph, staring out into the sunrise.

"Well, where to?" I asked.

"I know a place," said Romero.

"You're not going to tell us, are you?" Sonia asked, rolling her eyes.

Romero smiled. "She learns fast. I think we'll keep her. Set a course for the main island of Jahara. The Oracle awaits."

Rudolph nodded and took to the helm.

The seagulls rose and screeched proudly in victory over the city. The waves crashed against the shore, and Aerogapolis cast shadows over us.

Its dreams of perfection and happiness seemed lofty and out of reach. Inside, the bustling crowds and music echoed across the coast. The windmills churned, and the city lights blinked out one by one. It was a new day.

I thought I would find my family here. Romero squeezed my hand and Sonia bopped me one before placing her head on my shoulder. In a way, I did.

There was no sign of the suicidal moon. There was only a bright sunrise, beckoning us into the new horizon.

THANK YOU FOR READING!

Thank you for reading *Vestige: What Lies Beneath.* If you enjoyed this story, please leave an honest review on Goodreads or at your favorite retailer, wherever you purchased this book. It really helps the book do well. Thank you in advance.

For more of my books, please subscribe to my website to be the first to know when the next one will be released.

You can follow me at:

theantonioroberts.com
Goodreads
my Facebook author page

www.ingramcontent.com/pod-product-compliance
Lightning Source LLC
Chambersburg PA
CBHW060627260626
47161CB00008B/2823